Their relationship was so perfect, how could this happen?

The following day Jason went to the cafeteria and waited ten minutes for Philip to arrive. *He must be in surgery again.* He bought a sandwich and decided to make the quick walk to his own apartment to get a CD of Chopin piano pieces he had made for Dr. Glassman. He had learned from one of the other postdoc fellows that Chopin was Dr. Glassman's favorite composer, and he'd forgotten to pack the CD that morning. It was a crisp, clear, beautiful winter day in New York City, and although Jason was usually bothered by the cold, he didn't feel the freeze that day as he walked home. He'd been with Philip the night before and thought of him on the entire walk, how much he loved him, how lucky he was. He didn't notice the ice forming on the sandwich as he ate it. He didn't notice the people he passed in the street.

Jason opened the door to his apartment. The lights were on and standing in the middle of the room, naked with a towel, was Lucas Franklin, the anesthesiology resident he had met at lunch several weeks ago. Jason stood frozen, confused, as Lucas gasped.

"Did you say something?" Philip walked out of the bathroom with a towel around his waist.

All three men stood, paralyzed. The only sound was the outside traffic. Jason's heart began pounding, hard and slow. He felt light-headed and vomited his sandwich onto the floor as a wave of nausea overwhelmed him. He slowly walked into the kitchen, opened a roll of paper towels, lowered himself to his knees, and slowly wiped up the vomit. Lucas disappeared into the bathroom, and Philip stood motionless at the bathroom door, pale and silent, watching Jason.

When Jason Green begins his internship at Sinai Medical Center, there seems to be no limit to what he can achieve. Brilliant, hardworking, and driven by an intense desire to ease people's suffering, Jason has a knack for asking the questions that will lead to correct diagnoses. His efforts earn him the respect of his superiors—and the attention of Philip Olsen, a devastatingly attractive orthopedic surgeon.

But none of Jason's abilities can prepare him for the challenges he faces outside the hospital. Philip, with whom Jason has a seemingly perfect relationship, betrays him with another man. Dr. Fang, his dedicated but aloof research partner, guards a secret that might compromise their research. Can the problem-solving techniques that serve Jason so well in the medical world help him to repair the rifts in his relationships?

KUDOS for *The Intern*

In *The Intern* by John S. Daniels, Jason Green is a new doctor just starting his internship at a prestigious hospital in New York. Extremely bright, Jason is more concerned with patient health than protocol and he soon makes a name for himself as a diagnostician of the highest order. Jason is also gay, and he quickly falls in love with a gay surgeon at the hospital. In addition to his hospital work, Jason convinces one of the head doctors to let him work at his research lab where Jason solves several complicated problems for the team. But even though he should be on top of the world, trouble lurks just below the surface and it isn't long before Jason suffers some severe betrayals that shake his faith in both himself and his fellow man. Even though the book is quite technical with medical issues and terms, Daniels make it easy for lay people to understand, It's a complex love story woven through subplots of espionage and attempted murder. A great read. ~ *Taylor Jones, The Review Team of Taylor Jones & Regan Murphy*

The Intern by John S. Daniels is a young gay man away from home and family and embarking on a new phase in his life. Highly intelligent and a dedicated new doctor, Jason knows how things should be. Young and idealistic, he struggles with striking an acceptable balance between caring for his patients and obeying hospital protocol and regulations as he does his internship at the hospital. Even though he is somewhat awkward and doesn't like to draw attention to himself, he won't back down when a patient is at risk. Originally from Louisiana, he is out of his element in New York. He is learning quickly that things are far from perfect and rarely done the "right" way. Then he falls in love with a gay doctor at the hospital and his world is bright—until he discovers that relationships aren't perfect either. *The intern* is a heartwarming love story blended with mystery and intriguing for a compelling and thought-provoking book. ~ *Regan Murphy, The Review Team of Taylor Jones & Regan Murphy*

THE
INTERN

JOHN S. DANIELS

A Black Opal Books Publication

GENRE: GAY ROMANCE/SUSPENSE

This is a work of fiction. Names, places, characters and incidents are either the product of the author's imagination or are used fictitiously, and any resemblance to any actual persons, living or dead, businesses, organizations, events or locales is entirely coincidental. All trademarks, service marks, registered trademarks, and registered service marks are the property of their respective owners and are used herein for identification purposes only. The publisher does not have any control over or assume any responsibility for author or third-party websites or their contents.

THE INTERN
Copyright © 2015 by John S. Daniels
Cover Design by John S. Daniels
All cover art copyright © 2015
All Rights Reserved
Print ISBN: 978-1-626947-39-9

Published by Black Opal Books **http://www.blackopalbooks.com**

DEDICATION

*For Lauren, Melissa, and Julie (the joys of my life)
and for Lance (my Philip)*

CHAPTER 1

It was six in the morning on a hot and muggy first day of July in New York City, 2005. Jason Green sat chilled and alone at the ninth-floor nursing station, the hub of one of the general medicine units of the prestigious Sinai Medical Center, his heart pounding in anticipation. He was reading the tenth of fourteen patient charts he planned to review before the official start of his internship, which was in sixty minutes. Jason had just graduated from medical school the prior month, and his anxiety stemmed from knowing that he was entering one of the most sought-after internal medicine internships in the country.

He would be training and competing with some of the brightest young physicians coming out of the most prestigious medical schools, and he wondered how he would measure up to his fellow interns.

At seven o'clock, his resident, who had already been through a year of internal medicine internship and a second year of internal medicine residency, would arrive with two third-year medical students. They would work together as a team for the next eight weeks, and he was determined to be familiar with the patients assigned to his team before their arrival.

Jason's intense concentration was abruptly interrupted as a strikingly beautiful nurse bolted out of a patient room directly across from where he sat and yelled, "Doctor, come here now! I need your help!"

The nurse was frantic, and the pleading in her voice startled him. In addition this was first time he had been called "doctor" by anyone except for his father, and he was taken aback at the title.

Jason ran into the room to find the nurse breathing into the mouth of a pretty, middle-aged woman. The nurse looked up at Jason, wide-eyed, and shouted, "Call a Code Blue now, Doctor!"

Jason concluded that a Code Blue must be the same as a Code 9 at the University of Mississippi, the medical school from which he had graduated, but he had no idea how to initiate a Code Blue at his new hospital. He wasn't even officially an intern yet. He gently pulled the nurse away and told her to call the Code Blue. He got on top of the lady and started chest compressions. Five compressions and then one breath from his lungs into her lungs, repeated over and over. Jason could smell the Chanel No. 5 the woman must have recently applied. It had been his mother's favorite perfume.

After what seemed an eternity, Jason finally heard "Code Blue, room ninety-two zero four. Code Blue, room ninety-two zero four" echoing in the hallway. He was relieved. Help would soon arrive. Jason had practiced cardiopulmonary resuscitation on plastic dummies in medical school, but he had never participated in a real Code Blue and had certainly not expected to begin his internship under such difficult circumstances.

Within thirty seconds, the room was jammed with doctors in white coats; a nurse with a cardioversion device to deliver an electric shock; another nurse with a large cart on rollers filled with bags of fluid, medications, syringes, and tubing; and a respiratory therapist with a respirator. One of the doctors in a white laboratory coat seemed to take over. Jason noticed that he looked very young and was short and stocky, with curly brown hair. His nametag read Seth Goldberg, MD.

"Whoever you are, keep up the chest compressions," Dr. Goldberg calmly ordered Jason as he grabbed an endotracheal tube and scope. Jason resumed chest compressions as he watched Dr. Goldberg move to the head of the bed, insert the scope into the throat of the unconscious woman, and slide the endotracheal tube into the woman's trachea. He then took a syringe, inflated the balloon surrounding the tube to keep it in place, and began forcing air into the lungs of the patient with an Ambu bag, the handheld device used to inflate the lungs before a respirator is attached.

Jason continued the chest compressions, and his face flushed as he saw that several of the doctors and nurses were staring at him. He watched as a nurse quickly taped the endotracheal tube to the patient's face and attached the respirator to the endotracheal tube. Dr. Goldberg gave orders to the respiratory therapist for ventilator settings and at the same time quickly inserted a needle into the internal jugular vein so that medications could be administered. Jason then saw Dr. Goldberg silently motion for him to get off the patient. As Dr. Goldberg picked up the electric shock paddles and placed them on the bare chest of the woman, every eye in the room turned to the monitor. Jason looked over and observed only a flat line—no electrical activity of the heart.

"Stand back, everyone," Dr. Goldberg calmly ordered in a voice loud enough for everyone to hear.

He pressed the button on the paddle, and eight hundred volts of electricity surged through the woman's chest wall into the heart, causing the lifeless body to lift in a brief spasm. All eyes turned to the monitor—once again, there was only a flat line. Dr. Goldberg administered another

shock, again with no results. Although Dr. Goldberg remained calm, Jason could see that he was distressed at the
lack of response. He quietly ordered Jason to get back on
the bed and start chest compressions and then asked the
nurse for atropine, epinephrine, and sodium bicarbonate,
all of which he administered quickly through the jugular
line.

Only three minutes had elapsed from the time the
Code Blue had been announced over the loudspeaker.
The temperature in the room was noticeably warmer from
all the people jammed into the small space, and the intense stench of burned skin from the electric shocks startled Jason. But he was most impressed at the efficiency
and competency of this lead doctor.

After twenty minutes of repeated sequences of chest
compression, electric shock, and administration of several
different medications, Dr. Goldberg put down the shock
paddles, turned around, and said quietly, "Okay, stop.
That's it."

Jason noticed Dr. Goldberg's sad look, sweat dripping
from his brow, as he walked out of the dead lady's room.

Jason crawled off the bed and stood watching everyone silently file out of the room, the nurses and therapists
gathering and removing their equipment. The beautiful
young nurse who had first asked for his help was standing
in the corner, obviously shaken by the events. Jason went
over to her and asked her if she was okay. She nodded
with a sad smile, and then Jason left the room. He had not
even officially begun his internship, and he felt as though
he had already lost his first patient.

Jason sat down at the nursing station to continue his
chart review and noticed that one of his five remaining
charts was missing. He suddenly realized that the dead
woman would have been one of his patients and wondered if she had a son who would be as devastated as he

had been after losing his mother two years ago. Jason looked briefly at Dr. Goldberg who was sitting a few feet away intently writing a note in the dead woman's chart. The nursing station was once again quiet as Jason began reviewing the remaining four charts. A few minutes later, he was interrupted when Dr. Goldberg tossed the chart on the desk and looked up at Jason.

"Thanks for your help. Are you one of the new interns?"

"Yes, sir, I'm Jason Green. Y'all were—uh—you were amazing in there." Jason corrected himself, self-conscious about his deep southern accent.

"I'm Seth Goldberg. I'm your resident for the next eight weeks. Why are you here already? We don't meet till seven o'clock."

Jason saw that beads of sweat still covered Dr. Goldberg's brow, and his shirt was damp with perspiration.

"I wanted to familiarize myself with the patients before y'all arrived," Jason said, still shaken.

Dr. Goldberg grinned. "Well, you did good in there. But we're going to have to do something about that accent of yours. You're going to drive me crazy with it."

"What happened to that poor lady?" Jason managed to return his smile. "She looked awfully young."

"She was only fifty, with three children—one a medical student across town. She was going to have her aortic valve replaced today. We tried to get it done last week, but the surgeon said he couldn't get her on the schedule."

Jason saw that Dr. Goldberg was distressed and thought that perhaps his eyes had become moist with tears.

"She'd still be alive and probably home already had she been operated on last week. This was the classic nightmare scenario of someone with severe aortic stenosis waiting to have the valve replaced. Goddamn it, and the fix, it's so simple." He shook his head and looked down. After a noticeable pause, he looked back up at Jason. "By the way, Sheri, the nurse you were helping before we arrived—she couldn't take her eyes off you for the entire code."

"How could you possibly make that observation?" Jason asked in surprise. "You were completely immersed in running that code."

Seth smiled and wiped the sweat off his brow with his hand. "Well, I make a habit of observing people carefully, especially beautiful young women. I've been asking her—unsuccessfully, I might add—to go out with me for over a year. So already I don't like you."

Jason smiled too. "Don't worry, sir. She's not my type. I'm gay."

Seth laughed. "Well, that's a relief. Maybe I can set you up with my younger brother. I'll see you in a few. I have to call the patient's family and pick up the new students."

Jason wondered whether the medical team could have insisted on earlier surgery. He felt a mixed sense of sadness and anger at what happened to this lady, and he told himself that he would be aggressive in preventing anything like this from happening to any of his patients. The smell of burned flesh remained on his hands as he sat back down and read the remaining charts. His heart was still pounding, and he didn't know whether it was from the code or the anticipation of starting his internship.

At seven, Seth returned to the floor with two third-year medical students, just as Jason finished reviewing the last of the charts.

Jason stood up. "I'm Jason Green, your intern."

He shook both students' hands. The young woman had blonde hair, blue eyes, a nice smile, and was obviously shy. The other student appeared considerably older, tall and thin, with thick glasses, a rough complexion, and no suggestion that he even had the ability to smile. Jason guessed that because of his age, he was likely among those getting a combined MD and PhD and that he had been doing research for the past four or five years. He did not look happy to be there—perhaps, Jason thought, because he had to take orders from and be evaluated by a resident and intern who were several years his junior, or perhaps because he was more comfortable in a research lab than in a clinical setting.

Dr. Goldberg took the lead again, waving the group into a conference room just off the nursing station.

"Here's the plan for the next eight weeks." Dr. Goldberg was all business, looking at Jason and the two students with a serious expression. Jason watched as Dr. Goldberg told the students that they would be performing a history and physical on one new patient each admitting day and that they would be responsible for presenting that patient to Dr. Glassman during attending rounds the following day. "You had better know every detail of your patients' history and physical examination, every laboratory value, and everything there is to know about their medical problems. If you mess, up that reflects badly on me, and I will not put up with that."

Jason looked at the students who sat nervously, twitching their hands. Beads of sweat had formed on the PhD's brow. Jason wanted to say something to comfort the students but held back.

Dr. Goldberg turned to Jason. "Jason, you will work up every admission, including those that are assigned to the students. You had better be thorough but when you present to Dr. Glassman, be concise. We only have two hours with him every day, and we need to make good use of our time—"

Jason interrupted. "I'll do my best, boss."

The female student smiled at that remark, although Dr. Goldberg did not seem to be amused.

"I'm serious, Jason," Dr. Goldberg continued. "I don't know if you've even heard of Dr. Glassman. He's primarily a researcher and has received a Nobel Prize for his work. He's brilliant but very demanding, so unless you want to be the object of his wrath, you'd better take what I say seriously. And you're also expected to be at attending rounds everyday unless you have an emergency you need to tend to."

Jason nodded. In fact he was well aware of Dr. Glassman. It was Dr. Glassman's research that had piqued Jason's interest in Sinai Medical Center. He also knew that Dr. Glassman had the reputation of being very demanding, but he had become elated and excited when he learned during his intern orientation session that Dr. Glassman would be his attending physician for eight weeks. What luck, Jason had thought.

Dr. Goldberg continued his orientation, still addressing Jason. "The students may have two or three required teaching conferences each week with a professor or the chief residents. Otherwise they are here to help you take care of our patients. Don't be too easy on them. I'll be off the floor at resident teaching conferences and in the library at least half of every day, hopefully learning things that I can teach you and the students about our patients. But I'll give you my phone number, and you can call me anytime, twenty-four/seven." His gaze swept them once more. "If any of you three happen to be religious and have to attend mass or services on Sundays, I'm required to let you do that, although I won't be happy about it."

Jason laughed. "I guess you haven't met too many Jews from Mississippi."

Dr. Goldberg looked surprised. "I didn't know they allowed Jews in Mississippi."

Jason knew that Dr. Goldberg's comment was meant to be humorous, but it was a stark reminder that in his hometown of fifty thousand, with only sixteen Jewish families, the anti-Semitism was overt. Jason forced a smile.

"Okay, let's start rounds so we can finish by nine thirty," Dr. Goldberg continued. "Glassman is coming early since it's also his first day with us."

Jason gathered the thirteen charts and stacked them on a rolling cart, and the four went into their first patient's room. Jason knew that Dr. Goldberg had been on this unit for the prior month and was intimately familiar with all thirteen patients. Dr. Goldberg introduced an ill-appearing middle-aged man to Jason and the medical students.

Jason stepped forward and took Mr. Shepherd's hand, looked at him squarely in the eye, and said in his deep southern drawl, "It's a pleasure to meet you, Mr. Shepherd. We're going to continue the good care you're getting here and try to get you out of this hospital as soon as possible."

Jason put his hand on Mr. Shepherd's shoulder, turned around to his resident and the students, and proceeded to give a concise but detailed history, including all the pertinent laboratory results and the current diagnosis and treatment plan. He could see Dr. Goldberg's growing surprise—clearly he did not expect such a performance.

Mr. Shepherd had been admitted four days previous with pneumonia and sepsis, and although he had been critically ill when admitted, he was improving rapidly with antibiotics and fluids. After Jason finished his presentation, he performed a rapid physical examination, with Dr. Goldberg and the students looking on, stunned at Jason's confidence. Jason felt Mr. Shepherd's neck, listened to his lungs, asked the students to listen to

the abnormal sounds in his left lung, and finally palpat-
ed the abdomen. He asked Dr. Goldberg to feel his neck,
under the arms, and the abdomen, and then invited the
students to do the same.

"Mr. Shepherd." Jason smiled, taking his hand once
again. "From what I've read in your chart, your lungs are
sounding much better than when you first came in. You'll
be up and running before you know it. I'll be back a little
later to talk with you and answer any questions you might
have."

Mr. Shepherd smiled and nodded, and the group left
the room.

Dr. Goldberg stood silently for a moment, looking up
at Jason without expression, as the four stood in a circle
outside Mr. Shepherd's room. "Jesus Christ, Jason. How
could you know the patient that well? And you just found
some things on the physical exam that your predecessor
and I missed."

Jason felt his face flushing as he looked at the students
and explained, "He has some enlarged lymph nodes in his
neck and under his arms, and he has an enlarged spleen as
well. I suspect he has a lymphoma or some other underlying malignancy. It would explain why a previously
healthy man would get such a horrible infection." He
paused, his face feeling uncomfortably hot. "If you agree,
Dr. Goldberg, I'll order a CT scan of his chest and abdomen and then an ultrasound-guided lymph node biopsy.
That should give us the diagnosis. I'll sit down with him
and explain what we've found and our plan after we finish rounds."

"That sounds good." Dr. Goldberg nodded. "But my
name is Seth."

Over the next ninety minutes, the team went into each
of the twelve remaining patient rooms. Each time, after
being introduced, Jason took the patient's hand and pre-

sented a concise but detailed history of the patient's medical issues, treatment, and plans, followed by a physical examination. After leaving each room, Seth discussed various aspects of the patient's medical problems, and Jason eagerly took in everything Seth was teaching, frequently interrupting him with challenging questions.

During one lady's physical examination, Jason pointed out to Seth that her second heart sound was widely split, which Jason explained could be an indication of increased pressure in the pulmonary artery. The woman had been admitted with a bleeding ulcer but started complaining about shortness of breath two days after being admitted. Jason suggested that the abnormal second heart sound could be an indication of a significant blood clot in her lung, which could be causing her shortness of breath. Seth did not hide his look of surprise as Jason described his physical finding and agreed that a CT of the chest be ordered. Later that morning, the CT scan did show a large blood clot in the right pulmonary artery.

Following rounds, Seth directed the students to wait in the conference room for Dr. Glassman's arrival and turned to Jason. "Jason, you were quite impressive on rounds. But that accent of yours—I think some speech therapy might be in order."

Jason smiled as Seth chuckled at his own humor. Jason had learned in an orientation session the prior day that Seth had graduated first in his class from Harvard Medical School. He had developed the reputation of being the most brilliant resident in his group and was in line to become the next chief resident, a distinction that would open endless opportunities for his medical career.

Seth laughed. "C'mon, let's go try to calm the students down before Glassman gets here. They look like they are ready to fall apart."

Dr. Glassman arrived a few minutes later, shook

Seth's hand, and looked at Jason. "So you're Dr. Green. Your genetics professor at Mississippi, Franklin Deutsch, is a good friend of mine. He speaks pretty highly of you. I hope you don't make a liar of him."

Jason was surprised at Dr. Glassman's demeanor. There was not a hint of emotion and he certainly was not pleasant. "It's a pleasure meeting you, sir. I was—"

Dr. Glassman turned to the students, interrupting Jason. "And what are your names?"

The students introduced themselves, and then Dr. Glassman turned around and motioned everyone to follow him. "Let's go. Grab the charts. I want to hear about the patients. This is a dangerous time for patients in this hospital. Brand-new interns who know nothing and students who know even less. Dr. Goldberg, I expect you to be on this floor with Dr. Green and the students to make certain things go smoothly."

"Things will go smoothly." Seth chuckled as Dr. Glassman gave him a dour look.

Jason grabbed the cart with the charts, and they entered the first patient's room. This time around, Jason introduced the patient to Dr. Glassman, once again placing his hand on the patient's shoulder and presenting a complete but concise history of the patient's medical problems. He pointed out interesting findings on the physical examination and invited Dr. Glassman to listen and palpate. Dr. Glassman stared at Jason, stone-faced, during the entire presentation, except for a brief glance at Seth—who, Jason noticed, was smiling.

After leaving the room, Dr. Glassman asked Seth a few questions, and they went into the next patient's room. Jason repeated his performance for all the patients, each time talking to a stone-faced Dr. Glassman.

The patient presentations ended at noon, and Dr. Glassman looked at Jason. "Dr. Green, take the students and get busy. You have a lot of work to do. Walk back to my office with me, Dr. Goldberg."

Jason watched the two as they walked quickly toward the elevator.

"I thought this was the first day of his internship, Goldberg," Jason overheard Dr. Glassman say. He saw Seth respond with a few inaudible words and then laugh. Jason felt almost despondent at Dr. Glassman's lack of interaction with him, and his aloofness sent a chill through him.

Jason was already in Mr. Shepherd's room when Seth returned to the nursing station, and for the rest of the day, Jason went back into each patient's room, spending considerable time with each, answering their questions, and allaying their fears. He made mental notes on each patient, ordered necessary tests, changed antibiotics after looking at culture results on several patients, and saw that every patient was getting his or her needs met. He discussed each patient with the nursing staff to make certain the nurses were aware of the patients' problems. Jason also spent time with his two students, going over their assigned patients and discussing how to write a proper history and physical examination. Seth came to the floor several times during the afternoon to review patients with Jason and, at six o'clock, announced to Jason that he was going home. Jason had already let the students go home for the evening.

"You have my number," Seth said as he headed for the elevator. "Call me if you have any questions at all. And finish here soon, go home and get some rest. We're admitting tomorrow, and it will be hectic."

During the afternoon and evening, Jason attended three additional Code Blues. He was not familiar with the layout of the huge hospital, and by the time he arrived at each code, he found himself observing from the back of the room. But he was fascinated and eager to learn the resuscitation procedures. After each code, he went back to his nursing station and read about the various medications that had been given. He was, however, disturbed because not one of the patients in the four Code Blues he had attended survived, and even though he didn't know anything about these patients, the outcomes saddened him. Four codes, four deaths: Not a happy first day of internship.

By midafternoon, Jason noticed that the other intern on his floor, Zachary Kline, who was the admitting intern the first day and whom he had met at the intern orientation session earlier in the week, appeared to be very upset. Zachary had graduated from Stanford University School of Medicine near the top of his class and was obviously very bright. Jason approached him to ask if everything was going okay. Zachary said that he was having difficulty with an admission and that he couldn't find his resident to get advice. In fact, after further discussion, Jason realized that Zachary had three admissions and was having difficulty assessing all three cases. He appeared literally panic-stricken. Jason spent the next two hours with Zachary going over the three cases, helping him with a spinal tap on a lady who had been admitted with confusion and a high fever, and went over admission orders on all three patients. Zachary's resident finally returned at five-thirty, and Jason was able to return to his own duties.

At ten p.m. Jason finally sat down to write a daily progress note for each of his thirteen patients. He knew that he should have been finished with his duties and out of the hospital hours ago, but he couldn't leave Zach panic-stricken as he was. Jason's work had also been interrupted by numerous nurses who seemed to come from other floors in the hospital to ask him questions about their patients or borrow supplies from the floor. After another interruption at eleven p.m. by a nurse from a surgical floor, Jason approached the head nurse on his unit, a very pleasant middle-aged woman.

"Mrs. Connelly, nurses have been coming from all over the hospital asking me questions about their patients all afternoon and evening. Is that a common practice around here?" He worried that if these constant interruptions from nurses continued, he would have a problem efficiently completing his own tasks.

Mrs. Connelly started laughing. "Honey, have you looked in a mirror lately. You are gorgeous and single. You could earn a fortune as a highly paid model. All of these nurses are just taking a peek at the best-looking doctor at Sinai."

Jason's face turned bright red, resulting in further laughter and pat on the cheek from Mrs. Connelly. Jason knew that he had inherited his mother's good looks, but it hadn't occurred to him that all of these nurses had an ulterior motive for their visits.

Just before two a.m., with only one more note to write, Jason became overwhelmed with fatigue and laid his head down, his face resting on his forearm, his long dark brown curly hair covering the progress note that he was composing.

At two-ten a.m., Jason was startled out of a deep sleep by another Code Blue announcement. "Code Blue, room ten two fourteen. Code Blue, room ten two fourteen." He blinked, dazed, the intense fluorescent lighting making him squint. He looked, bleary-eyed, around the nursing station and saw that he was completely alone. He felt slightly disoriented from his fatigue and sudden awakening, but he took a deep breath and his head cleared. The silence on the floor was in conspicuous contrast to the constant chatter of doctors, nurses, therapists, patients, and patients' families in continuous discussion earlier in the day. Absent were the constant ringing of phones and beepers.

Code Blue. The echo of the announcement finally registered as the fog of exhausted sleep cleared. On each of the previous codes, the patient's room had been jammed with doctors and nurses. At each code, initial chaos had transformed into an orderly process because of a resident who took control of the resuscitation. The other twenty doctors and nurses had stood around, observing and occasionally making suggestions.

Jason yawned. He had not slept for almost twenty-four hours and still had one more progress note to write before he could go back to his apartment, sleep for a couple of hours, go for his three-mile run, and return to his unit to begin rounds with Seth and the medical students at seven a.m. He took a deep breath. He'd already been to four codes, and he surely would not be needed at this one. He began writing his final note.

At two-fifteen a.m., as Jason was finishing his final progress note, he heard over the loudspeaker: "Code Blue, room ten two fourteen." The announcement was repeated three more times. This time the voice was loud and with a sense of urgency, a marked contrast to the Code Blue announcement that had woken him five minutes ago. Jason put down his chart, realizing that the Code Blue was just one floor above him. It seemed strange to him that a code would have to be called a second time.

Uneasy, Jason hurried up the stairs and headed down an empty hallway for room 10214, expecting to see the usual throng of doctors and nurses resuscitating the patient. He walked into the room and halted. A young nurse was on top of a middle-aged man, compressing his chest and then breathing into his mouth. The room was otherwise empty.

She gave him one brief, frantic glance. "Please help me, Doctor."

Jason pulled her off. "Go fetch the code cart and make sure there are some endotracheal tubes and an Ambu bag."

The nurse ran off, and Jason resumed chest compressions and mouth-to-mouth respirations. Waves of guilt consumed him. His decision to not attend the Code Blue when it had first been announced would make him responsible for a bad outcome, and that thought terrified him. He had been having vivid nightmares since medical school graduation about making mistakes and causing harm to patients, and he wasn't sure how he would cope if he were responsible for this man's death. The nurse returned with a cart containing the electric paddles, endotracheal tubes, and medications.

"Take over the chest compressions, Ms. Chapman." Jason had read her identification badge before she had left to get the equipment. She appeared very upset, was sweating, and perhaps, Jason thought, even angry. He grabbed what looked like the right size endotracheal tube and the scope. He had never done this on a living human, although he had practiced on cadavers in his anatomy class four years ago. The vivid memory of that intense, noxious smell of cadavers preserved with formalin made him briefly cringe. He inserted the scope down the man's throat, saw where the trachea and the esophagus diverged, and inserted the tube into the trachea. He blew up the balloon with a syringe, quickly taped the tube to the man's mouth, connected the Ambu bag to the endotracheal tube, and began forcing air into the man's lungs. After a few seconds, he asked the nurse to take over the Ambu bag.

Jason ripped off the man's hospital gown, placed the paddles on the man's chest, and checked the monitor. He felt his stomach churn as he saw the squiggly lines that meant ventricular fibrillation, an absence of heart muscle contraction.

"Stand back, ma'am." Jason waited until Nurse Chapman was clear and then pressed the button.

The man's body arched up into a brief spasm. Electrical waves briefly returned as the heart began to beat once again, but they quickly flattened into the fatal rhythm. The now-familiar smell of burned skin brought a sense of urgency to Jason. The patient already had fluids running through an IV. Jason took lidocaine, atropine, and epinephrine off the cart and quickly injected each medication into the line.

"Stand back," Jason said again and pressed the button. Another spasm shook the man, and this time the heart erupted into a normal rhythm. Jason grabbed his stethoscope and listened to the heartbeat, which sounded normal. He listened to both sides of his chest and heard air rushing into both lungs as the nurse pressed the Ambu bag.

"Where's intensive care unit in this hospital?" Jason asked. Nurse Chapman continued pressing the Ambu bag but did not answer. "Nurse Chapman!" he said sharply.

"It's—" She swallowed. "—it's two floors down."

"Let's go. Keep pushing air into his lungs. I'll pull the bed." Jason grabbed the rail and started maneuvering the bed through the door.

"Doctor, we just can't just take him down there. We have to get permission from the resident who's running the ICU. They get *really* mad if we don't follow protocol." Her voice sounded almost fearful. Jason thought perhaps the nurses were reprimanded, or even fired, if protocol was not followed.

"I don't know anything about your protocol, but we're taking this man to the ICU now!" Jason took a deep breath and moderated his sharp tone. This was not her fault, after all. "Look, I'm new here. I don't know what this man needs now to survive, and we need to get him to someone who does." He pulled on the heavy bed and, after some difficulty, moved it into the hallway and then into the elevator. The orderlies made it look so easy.

Two floors down, they stood in front of the large doors that were the entrance to the intensive care unit. They were locked. Jason leaned on the buzzer next to the doors.

"Can I help you?" a sweet voice asked.

"Please open the door, ma'am. We have a critically ill man here we need to drop off," Jason calmly responded.

"You can't just bring a patient here." The sweet voice changed into a harsh pitch. "Have you cleared this with our resident?"

"Just open the door now, lady!" Jason didn't try to hide his fury and noticed Nurse Chapman's startled look.

A minute later, a doctor who Jason surmised was the ICU resident appeared at the door. He was in wrinkled blue surgical scrubs and was rubbing his eyes, obviously just awakened from a deep sleep.

He glared at Jason. "What do you think you're doing?"

"We need your help, sir. This man just coded. We resuscitated him, and he needs the intensive care unit and your expertise. C'mon, let's get him into a room. I don't even know if his heart is still in rhythm. He was in ventricular fibrillation."

The resident scowled for a moment and then opened the doors and helped move him into an empty ICU room. The ICU nurses attached electrodes to the heart monitor, replaced the now-empty IV bag hanging from the pole, brought in a respirator, and attached it to the endotracheal tube. The ICU resident gave orders to the nurse for the settings on the respirator. Jason saw that the man's heart rhythm was normal and that he was waking up and starting to become combative. The resident ordered the nurse to give him a sedative, and the patient became still once again.

The resident turned to Jason. "So what's the story with this patient?"

"I have no idea. I responded to his code, and Nurse Chapman and I were the only ones there. He was in ventricular fibrillation, I shocked him a couple of times, and he went back into a normal rhythm. Oh, and I did give him lidocaine, epinephrine, and atropine after the first shock. I guess I should write a note in his chart." Jason smiled apologetically at Nurse Chapman and asked her to go fetch the patient's chart.

The ICU resident was staring at Jason. "Who intubated him?"

"I did." Jason tried to keep the irritation out of his voice, but he was becoming angrier by the minute. "I don't understand. No one else came to this code. It was just Nurse Chapman and myself. Isn't there some sort of system when a code is called?" he asked.

"No, when a code is called, everyone is supposed to respond." The resident cleared his throat, not quite meeting Jason's eyes. "I guess I didn't hear the code over the loudspeakers, and the nurses didn't wake me."

"That's insane." Jason took a deep breath and closed his eyes briefly. "Where was the night float? I was told that there was a resident designated as the night float who was always in the hospital for emergencies." He couldn't understand why the night float had not come to the code.

"There is." The resident shrugged. "He was probably sleeping as well. But relax. You did good." He smiled and put a hand on Jason's shoulder. "It looks like he is going to be fine." The resident took the patient's blood pressure and listened to his heart and lungs once more and then turned around to face Jason. "You must be one of the new interns. I'm Sean Kennedy. What were you doing in the hospital this time of day?"

Jason managed to force a smile. "I'm Jason Green."

The nurse returned from the floor with the patient's chart, and Jason wrote a brief note recording the events. He ended the note by writing: *Nurse Chapman saved this man's life*. She still looked rattled as Jason handed the chart to her with a smile. "Thanks for your help, Dr. Kennedy." He paused at the door, looking back at the patient, and then left the ICU, distressed at what had occurred but thankful for what appeared to be a good outcome.

Jason hurried back down to his unit, finished writing his last progress note, and left the hospital hurriedly at three in the morning. He was still rattled and angry, mostly with himself for not going to the Code Blue at first call. And he needed to get over it if he wanted to sleep. He walked quickly to his apartment two blocks away, set the alarm clock for four-thirty a.m., and fell immediately into a sound sleep.

When the alarm woke him, he put on his shorts, T-shirt, and tennis shoes and went for his three-mile run, which he had mapped out on his first day of arrival a week ago. It was a humid and stifling hot early July morning, and most New York runners would be in an air-conditioned gym because of the heat. But for a boy from Mississippi, it felt like home, and he finished his run in twenty-two minutes.

The rotten smells of the garbage piled high on the sidewalks, the tall buildings that lined the streets, and the unending noise of the New York City traffic were foreign to him. The concrete slabs on the sidewalks were uneven, and Jason quickly learned to closely watch so that he didn't trip. He ran fast and took care to avoid running into other pedestrians. He had also learned on his first day in New York City that his salutations of "good morning ma'am," or "good morning, sir" to people he crossed paths with on the street were usually ignored or met with a nasty look. He had made it his private challenge to get a smile from the locals and so he persisted.

He returned to his apartment, showered, ate a bowl of bran flakes and a protein bar, and walked back to the hospital, arriving on the floor by six-thirty a.m., in time to visit a few patients before Seth Goldberg and his two medical students arrived.

CHAPTER 2

Morning, Jason." Seth approached with a wide smile. "Hope you had a good night's sleep. It's likely to be a hectic day."

Jason noticed that Dr. Goldberg used the same Calvin Klein Obsession cologne that he used. "Good morning to you, Dr. Goldberg," he said with a smile. He wasn't about to admit that he had gotten only a little over an hour of sleep.

"If you call me Dr. Goldberg one more time, I'll kick your ass. What time did you get out of here?"

"It doesn't matter. But I do need to tell you something. Zachary Kline—he's the other intern on the floor—struggled pretty hard yesterday." Jason frowned and hesitated. "And his resident was nowhere to be found. I helped him get through his admissions, but he needs his resident. I wonder if you would mind talking to him." He felt embarrassed and was obviously tentative, but he knew that Zach was in for a bad time unless he had resident supervision.

"What happened?" Seth's eyes narrowed. After a noticeable pause, Seth ordered Jason to tell him.

"It doesn't matter," Jason said matter-of-factly. "Suffice it to say, Zach's very bright and is a very nice guy, but he needs help. It's like my daddy says: it's a problem of not seeing the forest because of all the trees."

Seth chuckled. "Did you say 'daddy'?"

"I beg your pardon," Jason said in an exaggerated southern drawl. "My father."

"I'll talk to his resident. He has a reputation for disappearing. Any other problems yesterday?"

Jason paused. "Yes, one more thing. I went to five Code Blues yesterday. There were at least twenty people at every code except the last one."

Seth looked at Jason intently. "And what happened with the last one?"

"It was one nurse and myself. Apparently, when a code is called, people just show up. There aren't any designated doctors or other medical personnel who are notified and required to show up."

Seth nodded. "Yeah, I've seen that happen a few times in past few years. So what happened at the code?"

"It all ended fine. We got the patient down to the intensive care unit. But shouldn't there be a system that ensures that competent medical people will show up no matter what time of day or night?" Jason tried to stay calm but was unable to hide his anger as the two students walked quickly to join them.

Seth shrugged. "You're right. It's just been a tradition that when a code is called, anyone who can possibly break away runs to the code. And what you experienced happens only rarely. Look, after rounds, why don't you run over to the chief residents' office and tell them what happened? They want to meet you, anyway. C'mon, let's round."

Jason grabbed the thirteen charts, wondering why and concerned that the chief residents would want to meet him. He led the way, going into each patient's room with a good morning greeting and holding the patient's hand as he described to Seth the events that had occurred the prior day and what new orders had been written. Jason and Seth would then perform a brief physical examination, inviting the students to examine the abnormal findings. After each patient, the group would stand outside the door, and Seth would discuss various medical problems, citing statistics, diagnostic procedures, and the efficacy of various treatments. Jason listened intently, impressed with Seth's knowledge. Occasionally Seth would challenge Jason with a question, and Jason would immediately answer, citing an article from one of the medical journals. Jason noticed that Seth smiled and nodded each time he answered his questions.

After rounds, Seth reminded Jason to run over and talk to the two chief residents about the code situation while Seth talked with the students about their patients. Jason walked quickly over to the Department of Internal Medicine offices, intending to relate the problem but not offer any solutions. The offices were in an older part of the huge complex. The walls were lined with pictures of all the past internal medicine chief residents starting in the 1920s. He had met the current chief residents, Dr. Ryan and Dr. Santiago, only briefly at the intern orientation session the previous week. They both had the reputation of being brilliant as well as great teachers. Their door was closed, and Jason knocked lightly.

"Come in," one of them yelled.

Jason opened the door to a large office with two desks facing each other, a couch with two lounge chairs facing the couch, and two walls of shelves packed with books and journals. The smell of books and journals was familiar and reminded him of his father's library in Mississippi. On the couch sat the two chief residents, and on one of the lounge chairs sat Dr. Henry Stern, chairman of the department, whom Jason had not personally met. He recognized him from a National Institutes of Health conference at which Jason had presented data from his medical school research a year ago. Dr. Stern had asked him some difficult questions following his presentation, but Jason was certain Dr. Stern wouldn't remember him. It was just as well, he thought, since he recalled that Dr. Stern had not appeared satisfied with his answers. All three men stared at Jason, and the silence made him uncomfortable.

"I beg your pardon. I can come back later." Jason quickly turned to leave.

Dr. Stern stopped him. "Are you quitting already, Dr. Green?"

Jason turned around, surprised that Dr. Stern knew his name.

"You've just been doing this for one day."

"No, sir. I just wanted to make the chief residents aware of a potential problem. My resident suggested that I talk with the chief residents. I can do it later. I'm sorry to have disturbed your meeting." Jason could tell that the three men were amused by his southern accent as he turned to leave.

One of the chief residents smiled. "What is it, Dr. Green? Come in and sit down. We have the time."

Jason hesitated but then sat in the remaining lounge chair. He described concisely the first four codes that he had attended and then looked directly at each of them. "The last code that I attended, well, it was just one nurse and myself."

All three were silent, staring at him, and after another uncomfortable pause, Dr. Stern asked, "So what's the problem, Green?"

Jason tried to suppress his look of surprise at that question, but he knew he was not successful. "Well, the problem, sir, is that I doubt that an intern on his first day should be running a code by himself. I happened to still be in the hospital, but had I not been there, that poor nurse would probably still be down there by herself resuscitating that patient. I just think that in a hospital of this size and reputation, a nurse and an intern should not be the only ones at a code, no matter what time of day."

"Anything else, Dr. Green?" Henry Stern asked.

"No, sir. I'm sorry to have interrupted your meeting." He felt himself flushing as he got up and left the office. He felt foolish and was upset that he hadn't asked Seth to relate the problem to the chief residents.

Jason returned to his unit to find the students writing notes on their patients and Seth reading the progress notes that Jason had written on their patients.

"These progress notes are impressive. So how did your meeting go with the chief residents?" Seth inquired.

Jason tried not to scowl. "Not so well. Dr. Stern was there and didn't seem too pleased that a new intern was already complaining."

"You did the right thing. Honestly, Jason, I didn't tell you, but they were already aware of the situation, and they were particularly amused that your code was the only one that had a good outcome. I heard that your code was at two in the morning. What in God's name were you doing here at that time?" Seth seemed concerned. "You'll be no good to anyone today."

"I told you, I spent time helping Zach. His resident seemed to be invisible for the entire day," Jason answered sharply. He was still upset about his meeting, and he was starting the day fatigued.

A floor nurse approached the two doctors. "Dr. Goldberg, there's a new admission in ninety-two ten who is pretty sick."

"I'll go see the patient." Jason stood up, happy to end the uncomfortable discussion with Seth. "If the patient is okay, I'll break out and come to the conference room at ten to be with y'all."

Jason entered the patient's room to find a young woman, about thirty years of age, breathing rapidly and in some distress. He asked the nurse to start oxygen and sat down to take a medical history. He then performed a physical examination and found that she had the classic signs of congestive heart failure and a very large heart. He took her hand. "Miriam, you have a heart problem," he said confidently. "This is sometimes seen after a virus infection like you had two weeks ago. I'm going to put a needle into a vein in your arm, and the nurse will give you some medicine that is going to make you feel much better."

Jason continued to talk with her, explaining her problem and what she could expect. As he was talking, he inserted the needle and threaded a catheter into her vein without the patient even realizing it had been done.

He touched her cheek and smiled at her. "I'll be back a little later to see how you are doing. If you need anything at all, just press this button, and we'll come running."

The oxygen had already made her feel better. He found the nurse caring for her, explained her medical problems, and asked the nurse to administer furosemide, a diuretic, into her vein to remove the excessive fluid in her lungs. After he wrote the admission orders for the patient, he saw that he was already ten minutes late for attending rounds and hurried into the conference room.

"Good of you to join us, Green." Dr. Glassman's voice held a hint of sarcasm.

"I'm sorry, sir. I had an admission that I had to take care of."

"Let's hear about the admission, then."

"Sir, if it's all right with you and with Dr. Goldberg, I think this would be a very interesting patient for one of the students to work up and present to you at tomorrow's rounds."

Dr. Glassman didn't respond, and there was complete

silence in the room. Jason looked at Seth and noticed he wore a worried expression. He then looked back at Dr. Glassman and after an uncomfortable silence, continued, "Sir, I'll go over the patient with Dr. Goldberg after attending rounds to make certain I've made a proper assessment and haven't left anything out of her workup and care plan. But this is a great patient for the students."

"Then let's go see the other patients." Dr. Glassman was obviously displeased at Jason's challenge.

The team went into each of the other patients' rooms. Once again Jason gave a concise update on each patient as Dr. Glassman listened without expression. Outside each patient's room, Seth commented on various aspects of the patient's medical issues. Dr. Glassman would then ask probing questions, which Jason realized nudged their thought process in the proper direction, causing Jason to smile. Seth answered Dr. Glassman's questions, usually responding brilliantly and citing articles from the medical literature to support his answers. On the rare occasion that Seth seemed unable to respond, Jason would interject, citing an article complete with authors, journal, and date. Seth looked at Jason in surprise each time, but with a smile, while Dr. Glassman merely stared at him without emotion.

After rounds were completed, Jason returned to the nursing station to find two more new admissions awaiting him. Dr. Glassman, Seth, and the students returned to the conference room. Jason sat at the nursing station, concerned that he might have offended Dr. Glassman. It seemed pretty clear that Dr. Glassman didn't like him. Jason had never met a man who showed virtually no emotion in conversation.

What was most upsetting to Jason was that Harvey Glassman was the reason that he had chosen this medical center to do his internal medicine training. Dr. Glassman had won a Nobel Prize for pioneering techniques in genetic engineering. Jason had read virtually all of his research. Dr. Glassman had developed methods for transferring genes from one organism to another, such as the transfer of the gene responsible for making insulin into a bacterium. He had also developed methods for synthesizing genes of known structure and inserting them into the genetic code of a host organism. His work ultimately resulted in the development of insulin-producing bacteria in the early 1980s, which in turn resulted in an unlimited supply of insulin for individuals with diabetes. His research literally opened up whole new fields of research in medicine, agriculture, and industrial biotechnology.

Jason knew that Dr. Glassman was a pioneering genius, and, although aging, he continued to run a highly productive laboratory at the medical school that was funded by millions of NIH dollars and employed seven postdoctoral fellows. These postdoc fellows had already received a PhD in genetic engineering or a related field and were promising researchers in their own right. To be able to work as a postdoc fellow in Harvey Glassman's lab was tantamount to a ticket for a professorship at any academic institution of his or her choosing. Jason shook his head, wondering if he had made the right decision in coming to New York.

He was writing orders on another new patient he had worked up when he saw Seth, Dr. Glassman, and the students exiting the conference room at noon. Dr. Glassman walked quickly toward the elevators.

"Dr. Glassman?" Jason shouted as he ran to catch up with him.

Dr. Glassman turned around. "Yes, Dr. Green, what is it?"

"I would like to spend some time in your lab, if possible," Jason answered without hesitation.

"That wouldn't be possible, Green. Interns don't have the time for any meaningful experience in a research laboratory. It has never been done here or, as far as I know, at any institution. Forget it. Come to me after you finish your residency, and we can discuss it." Dr. Glassman turned around and headed once more to the elevators.

Jason walked behind him. "Sir, I can't accept that response. May I have just five minutes with you to try and convince you otherwise?"

Dr. Glassman turned and looked at Jason intensely for what seemed to Jason an eternity. "Come to my lab at six this evening, if you can break away from here. I have a meeting with my postdoc fellows you can sit in on, and then you can have your five minutes with me. But you're wasting your time. It's not going to happen." Harvey Glassman turned around and got into the elevator, staring at Jason as the door closed.

Jason returned to the floor. He presented the new admissions to Seth and discussed the old patients. Jason asked challenging questions about various medical issues, and Seth was almost always able to answer. When Seth didn't know the answer, he said he would find the answer at the library in the afternoon and report back. Jason could tell that Seth enjoyed their interchange, but interactions with Dr. Glassman had been disappointing for Jason.

He had learned from Sheri, the nurse whom he had helped during that first Code Blue, that Seth could be very tough. The nurses had told Seth that Dr. Kline had been almost paralyzed with his admissions and that Jason had to help him with physical exams, writing orders, and even performing a lumbar puncture. His resident had been absent the entire afternoon and evening. Sheri related to Jason with obvious relish that she saw Seth back Zach's resident against the wall and tell him that if he ever abandoned his intern again, he would personally make certain that he never finished his internal medicine training at this institution.

For the remainder of the afternoon, Jason completed admitting six patients to his service, involving the students as much as possible. He went back to each of his old patients, reviewed their charts, spoke to each patient about treatment and plans, and wrote orders. He discharged several patients who had recovered enough to leave the hospital. An elderly lady who had been admitted with pneumonia grabbed Jason and hugged him tightly after he had finished giving her discharge instructions.

Seth returned to floor just before five to make certain that the students had completed their assigned patient workups and then sent them home to study the medical issues related to their patients and to prepare their presentations to Dr. Glassman. Then he went over the patients on their service with Jason, making a few suggestions and answering the questions that he had been unable to answer earlier in the day.

"When did you last get some sleep?" Seth asked with concern in his voice.

Jason smiled. "I don't remember." But he was excited about his meeting with Dr. Glassman and would not miss it. "I think things are in order here. If it's okay with you, I'll head out and get some sleep. I know I'm supposed to be here till seven, but the nurse will call me if we get an admission before seven. I'm only a couple blocks away."

"Go on." Seth waved him away. "But don't spend too much time in Glassman's lab. It's a crazy idea. You're an intern, for Christ's sake."

That Seth knew of Jason's visit to Dr. Glassman's lab was a surprise for Jason. "Have a good night, Seth. Thanks for being such a great resident."

CHAPTER 3

Jason ran through the hospital lobby and into a hall-way that brought him to the research building that housed the labs of Dr. Harvey Glassman. His labs occupied the entire seventeenth floor of the all-glass seventeen-story Olsen Research Center. As he exited the elevator, he saw that the offices and the conference room looked out on western Manhattan Island. On the north, south, and east sides were seven separate laboratories, each headed by a postdoc fellow. Jason knew that each postdoc fellow had several PhD students and research assistants assigned to him or her. Men and women were scurrying through the halls, in and out of the various labs, and the sounds of computers, analyzers, centrifuges, and other electronic instruments brought back the familiar sense of excitement he had experienced doing research in college and medical school. Jason drew a deep breath, heart pounding. He knew that he would have to be very persuasive to convince Dr. Glassman to let him join one of the groups.

It was six-oh-five and the lab meeting had already begun. Jason carefully opened the door leading into the large conference room, closing the door behind him, and took one of the empty seats at the mahogany conference table, attracting looks of surprise from the seven postdoctoral fellows. Dr. Glassman glanced briefly at Jason without acknowledging him. The fellow on Dr. Glass-man's right was explaining the data from his experi-ments, describing the isolation of a new gene that he be-lieved regulated proglucagon gene expression, resulting in the production of a glucagon-like peptide. Dr. Glass-man asked several questions and turned to a Chinese re-searcher who headed the bioinformatics section of Dr. Glassman's laboratory.

Jason had read several articles on which Dr. Chao Fang had been first author, and since he was the only Asian postdoc fellow at the conference table, he assumed that he must be Dr. Fang. Jason was well aware that Dr. Glass-man had developed one of the most sophisticated bioin-formatics laboratories in the country, having created com-puter programs that were able to retrieve, organize, and analyze enormous amounts of biological data. Dr. Glass-man's bioinformatics lab collaborated with hundreds of laboratories from other institutions, including one lab at the University of Mississippi. This section of Glassman's lab had interested Jason the most.

Dr. Glassman turned to Dr. Fang. "Dr. Fang, have you analyzed all the data from Dr. Peterson's experiments?"

Dr. Fang responded in a heavy Chinese accent. "Yes, but the data does not meet statistical significance."

Dr. Glassman did not seem pleased. "Dr. Peterson, what do you have to say?"

"Dr. Glassman, I am certain of the data. I'm certain this is the gene I've been looking for. I may need to per-form several more studies before the data becomes statis-tically significant." Dr. Peterson's face tightened, and Ja-son noticed that he clenched both fists.

"You've spent a lot of money, and you have a lot of data there. If it's not statistically significant with the amount of data you have already accumulated, you need to stop wasting money and move on." Dr. Glassman ordered, his irritation clear. "Any comments from anyone?"

Jason understood Dr. Peterson's clenched fists. He had expected Dr. Glassman's response. Jason sat forward and, with a confident tone, said, "I would suggest changing the data analysis from binary to a natural logarithm with perhaps a base of three or five. I'm assuming that has not been done, in which case it is an easy transition, and frequently that conversion will clean the data up."

Everyone looked at Jason with a blank stare, including Dr. Glassman. The only sounds in the conference room were the hiss of air rushing through the ventilation ducts and the distant wail of an ambulance.

Dr. Glassman finally turned to Dr. Fang. "Can you do that?"

Dr. Fang glared at Jason. "I will have to get one of the programmers to work on it. I do not think that conversion will make a difference."

Jason looked at Dr. Fang, feeling his face get hot. "If your programs are Java- or Perl-based, I can do it for you in ten minutes."

Dr. Glassman turned to one of the other postdoctoral fellows and asked for an update without responding to Jason. Jason thought that perhaps he should have kept quiet, but he had seen similar problems easily solved by simple mathematical conversions and was surprised that Dr. Fang had not suggested it. Jason had taught himself statistics while doing research in college and medical school and had a profound understanding of statistical analysis that he guessed the other postdoc fellows didn't possess—or they were simply afraid to speak up.

Each postdoctoral fellow gave an update on his or her research efforts. There were questions from Dr. Glassman and discussions and suggestions from the other postdoctoral fellows. Jason kept quiet for the remainder of the session, although he noticed that Dr. Glassman glanced at him frequently during the discussions. After forty-five minutes, Dr. Glassman stood up.

"Okay, that's all. We'll meet as usual on Friday afternoon. Dr. Green, come with me."

Jason noticed that the postdoc fellows stared at him as he followed Dr. Glassman out of the conference room. He gave a faint smile and nod to them as he left the room.

Jason followed Dr. Glassman to his office. He looked to be in his seventies. He walked with a stoop but was quick paced. He was short, thin, and balding, with piercing hazel eyes. Jason had always thought he had the ability to sense an individual's emotions or thoughts when engaged in conversation, but Dr. Glassman gave no hint of what he was thinking or feeling when he talked, and that made Jason uncomfortable. Glassman walked into his office, sat down at his desk, and motioned Jason to sit in a chair across from him. His desk had two twenty-seven-inch computer monitors. Shelves packed with books and journals lined two full walls of his office. On the credenza behind his desk were framed pictures of his wife and three daughters.

Dr. Glassman looked tired. "So what are you wanting, Dr. Green?"

"Sir, I'm just wanting to spend some time in your lab. It is really your research and writings that made me want to come here."

"You are obviously from the South. Is your family still there?" Dr. Glassman asked.

"I grew up in Mississippi, sir. My daddy has a business there. My mother passed away two years ago. My sister lives in New Orleans. She is an elementary school teacher. I have a very small family, most of them are in Europe."

"What is your ancestry?"

Jason blinked, unable to hide his surprise at Dr.

Glassman's line of questioning. "German and Austrian. My eight great-grandparents and most of their offspring were all killed in concentration camps. My grandparents were first-generation Americans." Jason caught, for the first time, a hint of emotion in Dr. Glassman's expression.

"What's so interesting about my lab?"

"Well, I have some background in genetic research, which I accomplished in medical school. I can email you the papers I coauthored if you're interested. When I was in college, I majored in biomedical engineering and became interested in bioinformatics. I developed some software programs that helped analyze data that had come from research that I participated in. We were measuring the strength of various metals used in joint replacements. Anyway, I saw the power of computers in aiding with data analysis, and I know you have one of the best bioinformatics labs in the country. I just wanted to spend some time becoming familiar with your research, learning as much as I could, and hopefully after I finish my internal medicine training, perhaps convince you to let me join your lab for a few years. It's really that simple."

After an uncomfortable pause, Dr. Glassman replied, "I've read your articles, including your college articles. I was impressed with your presentation at the NIH last year. Why didn't you just get your PhD and forget about medicine?"

Jason didn't remember seeing Dr. Glassman at that NIH conference. "Never, sir. " He spoke quietly, but emphatically. "I love medicine, and I love taking care of patients. I'll always be involved in patient care. I don't want to sound patronizing, but I think you're the perfect role model in terms of how to mix research and patient care. Not that I expect to ever be as successful as you've been. But I'd like to try."

"Why didn't you do a combined MD/PhD program, then?"

"Sir, I thought it would be a waste of my time. I'm already quite familiar with methodology. I mean, you only have an MD, and you've won a Nobel Prize."

"Dr. Green, you were in the hospital until three o'clock this morning. How do you expect to spend any time in a research lab?"

Jason was shocked that Dr. Glassman would know how late he was in the hospital. "Sir, yesterday was very unusual, and I should have been out of the hospital by five or six. Unavoidable circumstances kept me in the hospital for a long time." He was very self-conscious of his deep southern accent, particularly when he talked rapidly, and he tried to slow down. "I know that my priority is taking good care of my patients and teaching the students. But I've learned to use my time wisely, and I'm fairly efficient in my clinical work. I think that I'd be able to spend a few hours in the evening on at least some of my non-admitting days and several hours on the weekend. Of course, only if y'all are also working on the weekends. I don't expect to be allowed in the lab by myself." He spread his hands. "And I doubt I will contribute much. I expect I will take much more than I can give."

There was a long pause. "Okay, Green, you and that charming southern accent have convinced me." Dr. Glassman opened a drawer and took out a key. He looked up at Jason, and said after another pause, "Dr. Green, it was no accident that I'm your attending these eight weeks. The professor who interviewed you for your internship here is a good friend of mine, and he told me of your interest in my lab. Well, anyway, here is a key to the lab. You need to pick one of the postdoc fellows and follow along with him. Did you have a favorite?"

"Well, I'm particularly interested in your bioinformatics program, so if you agree, I'd love to hang out with Dr. Fang, although I sensed he didn't like me."

Dr. Glassman smiled for the first time. "Don't worry about Fang. He doesn't like to be challenged. He is brilliant and a good choice. I'll let him know that he is to allow you to, as you say, hang out with him. But you are to leave this lab now and go home. I understand you haven't slept in about two days. No hanging out tonight."

"Thank you very much, Dr. Glassman. I *am* very grateful and won't disappoint you."

Jason got up and left the office. As he approached the elevator, he heard Dr. Fang behind him say, "Excuse me. I am Chao Fang." He shook Jason's hand, a flimsy handshake to be sure.

"I'm Jason Green. It's nice to meet you, Dr. Fang. I'm an intern over in the hospital but would like to spend some time with you in the lab over the next year or two."

"Did you say you could program my software to convert binary to natural logarithm?"

Jason had difficulty understanding his English. "Is your program in Java or Perl?"

"Java."

"It's very easy. I can do it for you now if you like."

Dr. Fang gave him a suspicious look. "Is there a risk of disrupting the rest of the program?"

"No chance at all." Jason shook his head definitively. "It's a simple addition to your current program."

"Come with me, then."

Jason followed Fang into the computer room. Fang entered the passwords, and Jason took over. He spent the next twenty-five minutes adding the necessary program. He then explained how to use the addition to Dr. Fang and demonstrated with a few examples.

They then ran Dr. Peterson's data through the logarithmic analysis. It was instantly clear that Dr. Peterson's data easily met statistical significance. Dr. Fang looked at Jason and smiled. As Jason was getting up to leave, he turned around to see Dr. Glassman standing at the door.

"I see that you were correct about Peterson's data, Dr. Green. But I expect that when you are in my lab you will do as I say. Get out of here now and go home."

Jason shivered inside at Dr. Glassman's cold tone. Jason rode down the elevator with Dr. Glassman, in silence.

"Do you need a ride to your apartment?"

"No, sir. I'm just a block from here. But thank you."

Jason went home, put on his shorts and running shoes, and went for another run. He showered and slept undisturbed until the alarm woke him at four thirty the next morning.

CHAPTER 4

Jason's move to New York City had not been an easy transition, mostly because he missed his father who had always been his closest companion, even before his mother had passed away. His father had taught him an appreciation and love for music, which Jason thought had always kept him grounded and sane. His earliest memories were of sitting on his father's lap on Saturday and Sunday mornings, listening to a Beethoven symphony or a Brahms piano concerto. Or to the Dave Brubeck Quartet's 1963 Carnegie Hall concert, which he had listened to obsessively since he was a young boy. His father would smoke a pipe or cigar as they sat and listened, and now just the aroma of cigar or pipe smoke would bring a sense of comfort to Jason. He had started piano lessons at age five, and, by the time he graduated high school, he had become a reasonably accomplished classical pianist, having won several state competitions.

His father had also encouraged him to read at an early age and had made a list of what he considered to be the greatest one hundred classic books. Jason and his father would read each book at the same time and discuss them, and, by the time he was sixteen, they had completed all one hundred books. When he had finished the final book, his father gave him his grandfather's gold Rolex watch, and Jason had worn it every day since. His favorite book had been Maugham's *Of Human Bondage*, which he had since reread dozens of times. Jason called his father daily, reporting his interactions with the other interns and residents, and particularly with Dr. Glassman, and he eagerly looked forward to his father's visit to New York City to spend Thanksgiving weekend with him.

Jason had been able to explore some of New York City the week before his internship began. The frenetic pace of the city was new to him: the constant noise of congested traffic, the quick strides of the pedestrians, the piles of garbage on the sidewalks, the endless potholes in the streets and the city workers trying to fill them, and the sulfur-scented steam seeping through cracks in the streets and sidewalks from sewers and subways. Jason wondered how anyone could remain sane living in such an environment. But many of the neighborhoods were beautiful, with turn-of-the-century façades and elegant doorways in front of which stood uniformed men to keep out the uninvited.

He got a last-minute ticket to see *Les Miserables* and was moved by the music. The story was already very familiar. He'd read Hugo's book in middle school. He spent hours at the Metropolitan Museum of Art and the Museum of Modern Art, overwhelmed by their collections, and he spent hours walking and eating in the Chinese district.

He went to a gay club his second night in New York City, his first foray ever into such a venue. There were no gay clubs in his small hometown, and, although he had been curious, he had never garnered the courage to visit gay clubs when he traveled to larger cities. He was struck by the energy in the club, the unending rhythm of the loud but tasteless music and hundreds of bare-chested men, eyes darting here and there, looking for their next liaison. Jason had never seen so many gay men in one place except on the news, usually in parades, and while he found the scene new and interesting, he felt out of place. He quickly realized that his model looks made him an object of unwanted attention, and he was approached numerous times. He even had a decent conversation with a surgical resident from another hospital, but the conversation ended with the resident wanting to take him home. Jason politely declined all invitations and left after an hour.

On his way home, he darted into a cigar bar and stood at the entrance, taking in the fragrance of the pipe and cigar smoke. A calm feeling returned, and he went home to his four-hundred-square-foot apartment that was barely affordable on his annual salary of forty-five thousand dollars. His apartment consisted of a small room that served as his bedroom and living room, furnished with a pullout bed, a small desk with a chair where his computer was kept, a small breakfast table, and a cabinet that housed his stereo system with speakers on either side. A tiny bathroom and kitchenette completed the small apartment. The $2,000 monthly rent would have gotten him a sixteen-hundred-square-foot modern apartment in Mississippi. But he quickly adapted. He cleaned the apartment meticulously, hung posters of Albert Einstein, Yo-Yo Ma, and Martin Luther King on his walls, and placed pictures of his father, mother, and sister next to his bed.

Jason's life became routine after the first week of his internship. He awoke to the alarm at four-thirty a.m., went for his run, ate a bowl of cereal with fruit that he picked up weekly at a nearby market, and was on his unit by six a.m. He would review the charts of all his patients until Seth and the students arrived, and on rounds he would give updates on all the patients, except for those that the students were following. Jason and Seth became great working partners. Jason knew that Seth made extraordinary efforts to find and teach him medical information that he had not yet discovered. Seth had exceeded all the expectations Jason had for a resident, and he felt fortunate after listening to the frequent complaints of his fellow interns with whom Jason would have lunch or supper at the hospital. Jason was extremely organized and efficient in his work, and while many of the interns wouldn't finish on their admitting days until nine or ten o'clock at night, he had usually completed all his work by five or six and would spend time with Seth or the students.

On non-admitting days, and even on some admitting days, he would go to Dr. Glassman's laboratory and work with Dr. Fang and the other postdoc fellows. He would leave the lab by nine or ten every night, occasionally dropping into a nearby cigar bar to briefly enjoy the aroma, and then go home. His days had become comfortable.

෴

Three weeks into his internship, one of Jason's patients, Ellie Shapiro, fell when she tried to move from her hospital bed to the bedside commode. Jason ran into her room after being called by the nurse and saw Mrs. Shapiro lying on the floor, obviously in pain. Mrs. Shapiro had been admitted to the hospital two days previously for a bleeding ulcer and had required four units of blood before the bleeding had finally stopped.

"Oh, Mrs. Shapiro, I'm so sorry. You know you should have called the nurse to help you." Jason was strong and lifted her by himself back into the bed, causing her pain to briefly worsen.

"I'm sorry, Dr. Green. I thought I could do it myself, and I didn't want to disturb the nurse. She works so hard."

Jason examined her and then ordered pain medication and a portable X-ray of her hip, which confirmed the fractured hip that he had suspected. He called the orthopedic department to request a consultation and then sat with her, holding her hand and explaining what would likely have to be done to fix the fracture. He touched her cheek and went back to the nursing station to call her family and write a note in her chart.

Thirty minutes later, as Jason was writing orders on another patient, he saw a doctor in green surgical scrubs walk into Mrs. Shapiro's room. He followed him into her room and was immediately struck by the surgeon's good looks. He was tall, with an athletic build, moderately long blond hair, deep-blue eyes, full lips, and a beautiful square face with a perfect, light complexion.

"Mrs. Shapiro, I'm Dr. Olsen, the chief resident on the orthopedic service. You've fractured your hip and are going to need surgery."

Jason watched him as he stood over Mrs. Shapiro, who was obviously frightened and upset. Jason saw the surgeon briefly glance at him.

"We're going to operate on you in the morning," Dr. Olsen went on, "and then, when the medical doctors say it's okay, we'll send you to a rehab facility to get you up and walking again. I'll have the nurse bring the consent forms for you to sign, and we'll bring you over to surgery sometime tomorrow morning." He patted her on the shoulder and turned around to walk out.

"Wait, Doctor," Mrs. Shapiro yelled, terrified. "Who is going to do the surgery, and what exactly is going to be done?"

Jason became upset as he watched Dr. Olsen stand impatiently at the door, obviously in a hurry to return to his previous work. "You don't have to worry about any of that. Everything is going to be fine. Let us do the worrying," Dr. Olsen said without emotion. He turned quickly and walked out of the room.

"I'll be right back, Mrs. Shapiro." Jason hurried out of the room and caught up with the orthopedic surgeon. He didn't try to disguise his anger. "Excuse me, sir, but what you just did in there was completely inappropriate."

The surgeon stopped and turned around to face Jason. "Who in the hell do you think you are?" He stood in front of Jason with an angry stare, close enough that Jason could smell the coffee on his breath and the Old Spice deodorant, the same that his father used.

"I'm nobody, and that's really not the question. I don't appreciate you treating my patient like she is an idiot. She's very intelligent—an editor for a publishing house—and she deserves to have her questions answered and to be treated with dignity. Why can't you take five minutes to sit down with her, reassure her, and answer all her questions? She is obviously terrified."

Jason noticed that several nurses had stopped their work and were watching with astonished looks on their faces. Jason was also aware of his exaggerated southern accent and flushed face.

The surgeon was trying to stare him down, but Jason stared back, not blinking or backing down. They stood face-to-face for twenty seconds in silence. The surgeon turned and walked back into Mrs. Shapiro's room. Jason followed him in, after getting Mrs. Shapiro's chart. Dr. Olsen sat down next to Mrs. Shapiro and apologized to her. He then spent twenty minutes explaining the surgery, recovery, and surgical team. He answered several questions as Jason sat and listened, writing in Mrs. Shapiro's chart as the two talked.

As they were finishing, he handed the chart to Dr. Olsen and returned to the nursing station to write orders on his other patients.

A few minutes later, the orthopedic surgeon left Mrs. Shapiro's room and came to the nursing station. The surgeon sat down with her chart and wrote a note. Jason caught occasional glimpses as he continued writing his orders on his other patients. Dr. Olsen finally put down the chart and looked up.

"Excuse me." He tapped Jason on the shoulder. Jason looked up and was, again, struck by his good looks. "I'm sorry for what happened. You were right to correct me."

"No apology necessary, sir. Thank you for going back in. I'm grateful to you, and I know Mrs. Shapiro is very grateful."

Dr. Olsen no longer had the angry stare, and Jason studied his face during a rather long pause. "I'm Phil Olsen."

"I'm Jason Green. It's nice to meet you, Dr. Olsen."

"It's Phil. You must be Seth Goldberg's intern."

"How would you know that?" Jason asked, surprised.

"Seth and I are good friends. He mentioned that his new intern was from the South, and I gather from your accent that you're from the South." Phil smiled for the first time. "There aren't too many people around here with that kind of accent."

"Well, I'll have to work on my accent, but yes, I'm Seth's intern." Jason gave what felt like a crooked smile. "I'm sorry if I seemed impertinent, but I figured you were in a hurry and that I wouldn't have a lot of time to convince you to go back in there. Thank you for doing that." He began flushing again. He hated that he flushed so easily.

They continued looking at each other, and after another uncomfortable pause, Phil said, "I was actually going to call you."

Now Jason was not only flushing but also confused. "Call *me*?"

"I was going to ask you to go to dinner with me. Seth said I would enjoy your company. Anyway, now I have an excuse to ask you. It would be a good way to apologize for the way I acted with Mrs. Shapiro."

"No apology is necessary, really." His face still felt warm, and Jason wondered whether he was being asked out on a date.

Another pause. "Are you busy this Saturday evening?" Phil persisted.

"I was planning on working in the lab—"

"Seth told me you were doing some lab work. I've never heard of such a thing," Phil interrupted. Jason didn't answer. "Well, you have to eat. How about if I pick you up in front of the hospital at seven?"

"You have a car in the city?" Jason couldn't keep the surprise out of his voice. Everybody used cabs or the subway.

"Yes, the restaurant I'd like to go to is too far away to walk to, and anyway, it's supposed to rain on Saturday."

"Is this a fancy place? Do I need to get dressed up and all? I really don't want to go to an expensive place. Medical interns don't get paid what orthopedic surgeons get paid."

Phil seemed impatient. "Don't worry about it."

Jason chuckled. "Now you're treating me like you did Mrs. Shapiro."

"Khakis and a nice shirt, and the restaurant isn't expensive. See you at seven?"

Jason nodded.

Phil turned and left Jason standing alone, wondering what had just happened. The head nurse, a middle-aged lady named Sharon, approached Jason. "You certainly put Dr. Olsen in his place. I enjoyed that immensely." She laughed out loud. "You were superb."

Jason looked at the surgeon as he walked away, feeling almost paralyzed by the encounter. "What's his story?"

"Oh, he's the chief resident in orthopedics. He's supposed to be a great surgeon, but he's known for his toughness, and the orthopedic residents are all afraid of him. I have to say, though, he is one gorgeous man."

"Well, I probably just ruined his day. I was pretty nasty to him, but he deserved it."

"Honey, from what I just heard, you didn't ruin his day at all." She winked at him, and Jason felt himself blushing again.

℘℘℘

On Saturday, Jason arrived at the hospital at the usual six-thirty a.m. and reviewed his charts prior to Seth's arrival. They had an unusually large number of patients, many with complex medical problems, and they spent the entire morning completing rounds. Dr. Glassman showed up unexpectedly during the middle of their rounds and joined the group for two hours, never saying a word or asking a question, just observing. Jason had come to deeply respect Dr. Glassman over the four weeks he had been his attending, not because he had extensive clinical knowledge but rather because he was such a clear thinker. When a problem had no obvious answer, Dr. Glassman asked a question that made the answer become obvious. Jason understood that what had made him a great researcher also made him a great clinician: he knew the right questions to ask.

"Jason, try to finish up and get out of here." Seth had excused the students, and Dr. Glassman had left without saying a word. "I'm going home to watch the ball game and drink some beer. You're welcome to come over, if you like."

"Thanks, Seth, but I can't. After I finish up here, I need to spend a few hours in the lab. Then I'm going out to dinner this evening."

"I wondered if you were going to tell me." Seth grinned. "I understand you're going to dinner with my buddy, Phil Olsen."

"He told me you were friends." Jason looked up, interested. "How do you know him?"

"He was two years ahead of me at Harvard Medical School. We had mutual friends and hung out together. We've stayed friends and have lunch together almost every week." Seth laughed. "He told me about the hard time you gave him. Sounds like he deserved it." Seth laughed and slapped Jason on the shoulder. "Anyway, I can tell you I've never been able to put him in his place. He always seems to get the last word and has certainly never offered to take *me* to dinner."

"Well, I think he felt bad about Mrs. Shapiro, so this is his way of apologizing. In any case, we are going Dutch. I'm not letting him pay."

"Have fun." Seth's smile had a puzzling quirk to it. "You're going to like him. And get out of here soon."

Jason arrived in Dr. Glassman's lab at two in the afternoon, and all seven postdoc fellows, several PhD candidates, and several lab assistants were busy with experiments. Nothing unusual for a Saturday. They were all driven in their work, at least in part because of the demands that Dr. Glassman placed on them. Jason had spent time with all seven fellows, learning about their projects and coordinating their data with the bioinformatics lab and Dr. Fang. Most of his time had been spent with Dr. Fang, learning the computer programs, entering data from the other fellows' experiments, and analyzing data and statistics that resulted from the computer analysis. Although Jason had never seen such sophisticated

had discovered and corrected sev-
he programming and changed the
that data would be analyzed in both
nic fashion. He had developed a good
p with Dr. Fang.
several times to prod Dr. Fang into
life in China, but it was clear he didn't
want to discuss it. Jason guessed that he had a troubled
past and didn't want to be reminded of it or was too
proud to talk about it. Anytime Jason would question him
about his personal life, Dr. Fang would either wave his
hand as if reprimanding him or deliberately turn his back
to Jason. He did learn that Dr. Fang had emigrated from
China after graduating from Tsinghua University in Beijing with a degree in computer engineering. He had then
spent the next six years at MIT obtaining a PhD in bioinformatics, after which he joined Dr. Glassman's laboratory. He seemed very shy and didn't laugh easily, but Jason
liked him and was grateful to him for his generous men-
toring. He had the feeling that Dr. Fang liked him as well.
At least they got along comfortably.

"Dr. Fang, I have to leave early this evening." Jason
stuck his head in the lab door on his way out. "I'm going
to dinner with a friend. See you tomorrow after I finish
with my patients." He wanted to go for a run, shower, and
return to the hospital entrance by seven.

"I will not be here tomorrow. But if you want finish
working on this program change, that will be excellent. I
wish to finish the statistics on Monday." Dr. Fang's English was difficult to understand.

The other postdoc fellows frequently teased Jason that
they didn't know which was more difficult to understand,
Dr. Fang's Chinese accent or Jason's southern accent.

Jason hurried home, put on his running shoes and
shorts, and ran his usual route for the second time that

day. Then he showered and dressed. He had a limited
wardrobe. He had never given much thought to his clothing, although his mother always tried to make him dress
nicely. He knew that his father made a reasonably good
living from the family department store, but they had always lived modestly, and Jason had never asked his parents for anything material. His father had given him an
expensive stereo system with McIntosh speakers for his
graduation from medical school, and he had packed them
in his eight-year-old 1997 Jetta and set them up in his
apartment, although he couldn't get the optimal effect in
such a small apartment without disturbing his neighbors.
He had with him his most prized possessions: his Rolex
watch, his stereo system, his computer, and his CD collec-
tion of classical and jazz recordings. He only missed having his piano, but he had decided that, when he was able
to save enough, he would buy an electronic piano that he
could keep in his apartment. He dressed in khaki pants
and a madras shirt with a black T-shirt underneath.

At seven o'clock, Phil drove up to the hospital entrance
in a gray Porsche 911. Jason opened the door and got in.

"I didn't know orthopedic chief residents were paid so
well." Jason smiled as he looked at Phil. Nurse Sharon
had been correct. He was one of the most handsome men
he had ever seen. Jason thought that his straight blond
hair, blue eyes, and perfect pale skin were so opposite to
his own dark-brown curly hair, dark eyes, and darker skin
tone. He chuckled to himself.

"What's so funny?" Phil asked.

Jason laughed. "Oh, nothing. I never expected to be
driving in a Porsche in Manhattan, that's all."

"Well, don't hold it against me. My parents gave it to
me when I graduated from medical school. It's four years
old, and I have less than three thousand miles on it. It sits
in a garage most of the time."

"You don't have to be defensive," Jason said. "There's nothing wrong with having wealthy parents. Where are we off to?" He tried not to stare at Phil, but it was difficult. He was unfamiliar with the cologne Phil was wearing, but it was subtle and smelled expensive.

"Well, it's my favorite Italian restaurant, Trattoria Del'Arte, on Seventh and Fifty-Sixth. You like Italian food, don't you?"

"Of course, but I hope your taste in restaurants isn't as expensive as your taste in cars."

"Let's not argue about that. I told you I'm taking you as an apology."

Jason sighed. He could see that Phil was serious, but Jason was going to pay his own way.

"No argument." Jason made his tone light. "I can afford it."

"Give a guy a break. I'm trying to be nice and convince you I'm not the horrible person you saw in Mrs. Shapiro's room."

Jason smiled. "I know you're not a horrible guy. I sensed you were a nice guy even initially, just a nice guy in a big hurry."

"So where did you get that accent?"

"I was born and raised in Mississippi. Does it bother you?"

"No, there is a charm to it. But one doesn't associate deep southern accents with brilliance, and the rumor around the hospital is that you're brilliant."

"I tend to ignore rumors. My daddy always quotes a Jewish proverb: 'What you don't see with your eyes, don't witness with your mouth.' Those rumors are silly."

"Well, there are also rumors that you are the best-looking doctor in the hospital, and that I've witnessed with my own eyes." Phil laughed for the first time as Jason felt himself blush. "And what's with this 'daddy' talk?"

"You New Yorkers seem to have a hard time with men calling their fathers 'daddy.' That's just the way it is in the South."

The small talk continued without interruption for the ten-minute drive to Trattoria Del'Arte. The traffic was light, and it was drizzling outside. A valet came to take the car, and Jason looked around. Across the street was Carnegie Hall. He stood staring at the building, oblivious as Phil called for him to follow him into the restaurant. Phil came back and tapped him on the shoulder, startling him.

"I'm sorry. I was just looking at Carnegie Hall."

They walked into the restaurant and the maître d' walked up to Phil with a big smile. "Welcome back, Dr. Olsen. We have your table ready."

The restaurant was bustling—crowded but elegant. There was a huge antipasto bar, and the walls were decorated with large, sculpture-like paintings of body parts. The maître d' led them to a table that was just below a ten-foot-wide sculpture of a pair of lips.

Jason looked around, wide-eyed and impressed by the surroundings. "They know you here."

"My parents come here often when they come to the city, and I've been coming here with them since I was a kid."

"Where are you from?" Jason tried not to stare at Phil.

"Wilton, Connecticut. It's about sixty miles north, so I would usually come to the city with my parents at least once a month when I was growing up. We would come to this restaurant and then walk down to the theater district to see a play. Then we would stay the weekend in our apartment."

"Your folks have an apartment in New York City?" Jason couldn't disguise his surprise.

"Yeah, I've been living in it during my residency. I might as well let you know, I grew up with a silver spoon in my mouth." Phil frowned, adjusting his napkin. "At my insistence, my father and I went every Saturday morning to a soup kitchen to feed homeless people until I left for college, and I probably broke a record at Harvard for participating in various charitable events. I don't know how convincing I was."

Jason thought that Phil might be blushing.

The waiter brought a bottle of Cabernet and showed the label to Phil, who nodded. The waiter uncorked the bottle and poured wine into their glasses.

Jason looked at Phil as the waiter left. "There's no need to apologize. No one picks their parents or the circumstances into which they were born. But I think it was Benjamin Franklin who said, 'Money never made a man happy yet, nor will it.'" He picked up the glass of wine. "So here's to happiness."

Phil smiled, and they touched their glasses.

The waiter brought a large plate of antipasto to the table followed by a Caesar salad. Jason was surprised, because no menus had been offered, and the food was served without them ordering it.

Jason asked Phil question after question about his family and his hospital duties. He learned that Phil had a younger brother and sister who were still in school.

His father had come from a long line of successful attorneys and was recognized as one of the most successful trial attorneys in the country. He had made a fortune litigating asbestos cases as well as a variety of other pharmaceutical-related class action suits.

His father had wanted Phil to continue the attorney tradition, but his aptitude was more in the sciences.

He was the quarterback of his high school football team but did not continue varsity athletics in college. He went to Harvard undergraduate and medical schools, and because he had always liked working with his hands, constructing models when he was younger and building houses as a volunteer for Habitat for Humanity in college, orthopedics was a natural transition from medical school. Jason could not take his eyes off him.

Phil sat back as the waiter set a plate of fettuccini Alfredo in front of him and a plate of grouper in front of Jason. "So all we have been doing is talking about me," he said. "What about you?"

"First of all, was this a set menu? Why didn't we order off the menu like everyone else in this restaurant seems to have done?"

"I took the liberty of preordering the meal."

"That was a bit presumptuous," Jason said with genuine surprise. "What would you have done had I said I disliked grouper?"

Phil laughed. "I knew you liked grouper."

"How is that possible? I've never talked about grouper with anyone within a thousand miles of New York City."

Philip shrugged. "Well, there is a famous story about you and your internship interview at the University of Chicago. At least it's famous at Harvard." Jason blushed and Philip laughed again. "Apparently, you and the chairman of the internal medicine department talked about your love of grouper. Tell me the story."

"I can't believe that story went around Harvard. And how could you possibly know that it was me at that interview?" Jason asked.

"Because the guy at that interview from Harvard was the roommate of one of my interns. And my intern somehow heard that you were an internal medicine intern here."

Jason blinked, surprised that he was the object of any-one's conversation. "Well, it was pretty funny. Apparent-ly, at the University of Chicago, the chairman of internal medicine interviews all the intern applicants, and—unlike everywhere else, where it's one-on-one—he interviews in groups of five. Anyway, five of us were sitting outside his office, and the other four were talking about their accom-plishments." He paused in thought and took a bite of grouper. "That's right, I remember now. One of the four was from Harvard. Anyway, each was trying to outdo the other with their accomplishments. It was pretty amusing, but I do have to say they were an impressive group. Any-way, the one girl, I think she was from Stanford, asked me where I was from, and when I told her the University of Mississippi, she started laughing, and the others sort of snickered. Anyway, just at that moment, the chairman opened his door and brought us into his office. After we each told him our name and school, he proceeded to have a thirty-minute conversation with me. He completely ig-nored the other four students. I don't know if he sensed that they had made fun of me, or maybe he had a hidden microphone set up outside his office, but the other stu-dents were obviously shocked. Anyway, we mostly talked about fishing and, yes, catching grouper in the Gulf. So now I understand how you know I like grouper." He didn't tell Phil that the chairman had offered him an in-ternship position at the time of the interview, a practice that was strictly forbidden by a protocol that all of the medical schools had established and agreed to.

Phil chuckled. "That *is* funny. Tell me more about you."

Jason had a hard time taking his eyes off Philip to eat and noticed that Phil could not take his eyes off him, ei-ther. "There isn't much to tell. My daddy talked my mom into moving back to Mississippi from St. Louis, where they went to college. I was the only Jew in my school, and sometimes that was difficult." He shrugged and poked at his perfectly cooked grouper. "Not only was I a Jew, I was gay to boot, although I wasn't really out until college. Anyway, I got a full scholarship to go to the University of Mississippi, and I wasn't going to take money from my parents to go to an expensive Ivy League school. I play a little piano, I ran track in high school and college, and I did some research in college and medical school. My mom became ill with breast cancer my senior year of college, and I wanted to stay close to home so I could visit her often." He took a bite of grouper and looked back at Phil. "And so I stayed in Mississippi for medical school. She died at the end of my second year of medical school." For the first time, he took his eyes off Philip to look down, fighting to suppress the tears. "That's really about it. I'm pretty simple."

The waiter brought a port wine and a cheese board to the table.

"When did you tell your parents you were gay?" Phil asked.

"Oh, I told them when I was in middle school."

"How did they react?"

"Well, they said they had always wondered why I was never interested in going to dances or parties and that they just wanted me to be happy. And they said they expected me to marry the man of my dreams one day and give them some grandchildren."

Philip laughed as he cut a thin wedge of blue cheese. "They must have been amazing parents."

"My daddy still is." Jason smiled. "He is the best human being I've ever known."

"So you were out in college and medical school?" Phil's piercing blue eyes were fixed on Jason's, and a fast growing connection between them was palpable.

"I didn't advertise it, but I never hid it either. I went out with a few boys in college and medical school but never more than a few times. I've just never found the right person."

"Well, I know you're not telling me everything." Phil smiled and took a bite of blue cheese followed by a sip of port. "You're being completely modest."

Jason frowned. "Why would you say that?"

"Because, for example, you said you ran track. You are so full of shit. You were an All-American in track at Mississippi. Everyone knows that about you. And Seth told me you did gene-sequencing research in medical school and have published four articles that are far too sophisticated for me to understand."

Jason blushed and looked at Phil as they were finishing the cheeses. "Well, speaking of modest, Seth tells me you were an all-state quarterback in high school, and the most popular person in college and medical school." He took a final bite of his cheese. "So, you never told me what happened to Mrs. Shapiro."

"You're changing the subject. But she is doing well. We put in a new combination metal polyethylene implant. She's already in a rehab facility. Believe it or not, I call her every day. We've become friends."

Jason smiled "I believe you."

"Do you know anything about these new hip implants? They're amazing."

Phil seemed excited to talk about it, and Jason was relieved to see the subject shift away from him. "I do know a little something about your implants." He immediately regretted revealing that. "So, tell me exactly how you do that surgery," he said as he took a sip of port, not taking his eyes off Phil.

Phil was obviously surprised. "Why in the world would you know anything about hip implants?"

"It's not important." Now Jason really wanted to change the subject. "I want to hear about Mrs. Shapiro, and I really want you to tell me exactly what you do when you put in one of these implants."

Phil shook his head. "Jason, you're not going to change the subject again. Now tell me why you know about these implants."

Jason hesitated, but saw that Phil was adamant. "Well, in college I was a biomedical engineering major and did some research in Dr. Osserman's lab. You may have heard of him. He's an orthopedic surgeon. Anyway, we developed some new techniques for studying the strength and torque of various metal alloys used in joint implants, and I even helped write a few articles about it."

Phil's face suddenly turned completely pale. He set the cheese down that he had been lifting to his mouth. "You have got to be kidding me. You are the J. I. Green on the Osserman review article on joint implantation?"

Jason felt himself turning beet red and focused on the piece of cheese he was eating. He could see the stunned look on Phil's face and was angry with himself that he had mentioned anything about his work with Dr. Osserman.

"Did you write that article? Tell me. You and Osserman are the only two authors of that article."

Jason remained silent.

"Jesus Christ, I've read that article at least once a year for the past five years. We require all of our interns and residents to read it every year." There was a pause. "Let's go." Phil got up abruptly and headed toward the exit.

"Wait, the check," Jason called after him.

"C'mon." Phil was walking quickly out of the restaurant.

The maître d' smiled at Jason and told him the check had already been taken care of. Jason followed Phil out onto the sidewalk, where he was waiting for the valet to return. Across the street, people were streaming out of Carnegie Hall.

"Would you mind if we went into Carnegie Hall before you get your car?" Jason asked Phil, who was staring down at his feet.

"Sure, why not?"

Jason could see that Phil was upset.

They crossed the street and walked through the open doors, making their way inside with some difficulty against the exiting crowd. They went into the main hall, and Jason walked quickly and deliberately down toward the front. He sat down as the last of the audience left the hall. Phil stood at the back of the hall, watching him. Jason stared at the empty stage for several minutes and then lowered his head, putting his hands over his eyes as the tears started to come.

After a moment, Phil walked down the aisle and sat next to him. "What's the matter?" he asked softly.

"It's nothing. Let's go." Jason tried to get up, but Phil held him down.

"You know, you're wonderful at listening but not very good at talking. I'm sorry about the way I just acted. Is that why you are upset?"

Jason smiled. "No, no. I'm just being maudlin. I grew up listening to Dave Brubeck, and he had—"

Phil interrupted him. "My father was at his 1963 Carnegie Hall concert. He said it was the greatest concert he had ever been to, bar none."

Jason looked at Phil, eyes still moist. "Well, I'd like to talk to him sometime about that concert. I've played it thousands of times and have fantasized about being there."

Phil laughed. "So that's what you fantasize about? But why the tears?"

"Oh, my mother knew how much I loved Dave Brubeck, and she would take me to New Orleans or Memphis every time he played a concert or a jazz club there. Being here at Carnegie Hall just brought back all those memories of being with my mother. I miss her a lot. Thanks for letting me come in here."

They sat for a while longer. Then Jason got up, and Phil followed him out.

They stood silently waiting for the valet to bring the Porsche.

"You did seem angry when we left the restaurant," Jason said as they drove off. "Did I make you angry for some reason?" He winced at how hesitant he sounded.

Phil looked over at him and smiled. "No, I'm not angry. I've just never been intimidated by anyone in my life. Ever. And now an intern, four years younger than me, is intimidating the hell out of me. It's just something new for me." Phil turned back to the front. "By the way, what does the *I* stand for?"

"What do you mean?"

"The *I* in your name."

Jason hesitated. "Itzhak. Philip, you are the only person other than my family who knows that." It was the first time that Jason had spoken Phil's first name, and Philip rather than Phil seemed, for some reason, more appropriate, perhaps more intimate. He laughed, happy that Philip had not been angry. "I'm entrusting you with that secret."

"Where does it come from?"

"It's Hebrew for Isaac. It was my father's paternal grandfather's name. He was killed in Bergen Belsen. Ironically, the name means *laughter*."

After a long pause, Phil asked, "Would you like to come to my apartment for a drink?"

"Thanks, but I'm admitting tomorrow, and it's already almost eleven. I have to get up really early."

Jason guided Phil to the front of his apartment building.

"Thanks very much for taking me. I'm irritated that you prepaid for the dinner, which was great by the way, particularly the grouper. I'll make it up to you, if you let me. I have a place I'd like to take you." He reached for the door handle and looked back at Phil. "Good night. Thanks again."

Phil leaned over and kissed Jason on the cheek. "Good night."

Jason blushed and smiled.

CHAPTER 5

Jason climbed into bed, his mind racing, going over every moment from the time Phil had picked him up in front of the hospital to the unexpected kiss on his cheek. He thought maybe he should have gone home with Phil, but he had never spent the night with another man. Jason admitted to himself that he was afraid, not because he was sexually inexperienced but because of his frequent night terrors. He closed his eyes briefly. The vivid nightmares were terrible: being thrown into a Nazi crematorium, the murders in *A Farewell to Arms,* Warren Henry's lonely and brutal death in *War and Remembrance.* Jason had avoided every sleepover invitation while he was a kid in school. He grimaced. He certainly didn't want Philip to think he was a psychiatric case right off the bat.

He remembered his parents taking him to St. Louis when he was nine years old for a neuropsychiatric evaluation at St. Louis Children's Hospital. After spending six hours with several different doctors, Jason sat with his parents as the psychiatrist explained that the vivid dreams were simply part of the remarkable memory and intelligence that Jason had been born with, and that likely, with time, the vivid dreams would diminish in frequency. They'd offered medications to help him sleep, but Jason's mother and father declined. The vivid dreams, mostly nightmares, never diminished, and Jason continued to be tormented by these nightmares, frequently awakening during the night in a panic.

Jason rolled over. He knew he should sleep. He was admitting tomorrow. But he could not stop thinking of Philip. Jason was physically attracted to him, sure, but what attracted him most was the person. What he liked most about Philip was that he was modest. Seth had told him that Philip was a star all-state high school quarterback and the most popular kid in his school. At Harvard, he had been one of the most talented chemistry majors in the undergraduate program and had coauthored several papers in major journals. In addition, his endearing personality made him a magnet for others, and he had been one of the most popular leaders in his class at Harvard. In medical school, he stood out in the clinical years as one of the best in his class, particularly in the surgical specialties. During his orthopedics residency he had astounded his professors with his surgical skills, and it was common for a professor to request that Philip scrub in on a difficult case. Philip had also invented several unique surgical instruments that had been patented by the hospital: a gift from Philip. He had asked only to be allowed to name the instruments. He had been offered the chief residency and then a professorship following his chief residency, a rare occurrence at any institution, particularly in an elite program such as Philip's. Jason shook his head in the darkness and smiled. He had learned all of this, not from Philip, but rather from Seth and a few of the orthopedic interns that he had met at lunch.

He wondered if Philip had really liked him, whether he was sophisticated enough for him, and whether Philip found him attractive. Jason certainly could have dressed better. Maybe he would let his father take him shopping when he came in over Thanksgiving weekend. And the scene he'd made at Carnegie Hall must have surely turned Phil off. Jason rolled over again. They had talked nonstop the entire evening, and Philip hadn't seemed bored.

Jason looked at the clock. It was already four a.m., and he had not slept a wink. He got up, put on his running clothes, and ran his usual route twice over. He showered, ate a light breakfast, and walked to a Starbuck's a few blocks away. He rarely drank coffee, but he had not slept, and it would be a very busy admitting day. He asked for the strongest brew they had and sipped it as he walked to the hospital, analyzing the previous night, wondering if Philip had been offended that Jason didn't have a drink with him after dinner, wondering if the Calvin Klein Obsession cologne that he wore was to Phil's liking.

Jason arrived on his ninth-floor unit at seven to prepare for rounds. He had gotten the expected buzz from the coffee, but it was not a particularly pleasant feeling for him.

Jason fell asleep at the nursing station just before Seth arrived at eight a.m.

Seth shook Jason's shoulders gently. "Hey, wake up."

"Oh, good morning. Just taking a snooze, waiting for you." He blinked up at Seth. "Where are the students?"

"They're on a class retreat today. It's just you and me, and maybe just me. You look awful."

"I didn't sleep much last night." Time to change the subject. "How was the baseball game?"

"The Mets lost as usual." Seth raised an eyebrow. "But the real question is, how was your dinner with Phil? Or maybe I should ask what happened after dinner? You look like you've been up all night."

"Well, if you think that I spent the night with Philip or that I went home with him after dinner, you're dead wrong." Jason could feel his face getting warm. "But you're right. I didn't sleep very much last night. I'll be fine today."

"So did you like Phil? He's a great guy. One of the few wonderful people I know."

"Yeah, I know that." Jason nodded and looked away. "I liked Philip a lot. But I doubt I'll hear from him again. I really gave him shit about Mrs. Shapiro, and I think I made a fool of myself last night with him."

Seth sat down, looking surprised. "Why? What happened?"

"Oh, I had a crying spell thinking about my mother during one of our conversations. It was stupid, and I'm sure he thinks I'm crazy." Jason sometimes wondered whether he might really be a bit off-center.

"Well, Jason, everyone's a little crazy, except me." Seth laughed. "You know, I think it's sweet that you call him Philip." He gave Jason a genuine smile. "Everyone else calls him Phil. By the way, you should know that he's very sensitive about his family's wealth. He doesn't want people thinking that his success is a result of family influence."

Jason stared at him, puzzled. "It's obvious that Philip is his own person. Why would anyone think that his success in medicine could have anything to do with his family?"

Seth chuckled. "You know that building that you go to almost every day to do your research?" Jason frowned at Seth, knowing that he was waiting for a response. "And by the way, you do know how ridiculous it is that you're doing any research this year?" He shook his head, pausing. "Well, anyway, do you know what the name of that building is?"

Jason stared at Seth for several more seconds and then almost yelled, "Jesus, the Olsen Research Center—that's Philip's family?"

Seth laughed. "You got it."

Jason couldn't believe he hadn't made the association.

After they made rounds, Jason insisted that Seth go to the library as he had planned. Over the next eight hours, Jason took care of discharges, wrote orders and progress notes on his old patients, and admitted seven new patients. He was somehow able to concentrate on his work, despite his fatigue and obsession about the previous night. He had never developed such an instant and strong attraction to anyone, and he felt uncharacteristically frightened and unsure of himself.

Seth returned and they reviewed all the patients on their service. Jason took Seth to meet the seven new patients, and, at six, Seth told Jason to go home and get some sleep. "I have to be here till seven anyway. I'm meeting a friend in the cafeteria for a quick bite, so I'll take care of anything for the next hour."

Jason thanked him and walked over to the Olsen Research Center. He read the plaque in the lobby, which he had not previously noticed. *This research center was made possible by the generosity of the John D. Olsen Foundation, February, 1998.*

The lab was empty except for one of the postdoc fellows and one of his research assistants who was removing gels from an incubator. Jason logged on to the main bioinformatics computer and began working on the program in which he and Dr. Fang had found errors. Jason had come to like Dr. Fang and had even talked him into going to Chinatown where they had a meal at a genuine Chinese restaurant that Jason's adopted uncle Harold Lin, a close business associate of his father and close family friend, had written to him about. Jason had not eaten real Chinese food since he had last been in Hong Kong years ago.

Apparently, the other postdoc fellows were genuinely

stunned that Fang had agreed to go out with Jason. Fang was a dedicated loner, they had all told Jason. Well, Fang hadn't talked much about himself at dinner, but he had really seemed to be happy with the food, and Jason felt that he had broken through a barrier.

Jason finished the corrections over the next hour, opened up the top drawer of the desk, and found a note-pad to write down the changes he had made to the code. As he replaced the pad, he noticed a plastic bag with two USB memory sticks in it. Why memory sticks? Overkill, he thought, as he closed the drawer. All the computer da-ta was automatically backed up to an offsite computer under a contract with EMC Corporation. Dr. Fang must not trust automatic backup. Or maybe this was data that he'd been sent from an outside lab. *He should label them, though*, Jason said to himself. *Someone might grab one, thinking they were empty*. Exhausted, he left the lab, stopping in front of the plaque once more, wondering if he would ever be with Philip again.

Jason arrived at his apartment to find a package sitting at the entrance to his apartment. Probably another care package from his father, he thought, although it was strange that it had been delivered on a Sunday. He carried it inside and sprawled out on his couch, exhausted. An hour later, a screaming ambulance woke him. Jason had become desensitized to the noise of traffic and sirens, but the couch was uncomfortable. He ate some canned soup and a turkey sandwich and then casually opened the package.

He immediately recognized the vinyl record album cover. It was the Dave Brubeck Quartet's Carnegie Hall concert. On the back was a line of cursive script, obvious-ly written by an elderly person: *To Jason Green, my big-gest fan. Dave Brubeck*. He sat back down on the couch, puzzled, and opened the card. On it was written: *Jason, I*

*can't stop thinking about you. Meet me for lunch in the
cafeteria at noon tomorrow. Phil.*

Tears came to Jason's eyes. He had always cried easily and had never been able to overcome it. His father
cried easily as well, and Jason had often joked with his
father that his goal in life was to isolate the crying gene
and obliterate it from his own gene pool. He blinked
away the tears, looked at the record and the note from
Philip, and thought that perhaps he was just having another vivid dream. How could Philip have gotten a relatively rare vinyl album and also have it signed by Dave
Brubeck? It had to be a prank, although the vinyl record
was real. His father had the same vinyl album, and it was
clearly superior to the digital recording. Jason looked at
Philip's note and read it over and over. Finally, he pulled
out the bed, set the alarm for four a.m., and fell into a
deep sleep. He was startled when the alarm woke him. He
was still in the same position as when he had fallen
asleep.

After his run and breakfast, Jason went to his unit and
prepared for rounds with Seth and the students. He had
watched with great satisfaction the students becoming an
integral part of the medical team, contributing to rounds
and patient care. Despite Jason's anticipation of lunch
with Philip, he remained focused during rounds, and the
give-and-take among the four was lively and construc-
tive. Jason spent the first hour of attending rounds with
Dr. Glassman, introducing him to the seven new patients
he had admitted the day before. Jason excused himself
from the remainder of rounds at eleven-ten.

"Stay with us, Dr. Green. You don't admit today. You
should have time," Dr. Glassman said.

"I'm sorry, Dr. Glassman. I have several orders I have
to take care of, and I have a lunch meeting today that I
can't miss." Jason was perplexed by Dr. Glassman's invi-

tation. That had never happened in the six weeks that Dr. Glassman had been his attending.

Dr. Glassman smiled wryly, and Seth looked puzzled.

"I bet you do," Dr. Glassman said, turning and walking into the conference room. Jason stood still, wondering what that had meant.

At noon, Jason went to the hospital cafeteria where he usually ate his lunch in five minutes. He immediately saw Phil in his surgical scrubs, seated at a corner table, watching him as he entered the large dining room filled with noisy hospital personnel and patients' families. Philip did not take his eyes off him as he walked over to the table.

"I wasn't sure you would show up," he said.

Jason realized that he was serious, even worried. "Philip, after our dinner I thought you would never want to see me again. I didn't sleep the entire night." He dropped into the seat across from him. "The only respite I've gotten from thinking about you since Saturday night was the result of sheer exhaustion last night."

"This has never happened to me." Phil seemed almost desperate. "I don't want to sound glib. I've never told another human being that I loved them, except for my parents and maybe my brother and sister. But I'm telling you, I may be in love with you! I know I sound crazy. It sure sounds crazy to me."

"You barely know me." Jason swallowed as emotion surged through him. "We spent one evening together. There are things about me that *would* drive you crazy, and I promise, you can do better than me. Besides—"

"I know you." Phil interrupted him. "I know who you are, and I know this sounds crazy. But I'm going to do my best to get you to fall in love with me."

"You are mistaking love for lust." Jason smiled as his face began to get hot. "Your testosterone levels are just very high, and I'll tell you—"

"You've got it wrong." Philip interrupted again. He paused and looked down and then looked at Jason again. "I'd be lying if I told you I didn't want to get naked with you. But my feelings are not related to my testosterone levels. I've never met anyone like you, and I'm sure I never will again."

There was a long silence. "Your card took my breath away." Jason said it softly as he looked into Philip's eyes. Suddenly the noisy cafeteria seemed to have gone silent.

"I thought the album might do that, but I didn't have high hopes for my card."

Jason put his hand on Phil's forearm. "Whose signature is that on the album cover? And where did you get the vinyl album? I don't think that album is easy to find."

"You probably don't know this, but Dave Brubeck has lived in Wilton for at least the past thirty years. My parents know him very well, my father has done some work for him, and he's been at our house several times for small parties. When I dropped you off, I drove home and asked my father for a favor."

"Did you tell your daddy who it was for?"

"I tell my father everything. I'm very close with my parents." Philip held Jason's gaze. "They know everything about me, and now, about you."

"Do they know that I'm a Jew?"

"Jason, if they have an ounce of bigotry in their bones, I'm not aware of it.

"It's just that the anti-Semitism that I endured growing up still haunts me. It's hard to imagine a very wealthy gentile family accepting that their gay son might be bringing his boyfriend home for dinner, and that he's a Jew to boot."

"Sounds like the making of a good movie." Phil laughed, and Jason found himself joining in. "Jason, I want to be with you, as much as possible. Give me a chance."

"Can you go to dinner with me on Friday? I'm not admitting patients on Friday, and—"

"Of course, but I don't think I can wait that long to see you." Phil once again looked desperate.

Jason paused, taking his time. "Do you know where the phrase 'absence makes the heart grow fonder' originated?"

Phil forced another smile. "Teaching me something again?"

"It comes from the Roman poet Sextus Propertius. He said, *Always toward absent lovers love's tide stronger flows*." Jason paused. "Well, anyway, meet me at the subway entrance at Ninety-Sixth and Lexington at six Friday evening. No Porsche is necessary."

Jason stood up, watching Philip.

"You haven't eaten lunch," Philip said.

"I've just had dessert." Jason smiled and walked away, leaving Philip sitting alone, their eyes meeting one more time as Jason turned the corner to leave the cafeteria.

CHAPTER 6

Each evening after completing his patient work, Jason went to the lab to work primarily with Dr. Fang, although he did spend significant time with each of the other postdoc fellows. They had all recognized Jason's ability to work through problems involving methodology and statistics and frequently sought his advice. Dr. Fang and Jason had continued with their strong working relationship, and he had even opened up to Jason in a small way about his personal life. Dr. Fang confided that his sister was in graduate school in San Francisco and struggling financially and that he sent her money every month in order for her to live comfortably. His parents still lived in Beijing, and he was hoping to return to China once he finished his postdoctoral training. He missed his family and wanted to go back to China to live a simple life, teaching. He admitted that he was uncomfortable with American culture.

Jason found it strange that Dr. Fang wanted to complete a prestigious postdoctoral fellowship if his goal was only to teach and not continue his research. Jason had also decided not to reveal to Dr. Fang that he spoke fluent Mandarin, because he did not want to get into the habit of speaking Mandarin with Dr. Fang in front of the other postdoc fellows. It would be pretentious and unseemly, and Jason knew, based on previous experiences with other Chinese nationals, that Fang would insist in talking in Mandarin. Besides, Fang needed to practice his English.

On his non-admitting days, Jason usually arrived in the lab by six, after eating a five-minute supper in the cafeteria, and on his admitting days he usually arrived by seven.

Dr. Glassman was always there until at least seven-thirty p.m., except on Fridays. One of the postdoc fellows had told Jason that Mrs. Glassman insisted that Dr. Glassman be home by six p.m. every Friday to have Shabbat dinner with his family, which included his three daughters and their husbands as well as eight grandchildren.

Dr. Glassman rarely acknowledged Jason's presence in the lab, and Jason had assumed that Dr. Glassman had no idea of his laboratory activities. It didn't bother him. He was learning more than he'd ever imagined.

On the Thursday evening before his second date with Philip, Jason was finishing downloading data from an outside lab for analysis. He sensed someone standing behind him at the door and turned around to see Dr. Glassman staring at him.

Jason could not hide his surprise—it was a first since working in his lab. He had developed a profound appreciation for Dr. Glassman's questions during their daily patient rounds, but, in all the time he had been his attending, not once had he ever made a comment or questioned Seth, the students, or Jason about personal issues. In fact, Jason could not think of a single instance when Dr. Glassman had spoken of anything other than patients or research, except for that first interview with him.

"Good evening, Dr. Glassman." Jason waited as Dr. Glassman continued to stare down at him for what seemed an uncomfortably long time.

"Jason, would you like to come to my home tomorrow

evening for dinner with my family? You could probably use a good meal."

Jason blinked in surprise. "Oh, thank you so much for the invitation. I'd love that, but I have a prior engagement I can't break."

There was another pause. "Phil Olsen is a genuinely good person, and smart. I suspect you two are a good pair."

Jason could not hide his surprise. "Jesus Christ, sir." The words erupted before he could stop them. "How could you possibly know about Philip and me?"

Dr. Glassman smiled. "His father gave me the money for this lab. I know the family quite well. He called me last Sunday after your dinner with Phil to find out more about you. He's very protective of Phil. Good night, Jason. Thank you for your contributions to this lab. We'll make dinner another night."

Dr. Glassman turned and left. Jason stared after him, stunned at the revelation.

After a minute of shock, he smiled. So Dr. Glassman actually had feelings and emotions, after all. Still smiling, Jason returned to his work.

ℰℑℰℑ

On Friday evening, Jason arrived at the subway entrance ten minutes early, pacing back and forth. He spotted Philip two blocks away, and for the entire two blocks their eyes were fixed on each other. Philip stopped in front of Jason, saying nothing. Jason was completely unaware of the frenetic movement of traffic and people about them.

The smell of that expensive cologne and Philip's face aroused Jason as they continued to look at one another.

Philip finally broke the silence. "Someone said time

moves slowly for those who wait. This week has been the slowest of my life."

"Henry van Dyke said that." Jason smiled, put his arms around Philip, and hugged him tightly. Still holding him, Jason whispered in his ear, "That verse ends, 'For those who love, time is eternity.'"

Philip pushed Jason back. "How could you possibly know that?" His expression said that he was really expecting an answer. "I want to know. You're a scientist and a doctor, and yet you quote obscure poets."

"C'mon." Jason took Philip's arm and led him down the subway stairs. "Van Dyke isn't obscure."

They got onto the subway, but Philip wasn't willing to let it go. "How could you remember that poem?"

"I don't know. I have a good memory." Jason shrugged. "I rarely forget things that I read. Believe me, it can be a curse." He paused. "Philip, I'm a little crazy. I have vivid memories of scenes from all the books I've read, and I have frequent, vivid nightmares and sometimes wake up in a panic." He looked away. "I wanted to get that off my chest. I told you there were things about me that would make you run away from me."

"Where are you taking me?" Philip didn't sound at all disturbed.

"Well, we're going to a restaurant in Chinatown. The subway is probably a new experience for you." Jason smiled. "And I promise the meal will be something you've never experienced."

They sat close to each other, legs and arms touching, and Jason smiled at the warmth of Philip against him.

"I hope that you like Chinese food—I mean real Chinese food."

"Contrary to what you might think, I *have* been on a subway once or twice." Philip cocked an eyebrow. "And

I've been to Chinatown many times and have eaten in most of the good restaurants there."

Jason chuckled. "You haven't eaten where I'm taking you."

Philip pushed his arm against Jason, and Jason pushed back. For the next ten minutes, they sat in silence, subtly pushing each other's arms and legs, like two teenagers in love, trying to be inconspicuous. Jason smiled at himself.

"Come with me." He pulled Philip through the subway exit. The area bustled with Asian residents, American tourists, Chinese food markets, street vendors, and many restaurants with large neon signs. After two blocks, they turned into a narrow, dead-end street. Halfway down the street, they reached a small door that had no sign, walked down two steps, and entered a room that had twelve tables, all but one filled with Chinese couples or families.

They waited at the entrance as an elderly man with a wide smile and yellowing teeth approached them. *"A, zhǔrén jié sēn, huānyíng xuǎn gòu. Yīncǐ, zhè shì nǐ tèbié de péngyǒu?"* He smiled widely at Jason. "Ah, Master Jason, welcome." He continued in Mandarin. "So this is your special friend? He is a very handsome man. Does he speak Mandarin?"

Jason took the owner's hand, speaking in Mandarin as well. "It is so good to see you again, Mr. Zhao. It has been too long since I've been here, and I miss your food. Yes, this is my special friend, and no, he does not speak Mandarin. At least I don't think he does." Jason looked at Philip, who looked rather shocked. Jason laughed and continued in Mandarin, "No, he doesn't speak Mandarin. I want to show him how real Chinese food tastes."

The owner took Philip's hand. "I am so glad you both here," he said in broken English. "I have prepared special meal for you."

They were led to the only open table, in the far corner

of the restaurant. The aroma in the small restaurant was unfamiliar to Philip but pleasant. The tables were small but elegantly set with beautiful authentic chinaware and linens. The owner had put forks and knives on their table as a courtesy, although Jason used chopsticks.

They sat facing one another.

"You speak fluent Chinese?" Philip looked surprised.

"I learned it when I was very young. My father's main supplier for his business is Chinese, and I spent time with their family in Hong Kong. I'm excited for you to try this food." Jason smiled widely. "I promise that you've never had this kind of Chinese food."

For the next two and a half hours, the owner brought ten courses of the best food that Philip had ever eaten. Much of it was delicate, flavored with spices new to Philip—honey garlic pork ribs, boiled dumplings, mandarin crepes, pot stickers with prawns, steamed pork buns, and mango pudding. The owner would explain each course to Jason, who would then translate for Philip. At the end, neither Jason nor Philip was uncomfortably full and both knew they had eaten a meal few other Americans would ever experience.

Jason and Philip did not take their eyes off one another the entire meal. Philip asked about Jason's week, and, after a brief reply, Jason insisted on knowing everything that had happened in Philip's surgical world. He wanted details about each surgical procedure, details about his residents and interns, how he handled them, what the attending doctors were like, and what his specific duties were. Each time Philip asked Jason a question, Jason answered quickly and then asked Philip more questions about his work.

"By the way," Jason finally said, "your daddy has been checking up on me."

"Jason, my *daddy* is very protective of me. He worries

about me. So don't take it personally. He knows I've fallen head over heels for you, and all he knows about you is what I've told him." Philip shrugged and forked up a bite of crepe. "He wanted an independent opinion, so he called Dr. Glassman."

"I know. Dr. Glassman told me he called."

Philip's eyes glinted with amusement. "He probably didn't tell you what he told my father."

"No, and I don't want to know."

Philip smiled. "Suffice it to say, my father is no longer worried."

At the end of the meal, Mr. Zhao brought a small scroll tied with string and handed it to Philip. Jason took Mr. Zhao's hand, and they spoke in Mandarin for several minutes. When they finished, Philip shook hands with Mr. Zhao. Then Philip and Jason left the restaurant, which was still filled with Chinese diners.

"You didn't pay for the meal."

"It was preordered and prepaid." Jason gave him a sideways glance. "I'm a good learner."

They walked up the stairs into the street. Philip opened the scroll, and on it was inscribed a series of Chinese characters.

"What does it say?" Philip asked.

"It says, 'A flower cannot blossom without sunshine nor a garden without love.'"

They walked quietly toward the subway. Phil waved an empty taxi over. "C'mon, this is on me."

They got into the taxi, and Philip gave the driver the address of his apartment, an address that Jason had gotten from Seth under the pretense of needing to send a card.

"Philip, I'm admitting patients tomorrow, and I have to get up early." Jason shifted a bit uneasily on the seat. "I get up at four thirty and run three miles, and I have to be on the floor by six."

Philip shook his head. "Tomorrow is Saturday, and you don't have to be there until seven. I'll get up at five and run with you, and I'll have you at the hospital at seven. And there will be no sex if that is your worry." He touched Jason's hand lightly. "That's not why I want you to spend the night. I just want to be close to you."

They both looked at the driver, who was smiling in the mirror. Jason took Philip's hand. It was the first time they had held hands and Jason laughed.

"What's so funny?"

"Did you see *Sleepless in Seattle*? The radio psychologist asked Tom Hanks what was so special about his wife who had passed away. And he answered, "When I first held her hand, I knew; it was like...*magic*." Jason was dramatic when he paraphrased the scene.

They both laughed, and Jason drew a deep breath, becoming serious once again. "I've never in my life spent the night with someone else. I told you about my vivid dreams and night panics. I don't want you to think I'm crazy if that happens to me." He risked a glance at Philip. Philip's smile didn't falter as he squeezed Jason's hand.

The taxi stopped in front of a vintage World War II-era building with a beautiful façade across from Central Park. Philip pulled on Jason's arm, and they went to the entrance. Philip entered a code, and the door snapped open. In the entry sat a middle-aged man.

"Good evening, Dr. Olsen. A package is here for you." He handed it to him.

"Thanks, Mr. Gregory."

The two took the elevator to the seventeenth floor. Philip's spacious apartment had a stunning view of Central Park and was beautifully decorated with traditional plush furniture. The art was original, and Jason recognized several of the artists as early twentieth-century American. As Philip was turning on lights, Jason went to

Philip, quietly took the package from his hands and set it down, put his hands on the back of Philip's neck, and slowly pulled him close. After looking at him for a moment, he closed his eyes and, for the first time, kissed Philip, lightly at first, and then passionately. The kiss lasted several minutes and was the sweetest that Jason had ever experienced. He had kissed only a few boys in his life, but this was the first kiss that had really mattered. He loosened his grip on Philip's neck, opened his eyes, and saw tears in Philip's. They stood silently, holding each other for several more minutes. Philip turned around, quietly finished turning on lights, and sat on the couch. He picked up the package and opened it. In it were two compact discs and a card.

Jason watched as Philip opened the card. On it was written: '*Music is the mediator between the spiritual and sensual life.*' *Beethoven wrote those words. Music has been the core of my spiritual life, but until I met you I did not understand the meaning of those words. Jason.*

Jason had made a CD of some of his favorite music: several Dave Brubeck songs, Barber's *Adagio*, Rachmaninoff's Prelude in C Sharp Minor, several Barbra Streisand songs, two songs by Brian McKnight, Michael Jackson's "Man in the Mirror," and another twenty pieces of diverse genres.

Philip got up, took Jason into his bedroom, went into the bathroom, and turned on the shower. He undressed and then went to Jason and undressed him.

"Don't worry, no sex," Philip said softly.

They showered together; washed each other, laughing; explored each other with their eyes; and kissed passionately. When they had finished drying, they got into bed and held each other. Jason fell into a deep sleep almost immediately, aware of Philip's smile and his arms around him.

Jason awoke to an empty bed with the sound of an alarm at five a.m., relieved that he had not embarrassed himself with one of his night terrors.

"Let's go running," Philip said as he walked into the bedroom and tossed running shorts, a T-shirt, socks, and a pair of tennis shoes onto the bed. "These shoes should fit."

Jason sat up, still bleary-eyed, and looked at Philip, who was already dressed to run. Jason went into the bathroom, washed his face, brushed his teeth with a new toothbrush Philip had left out, walked into the kitchen, and pulled Philip back into the bedroom. For the next hour they made love as passionately as any two could. It was a joining of souls, a desperate act of communication, passionate, gentle, inexplicable.

They lay together for several minutes afterward, breathing deeply and synchronously, looking at each other.

Jason smiled. "I didn't dream having sex could be this good."

"This was more than sex, at least for me. This is the first time in my life that I've made love." Philip paused, looking at Jason seriously. "You're always surprising me. This was the most passionate sex I've ever had. I've fantasized about you since the day I met you, and my fantasies didn't come close to the reality."

"What happens when I stop surprising you?" Jason made his tone glib, hiding a pang of fear.

"You worry too much. The mere fact that you're with me will always be surprising to me." Philip stroked his face gently. "I intend to grow old with you."

"Do you always get what you want?"

"Usually, but I sense a challenge with you. I know you think this is fast." Philip grew suddenly pensive. "Frankly I'm scared."

Jason could sense that Philip's fear was genuine. "Philip—"

"Quiet." Philip put his hand over Jason's lips. "We should go to work."

CHAPTER 7

Philip had asked Jason to meet him every day for lunch at noon, and Jason readily agreed. It was understood that if one didn't show, the absence was because of inescapable duties. Philip managed to break away for lunch with Jason every day during the next week, except on Wednesday, when he had to remain in surgery to help a professor with a difficult cervical spine case. Philip had almost begged Jason to move in with him, but Jason had declined, stunned by the offer. He wanted to. But it wouldn't be practical because of his work in Dr. Glassman's lab. He enjoyed the lab immensely and often didn't leave until ten.

The three-minute walk to his apartment allowed a good night's sleep. The walk back and forth to Philip's apartment each day would take away another hour of his day. Jason also admitted to himself that he was still concerned about his night terrors, although Philip seemed unperturbed. Philip made it clear that he was unhappy with Jason's decision, but Jason thought that, not only was time an issue, but also he and Philip did not know each other well enough for such an important transition.

He had only one more week on his eight-week rotation with Seth and Dr. Glassman. After that, he would transition to the intensive care unit. Even though the eight-week ICU rotation was intellectually demanding, interns

were only required to work Monday through Fridays
from seven a.m. to seven p.m. with weekends off. Jason
had promised to spend every weekend with Philip during
his ICU rotation.

Jason had learned a lot about what Philip did on a daily basis, mostly by dragging information out of Philip and
from conversations with Seth. He knew that Philip was
completely responsible for organizing and running the
orthopedic training program for the academic year, and
he was in the operating room every day, usually supervis-
ing residents and helping professors with difficult cases.
He was responsible for making certain that the interns
and residents did their jobs and had learned early on that
he had to be tough because, even though his interns and
residents were among the most elite surgical trainees in
the entire country, many would shirk their duties if left
alone. If an intern or resident took a shortcut working up
a patient in preparation for surgery, or if the postoperative
care was not meticulous, he was merciless in his criticism
and did not hesitate to embarrass the young surgeon in
front of his colleagues or professors.

On the other hand, Jason also learned that Philip had
the reputation of being a great mentor to those young surgeons, and he gave completely of himself to help them
with their training. The professors were, without excep-
tion, in awe of his surgical abilities and confidence. That
he was gay was widely known and did not diminish the
respect that he had garnered from everyone who knew
him. He had always been careful not to socialize with any
of the surgical trainees, and the several times that he had
been approached by a gay intern or resident—and even
once by a female resident who apparently did not know
or care about Philip's preferences—he had rebuffed the
invitations politely.

Jason was saddened at the prospect of no longer being

with Seth, who had been a mentor beyond all his expectations. And although he would continue to have contact with Dr. Glassman through the lab, it wouldn't be the same. Jason had learned a lot from the questions Glassman had asked on daily clinical rounds. Glassman had not once offered clinical data, but the clinical insights Jason had gained from his questions were enormous. Information was readily available. The difficult part of medicine, Jason realized, just as in the scientific laboratory, was learning how to ask the right questions. Jason knew it was a lesson that most physicians did not understand.

On the last day of his rotation, Jason brought Seth a CD of his favorite classical music with a note that said: *To the greatest resident an intern could hope for. Thank you for everything. Jason.* Seth gave Jason a big bear hug just as Dr. Glassman was approaching for his last clinical rounds with the team.

"What's going on here? Goldberg, if you are trying to cause trouble between Green and Olsen, stop it now." Dr. Glassman laughed with gusto, a laugh that neither Jason nor Seth had ever heard.

Jason laughed. "Good morning, Dr. Glassman. No, Seth is as straight as an arrow. He just couldn't control himself. No one has ever given him a gift before. This is for you, Dr. Glassman, to thank you for being such a great attending." He had also made a CD of what he imagined would be Dr. Glassman's two favorite classical pieces, although he had no idea what his tastes really were: Brahms's first piano concerto performed by Emanuel Ax and Mendelsohn's Violin Concerto in E Minor performed by Jascha Heifetz. On the card, he had written: *Thank you, Dr. Glassman, for the opportunity to learn from you, and thank you for trusting me to work in your lab. Jason.*

Dr. Glassman smiled, obviously touched. "Well, Dr. Green, this is a first for me as well. In forty years, I've never received a gift from an intern or a resident."

After rounds, Dr. Glassman paused before he left them. "Goldberg and Green, I want you to come to my home this evening for dinner. I won't take no for an answer, and Jason, you bring Phil. I would like to see him again. Six o'clock. You know where I live, Goldberg. Give them directions." Dr. Glassman turned and, as he walked toward the elevators, Jason noticed that his gait seemed more spritely than usual. Jason smiled. It was rare that Dr. Glassman used his first name. Jason and Seth looked at each other with stunned expressions.

Jason and Philip had each other's cell phone numbers, although Jason rarely called Philip because he was usually in the operating room. On the other hand, Philip called Jason several times a day. The conversation would always be similar.

Philip: "Hey, what are you doing?"

Jason: "Saving lives. How about you?"

Phillip: "Thinking of you, wanting to get into bed with you now."

Jason: "I told you this was all testosterone."

Philip: "Move in with me."

Jason: "See you later. I'm standing here with an erection, and I'm going to embarrass myself."

This time Jason called Philip expecting to leave a voice message and was surprised when he answered.

"Hey. Dr. Glassman has invited Seth, you, and me to his house for dinner tonight, and he won't take no for an answer."

"I was hoping to have you to myself tonight, but I guess Glassman the Great can't be denied." Philip gave a theatrical sigh, but Jason could tell he was smiling. "What time?"

છજ્ઞ

Dr. Glassman lived in a beautiful older apartment building across from Riverside Park on the Upper West Side. He had bought it at a time when those apartments were affordable. They now cost in the millions.

Mrs. Glassman answered the door with a big smile and gave them each a hug. "Seth, it's so good to see you again. You must be Dr. Green, and of course I know you." She smiled at Philip. "Welcome back, Phil. It's so good to see you."

As they entered the home, Jason could see that it was very spacious, with three bedrooms, a large living and dining room, a study with three walls filled with books, and a decent-sized kitchen, all decorated with antiques and furniture that had probably been there for the forty years the Glassman family had occupied it. The apartment had a beautiful view of the park and the Hudson River.

In the living room, a large table had been set for two of the three Glassman children, their spouses, and six of their eight grandchildren. The other daughter, her husband, and two children were out of town on a vacation. The atmosphere was jovial, the talk mostly about politics and theater. The grandchildren ranged from seventeen to twenty-six years, and the two daughters appeared to be in their late forties or early fifties. Jason knew that the Glassmans were not religious Jews, but they had made a tradition of having Shabbat dinner every Friday night with their family from the beginning of their extraordinarily happy marriage.

The smell of brisket and the atmosphere in the home reminded Jason of how it was when his mother was alive, and a wave of sadness suddenly overwhelmed him. Jason quickly realized that Mrs. Glassman and Philip both noticed this sudden change, and Philip, who had not taken his eyes off Jason since arriving, immediately went to him.

"Is everything okay?"

"Of course. I just started thinking about my mother. Sorry."

"Okay, everyone to the table," Mrs. Glassman announced loudly. "Sit where you like, except at the ends." After everyone was seated she looked around, smiling. "Okay, who would like to light the candles and say the prayers? It's someone else's turn."

Jason, who was seated next to Philip, stood up, walked around to the buffet, lit a match, and, in a soft, almost perfectly pitched tenor voice, slowly sang the Sabbath prayers:

"Baruch atah, Adonai, Eloheinu, melech haolam, asher kid'shanu b'mitzvotav, v'tzivanu l'hadlik ner shel Shabbat.

Baruch atah, Adonai Eloheinu, Melech Haolam, borei p'ri hagafen.

Baruch atah, Adonai Eloheinu, Melech haolam, asher kid'shanu b'mitzvotav v'ratzah vanu, v'Shabbat kodsho b'ahavah uv'ratzon hinchilanu, zikaron l'maaseih v'reishit. Ki hu yom t'chilah l'mikra-ei kodesh, zecher litziat Mitzrayim. Ki vanu vacharta, v'otanu kidashta, mikol haamim. V'Shabbat kodsh'cha b'ahavah uv'ratzon hinchaltanu. Baruch atah, Adonai, m'kadeish HaShabbat."

Jason noticed the room was completely silent when he finished, and everyone was staring at him. He returned to the table, his eyes annoyingly moist.

Dr. Glassman broke the silence. "Jason, that was beautiful. I didn't know you were observant. I understand you've been in the lab every Friday, sometimes very late, so I assumed you didn't observe the Sabbath."

Jason looked around the table. He had a sudden feeling that he had turned the mood of the evening in an unwelcome direction. "Oh, I'm not religious." He kept his voice light. "I'm actually an atheist. When my mother was alive, she insisted on lighting the candles and saying the prayers every Friday, and this just brought back good memories."

The banter resumed immediately, and for the remainder of the dinner Jason and Philip engaged the Glassman family in lively conversation, Philip occasionally pushing his leg against Jason's and Jason pushing back. Jason could see that everyone at the table had noticed their gestures, their simultaneous smiles, and occasional chuckles.

CHAPTER 8

Over the next eight weeks in September and October, Jason spent his rotation in the medical intensive care unit learning critical care medicine. It was an exciting rotation for him—one crisis after another, rapid changes in patient conditions, diagnoses changing by the hour, and frequent changes in treatment plans. It became clear to Jason that asking the right questions was even more important in this setting. The critical care fellow, a physician who had already completed his internship and residency in internal medicine and was now training in the subspecialty of critical care medicine, and three residents manned the unit twenty-four/seven. Jason found them all to be extremely bright. They knew the fine details of each patient and could spew out medical facts as impressively as anyone could. His attending physician was a new, young critical care professor from Harvard who was meticulous during rounds, wanting to know every detail down to the settings on the ventilator. However, he never asked a question unless it had to do with a laboratory value or a ventilator setting.

Jason took on the role of asking the right questions, just as he had learned to do from Dr. Glassman. Jason frequently caught the looks of surprise on the faces of his superiors when his question resulted in a new diagnosis and a change of plans. Jason also performed meticulous physical examinations, and rarely did a day go by that he didn't surprise his attending and residents, not only by knowing the fine details of each patient and developing close relationships with his patients and their families, but also by making astounding diagnoses based on physical findings. And, yet, Jason was always modest in his presentations and was deliberate in giving credit to his residents and fellow.

Jason continued to go to Dr. Glassman's lab every evening, arriving by seven-fifteen during the week and remaining until ten, and going in for several hours every Saturday and Sunday. He continued to deliberately develop his relationship with Dr. Fang, who now seemed much more at ease with him, particularly after Jason revealed to Dr. Fang that he spoke fluent Mandarin. The two were able to make significant improvements in the computer programs, resulting in more rapid data analysis. In the conferences, Jason always let Dr. Fang present and never took credit for his work. Dr. Fang talked with Jason frequently, and even smiled, much to the surprise of the other postdoc fellows with whom Fang remained aloof.

"Dr. Fang, I've been working on a new idea, and I want to know what you think of it," Jason told him one evening after Dr. Glassman had left the lab. Dr. Fang looked up, obviously interested. "A lot of new information has come out recently about unique proteins that have been discovered on the surfaces of tumor cells. What if we could develop computer models of antibody-like molecules that have a high affinity for these surface proteins? What if we could attach a molecule of a chemotherapy agent to the opposite end of the molecule, one that would detach when the molecule became attached to the cancer protein? It would be a way to deliver chemotherapy specifically to the cancer cells, leaving normal cells unexposed. There's already a lot of work going on with antibodies to specific cancer proteins, but not in terms of delivering chemotherapy agents specifically to the cancer cells."

Dr. Fang brightened. "Why you so interested in this?"

"Well, my mother died of breast cancer, and I've always wanted to help make some contribution to curing cancer."

"Where do you find such a computer program to develop these protein models?"

"The basic programs already exist. They just need to be tweaked to suit our needs. Specifically we need to develop affinity models, and I can do that if I'm allowed to use our computers to develop this new program. We would probably need to purchase more memory, or even another computer to tie in to the mainframe. I would just need your help and Dr. Glassman's approval for the purchase. I want this to be your project, and I will help you on it."

Dr. Fang nodded with enthusiasm, clearly excited at the prospect of his own program. "I will speak with Dr. Glassman about it tomorrow." He smiled and patted Jason on the shoulder, the first time there had been physical contact between the two except for that first flimsy handshake.

Jason guessed that a major barrier had been broken. Dr. Fang had always seemed very tense and worried. Almost every evening he received a phone call at precisely eight o'clock. At each call he would walk out into the hall, speaking in quiet and rapid Mandarin that Jason couldn't hear. After each conversation he would return to the computer room visibly upset. When Jason asked if everything was okay, Fang would dismiss it quickly, saying that his sister continued to have problems.

Clearly Jason could see that those calls were personally distressing. Dr. Fang was an enigma to Jason. He had opened up to him somewhat, but he continued to decline any social invitations to eat dinner with Jason and Philip, apparently preferring to remain alone. He dressed in the same clothes every day, and Jason thought that he must wash his limited wardrobe almost nightly. Dr. Fang had told Jason that he sent his extra money to his sister in California. However, he carried a very expensive leather Tumi briefcase with his initials branded on one of the pockets. In fact, he had two different but identical Tumi briefcases, one with his initials and one without his initials, which Jason thought was very strange, considering his limited finances. They cost almost a thousand dollars each. Jason's father sold them at his department store. He guessed they must have been presents to Dr. Fang.

Jason spent every weekend during his eight-week intensive care unit rotation with Philip, who complained frequently to Jason that he should spend less time in the lab and more time with him. Jason recognized that the complaints were just to let him know that Philip wanted to be with him all the time. They ate lunch together during the week almost every day and were inseparable on the weekends. Their sexual relationship, although passionate and frequent, did not compare to their emotional relationship. Jason was falling deeply in love with Philip, and he could sense that Philip had the same feelings. Jason couldn't believe that such a brilliant, accomplished, and genuinely good human being could be interested in him, and he constantly worried that Philip would tire of him and move on. Philip was physically beautiful and drew looks from men and women whenever they were out. He could have anyone he wanted. Jason had also woken up several times with night terrors in Philip's bed, but each time Philip held him tightly, and Jason fell immediately back to sleep.

On their three-month anniversary, toward the end of

his intensive care unit rotation, Jason walked into Philip's apartment at seven-fifteen skipping his usual lab time that Friday evening to celebrate with Philip. They had long since given each other keys to their apartments, and occasionally Jason would surprise Philip during the week, or Philip would surprise Jason. Usually, on such occasions, they made love and slept over, making it necessary to keep some clothing at each other's apartments. Jason handed Philip a small package, which he opened sitting next to Jason on the couch. In it was a CD of Ravel's *Bolero* and a card that read, *Mrs. Shapiro's misfortune brought you into my life, and never a day goes by that I don't silently thank her. After I met you, I was afraid to talk with you. After we talked, I was afraid to kiss you. After we kissed, I was afraid to love you. And now that I love you, I'm afraid I will lose you. Yours always, Jason.*

Philip kissed Jason passionately and held him tightly.

"Are you telling me that you love me?"

"To the core."

Philip sat silently, trying to remain composed. "Why *Bolero*?"

"It's a very erotic piece, and I've fantasized making love to you with that music in the background."

Philip laughed and stood up. "Well, it'll have to wait. We're driving up to my parents' house. They would like to meet you, and I want you to meet them. And no excuses—you're off this weekend."

Jason stood up and started pacing, trying not to hyperventilate. "What if your parents don't like me? What if I don't like them?"

Philip laughed. "Relax, they're going to love you, and I promise that you'll like them as well."

They left without taking any clothing or toilet articles. Philip assured him there would be plenty at his parents' house since they wore the same size. Jason fidgeted the entire drive, and Philip held his hand in an attempt to calm him. It helped only slightly. They arrived when it was dark and pulled up to what appeared to be a huge, three-story mansion. Philip's younger brother and sister were away in graduate school, and Jason couldn't imagine two people living in such a large home.

Jason followed Philip through the front door, and a tall, handsome man with graying blond hair quickly got up from the living room couch, walked quickly to Philip with a wide grin, and gave him a kiss on the cheek and a tight bear hug that turned Philip's face red. "Dad, it's great to see you. This is Jason. Where's Mom?"

"She's finishing the dinner." Mr. Olsen turned to Jason and smiled. "So this is the young man who has made you so happy. Dr. Green, is it?" Philip's dad gave Jason a bear hug as well.

"Yes, sir, and it's Jason. Thank you so much for inviting me into your home." Jason still felt nervous but was pleasantly surprised by Mr. Olsen's warm greeting.

Mrs. Olsen walked in at that moment. She was stunning to look at, tall, with Lauren Bacall looks and a beautiful smile. Jason now understood why Philip was such a beautiful specimen. "Phil, I've missed you so much." She reached up and kissed him. "And Jason, I've been so looking forward to meeting you." She kissed Jason on both cheeks. "I hope you two haven't eaten. I've prepared Phil's favorite meal."

Jason smiled. "I'm actually starved. I forgot to eat lunch today. Mrs. Olsen, thank you for inviting me into your home."

They ate at the kitchen table, which relieved Jason. He could see the dining room table as they walked into the kitchen, and that table was large enough to seat fifteen or twenty people. In the center of the breakfast table were two unlit candles.

Mrs. Olsen handed Jason some matches. "Jason, would you light the candles and say the Sabbath prayers? When we have our Jewish friends over on Friday nights, we always do this. It's a tradition."

Jason smiled. "Mrs. Olsen, that's very considerate, but it really isn't necessary. I'm actually an atheist, so lighting the candles is really not important to me."

"Atheist or not, young man, you need to remind yourself why your great-grandparents were killed." She gave him a mock stern look. "Now, light the candles."

Jason looked at Philip, who was smiling. For the second time in front of Philip, Jason sang the Sabbath prayers, causing Mrs. Olsen's eyes to moisten.

She smiled. "Thank you, Jason, that was beautiful. I've never heard them sung before."

The dinner conversation was lively. Mostly, the conversation was about politics and the economy, with Philip's father doing most of the talking. Mrs. Olsen had prepared a roasted tomato caprese salad, followed by filet mignon with garlic mashed potatoes and green beans almandine. Desert was homemade apple pie. Jason realized that he and Philip had never discussed politics and that he had no idea of Philip's political leanings. It was obvious that Philip's father was a staunch Republican, and a picture of Mr. Olsen with the president hung on one of the kitchen walls.

"Well, Jason, you've been quiet during this conversation. How do you think the Republicans have been doing these past six years?"

"Mr. Olsen, I'm not politically passionate." Jason paused and continued to eat, wanting to avoid further political discussion.

"You must have some opinions," Mr. Olsen persisted.

Jason looked at Philip for help but saw that he was

just smiling and would not intervene. "Well, sir, to answer your question, not so well. The Iraq War is a disaster, and I'm afraid there are bubbles forming in the derivatives market that are going to result in an economic disaster."

Philip looked at Jason with a surprised expression.

Philip's father asked Jason to explain his views on the economy. Again Jason turned to Philip with a subtle but pleading look to get him out of the conversation, but Philip continued to smile and remained silent.

"Sir, I'm not an economist, but I think the Republicans and Democrats have been shortsighted for many years. Nixon did away with the gold standard in 1971, and the Federal Reserve started printing money. Then the Democrats came to power and forced the banks to relax loan standards, resulting in mortgage loans to millions of people who couldn't afford them." He shrugged. "And now the banks have gotten greedy and are selling these leveraged loans all over the world as if they are investments without risk. I'm pretty simpleminded when it comes to the economy, but it seems to me that the Federal Reserve, the government, and the banks all believe that money grows on trees. I think the economy is a house of cards, and it's all going to come tumbling down, sir." He felt his face heating. "I'm sorry. I'm rambling."

"So where would you invest your money?" Philip's father asked.

"Sir, right now I invest my money in food." He smiled crookedly. "They don't pay interns very much."

Everyone laughed.

"Well, what if you won the lottery? What would you invest it in?"

"I would buy gold and silver and put it away in a safe place."

"That doesn't sound so simpleminded to me, Jason." Mr. Olsen seemed quite serious. "Where do you get your information?"

"My daddy and I have read a variety of books on economic theory, the Keynesian theories, and the Austrian School. I think it was started by a man named Mises. We like to read the same books and discuss them. My daddy also—" Jason felt himself blush again. "I've not lost my southern dialect yet. Philip teases me about it. Anyway, my father subscribes to a lot of finance magazines as well, so I've scanned articles over the years. Honestly, I probably have no idea what I'm talking about."

"And what of the war?" Mrs. Olsen inquired.

"I'm basically antiwar unless the reasons are certain. Republicans and Democrats have spent fortunes and lives on unnecessary wars, starting with Vietnam. I wish I could understand the real motivations for these wars." He suddenly realized what he was doing and felt his face getting even hotter. "Mr. and Mrs. Olsen, I feel terrible and am very sorry I'm talking this way. I can see you are friends with the president, and the last thing I wanted to do was to come into your home and insult you. Please forgive me."

"Jason, you're not insulting us," Mr. Olsen reassured him. "Everything you've said makes sense. I'm going to have to read about the derivatives market. You've piqued my interest. Why don't you and I go into the living room and talk while Phil helps his mother clean up?"

Jason stood, relieved that there were no hard feelings. So far! "Mrs. Olsen, thank you for the wonderful supper."

Mr. Olsen and Jason went into a spectacular living room, with large oversized couches covered in Japanese silk floral design material, oversized leather chairs in front of a beautiful stone fireplace, walls lined with museum-quality paintings that Jason recognized again as early twentieth-century American. In the corner was a beautiful concert grand piano.

"Mr. Olsen, again, I'm very sorry if I offended you. I hope Philip isn't angry with me." Jason took a deep breath, hoping his face didn't betray his worry too much. "You know, Philip and I have never discussed politics. Sometimes I get carried away."

"Believe me, I wasn't offended. I understand that you are a brilliant scientist. I'm just surprised you know so much about the economy." Mr. Olsen sat down in one of the chairs and indicated Jason should seat himself. "And Philip isn't angry. He was smiling the entire time you were talking. He and I argue politics all the time. I'm afraid he hasn't inherited my political views." Mr. Olsen laughed and then paused. "You know, Phil has been an intrinsically sad young man for his entire life. It was hard for him to come out, and he's always believed he would never meet someone with whom he could spend the rest of his life. I've never seen him as happy as he has been these last few months. So I thank you for that."

Jason blushed again and changed the subject. "Do you play the piano, Mr. Olsen? I haven't seen a piano like that since I saw Emanuel Ax play with the New Orleans Symphony five years ago. It's spectacular." The piano was a rare nine-and-a-half-foot Bösendorfer grand that one would usually find only in world-class symphony halls.

"No, I don't play, and unfortunately, we didn't insist that our children learn. It's there for show and for the occasional dinner parties we have. Do you play?"

"A little."

"Will you play something for me? I haven't heard my piano played in a long time."

"Sir, I shouldn't."

Mr. Olsen got up and led Jason to the piano. "Phil didn't tell me that you played. Please."

Jason hadn't practiced since he had left home four months ago but didn't want to offend Mr. Olsen. He decided to play the first movement of *Moonlight* Sonata, which he had played since he was a child. It was one of his favorite piano pieces and was easy to play. He had never played on such a fine piano. The sound was brilliant, and the keys felt perfect. As he was playing, Mrs. Olsen and Philip interrupted their cleaning and came into the living room. Philip looked surprised and was smiling.

"That was beautiful," Mrs. Olsen said. "Phil didn't tell me that you played piano."

"I didn't know that he played piano that well." Philip laughed. "I wonder what else I don't know about you." He looked at Jason. "Mom, Dad, do you mind if we go to bed? We're both exhausted, and we have all day tomorrow and Sunday to spend with you."

Mr. and Mrs. Olsen both kissed Philip and Jason, and the two went to Philip's room, which was still decorated with high school memorabilia. They fell asleep in each other's arms before Mr. and Mrs. Olsen had finished cleaning the kitchen. For the next two days, Philip and Jason spent most of their time with Philip's parents.

Jason avoided talking politics, for fear he would be offensive, but Philip challenged his father frequently. "How could you belong to a party that claims to be the party of small government and individual liberty when they try to pass amendments banning same-sex marriage?" he argued over lunch on Saturday. "If that isn't big government, what is?"

Mr. Olsen admitted that the Republican's social policies were distressing, but he asserted that politics was always a compromise and that the economy would be ruined if Democratic programs were enacted. He looked at Jason for a response.

"Sir, I agree with you." Philip looked surprised at Jason's answer, and Jason gave him a brief smile. "But the problem is that both the Republicans and Democrats love to spend money. The spending curve has been straight up since World War II, and the slope of the curve hasn't changed, no matter who's been in power. They just like to spend on different things, and frankly, if we are compelled to spend, I would rather not spend it on cruise missiles."

Mr. Olsen smiled at that, and Philip laughed outright.

Jason became comfortable over the weekend. Philip's parents had a wonderful and loving marriage, and they obviously adored Philip. They seemed to genuinely like Jason as well. On Saturday night, the Olsens had a dinner party and invited seven couples, including two of Philip's high school buddies, both of whom were married with children. Philip's parents introduced Jason to everyone as Philip's partner, and Jason engaged everyone in easy conversation. He uncharacteristically consumed several glasses of wine, and when Mr. Olsen asked Jason to play a piano piece for the guests, he didn't hesitate, primarily because he was slightly intoxicated. He decided to play the same dramatic Rachmaninoff Sonata in C Sharp Minor that he had played for a skeptical professor during one of his internship interviews. He made several mistakes, thanks to the wine, but was satisfied with the performance. The guests applauded enthusiastically, and Jason blushed as he got up to join Philip. Philip kissed him unabashedly in front of everyone.

Jason called his father from the Olsen house as he walked alone in the large backyard of the estate on Sunday morning. He had told his father from the first day he met Philip that he believed he had met the love of his life.

He described Philip's parents as loving but had never mentioned their wealth or politics. Jason knew that his father was relieved that he had found happiness, both in his internship and relationship. He had avoided visiting him because of his schedule but was looking forward to coming for a visit in less than a month for Thanksgiving. He had already made reservations at the Waldorf Astoria.

Philip and Jason returned to the city Sunday evening. Both Mr. and Mrs. Olsen warmly embraced Jason as they left. Mrs. Olsen gave Jason a picture of Philip and Jason that she had taken on Saturday with her digital camera. It was a beautiful picture with perfect lighting and a background of evergreens in their backyard, and she had framed it in sterling silver.

The weekend had been wonderful for Jason. He liked Philip's parents and could see much of his father and his mother in Philip's physical and mental being. They made love Sunday evening, as they did most evenings they were together, and for Jason, life could not have been more perfect.

CHAPTER 9

Jason and Philip had settled into a comfortable routine during Jason's two months in the ICU. Most days, they had lunch together in the cafeteria, frequently interrupted by orthopedic surgery residents or professors. It was obvious to Jason that his relationship with Philip had become common knowledge, and, according to Philip, all of his colleagues wanted to meet his attractive and brilliant partner. Seth joined them at least once weekly, and each time Jason hugged him and told him he missed being with him.

Although they spent every weekend together, Jason continued to insist that he remain in his own apartment during the week. Their time on the weekends was spent making love, reading together on the couch, taking their daily six-mile run around Central Park, and occasionally going out for a meal. Philip was a natural athlete and was stronger than Jason, but Jason's running skills were superior, and he had to hold back. For him, sitting next to Philip with music playing softly in the background, reading medical or scientific literature, looking up occasionally to a beautiful view of Central Park, and looking at Philip sitting next to him was heaven, or as close as he would ever get to it.

The first of November, Jason moved on from the intensive care unit to a four-week rotation on the cancer unit. Each team consisted of an oncology fellow, an internal medicine resident and intern, and an oncology professor who had ultimate responsibility.

Jason was an eager learner. He continued to develop very close relationships with his patients and their families, performed meticulous examinations, and continued to ask the right questions. He also had a keen interest in the mechanism of action of the various chemotherapy agents, particularly since it related to the project that he had proposed to Dr. Fang and for which Dr. Glassman had given his blessing.

Jason had learned on the first day of his rotation that he would be able to leave most days by five, since patient duties were usually completed by then except under unusual circumstances. He was particularly happy about that because it was an extraordinarily productive time in Glassman's lab. Dr. Fang and Jason had been receiving huge volumes of data from the other postdoc fellows and from outside labs for analysis, and the amount of information they analyzed had been enormous. In addition, he had been working with Dr. Fang on their new computer program, which would allow them to design antibody-like proteins that had a high affinity for cancer cells.

On the first day of his rotation, Jason stopped in the cafeteria for his usual five-minute supper, and to his pleasant surprise, Philip was sitting at a far table in his scrub suit talking with another surgeon in scrubs.

Jason leaned over Philip's shoulder, surprising him. "Am I interrupting?"

"Of course not." Philip stood up and kissed Jason on the cheek. "Jason, this is Lucas Franklin. He's an anesthesiology resident who is thinking of changing to orthopedics. I'm trying to talk him out of it," he said with a laugh.

Dr. Franklin shook Jason's hand. He was very handsome and wore a wedding ring.

"Nice to meet you." Dr. Franklin said as he stood up. "I'll leave you two. I should get back to work."

He seemed a little nervous, and Jason stopped him. "No, no, don't go. I'm going to scarf this down in two minutes. I'm headed over to my lab. I just wanted to say hi." He finished his tuna sandwich quickly and gave Philip a kiss on the cheek. "Nice meeting you, Lucas."

Jason arrived in the lab at five-twenty to find an envelope lying on his desk. In it was a payroll check made out to him for $800.00. He walked down to Dr. Glassman's office and knocked on the door, which was open.

"I'm sorry to interrupt, Dr. Glassman. There's been a mistake. Someone has made a check out to me. I'm returning it." He held out the envelope. "Maybe you can correct the problem."

"There's no mistake." Dr. Glassman smiled. "You've worked hard in this lab. I managed to get you an eight hundred per month stipend as a token of my appreciation. I worry that you are working too hard and not taking any time for yourself." He looked at Jason with concern and, after pausing, continued, "Having said that, how is the new computer program coming along? Your idea is very intriguing."

"It's coming along well. The program is almost finished. Dr. Fang is amazing, and I think it has real potential. But the paycheck is completely unnecessary." He offered the check again. "I'd gladly pay *you* to work here. I'm taking away much more than I'm giving."

"Forget it." Dr. Glassman waved his hand, and Jason put the check in his pocket. "How are things with Phil?"

"They couldn't be better, sir."

"Good. Get back to work."

Jason turned to leave, smiling to himself about Philip and grateful for the extra money.

☙❧❧

Over the next four weeks, Jason worked in the lab every weeknight and usually on Saturday mornings. He saved Sunday for Philip, who rarely went to the hospital unless there was an emergency surgery that required his presence. The pace in the laboratory had become frenetic. Unlike the other postdoc fellows, Dr. Fang had no PhD candidates or lab assistants working with him, since his work was strictly computer-based. Dr. Fang actually depended on Jason to help with the data that was coming in at an almost incomprehensible rate from hundreds of collaborative labs, as well as Dr. Glassman's postdoc fellows. Jason wondered how Dr. Fang would have managed all the data without his help. He supposed Dr. Glassman would have had to hire an assistant.

Jason had also reviewed and contributed to several papers written by the various postdoc fellows that used data derived from some of his data analysis. Jason learned that he would be listed as a coauthor on several of the papers, giving him great satisfaction that he really was contributing to the lab.

Dr. Fang still declined Jason's numerous invitations to have dinner with him and Philip, and, at times, Jason was quite worried about him. He continued to get the eight p.m. phone calls, and, after each call, he would usually return to the computer room visibly shaken. Jason thought that his sister must have serious problems. He offered to help but was always waved off without a response. When Jason mentioned to Dr. Glassman that he was worried about Dr. Fang and that his sister in the San Francisco area was having problems, Dr. Glassman had looked surprised. He'd told Jason that as far as he knew, Dr. Fang was an only child and had no relatives in the United States. That surprised Jason, who concluded that Dr. Fang probably had had an affair that resulted in a pregnancy. He wished Dr. Fang felt comfortable enough to confide in him.

The oncology fellow told Jason to take the Thanksgiving weekend off since the oncology service was lightly populated with patients during the holiday and Jason had worked harder than any other intern with whom he'd been associated. Jason didn't argue with him and picked his father up from LaGuardia Airport on Wednesday evening in his Jetta, which he was driving for the first time since he'd arrived in New York City. He had left the car parked in the hospital parking facility for the entire time and was relieved when the engine started.

He ran to his father as he exited the security area, hugging him tightly. "I'm so happy to see you, Dad."

His father was crying, which Jason had expected.

Jason laughed. "I'm a chip off the ol' block. I wish you hadn't given me that crying gene of yours."

They both laughed as Jason picked up his father's carryon and they walked to the car.

Jason had arranged for Philip to meet them at an Italian restaurant near the Waldorf Astoria at eight. They would be driving to Wilton on Thursday morning to have Thanksgiving with the entire Olsen family. Philip was waiting outside the restaurant as Jason and his father pulled up in his Jetta. Philip opened Jonathan Green's door, and, as he got out, Philip put his hand out to shake hands.

Instead, Jason's father put his hands on Philip's shoulders, looked at him, and then hugged him tightly. He pushed him gently back, looked again at him, and smiled. "You're as handsome as Jason has described. I told him no one could be that handsome, but as usual, Jason is right. It's so good to finally meet you."

"It is so nice to meet you as well." Philip was beaming. "And thank you for bringing Jason into this world."

Philip hugged Jason, and they went into the restaurant as the valet took the car. The conversation was easy, with Jason's father asking Philip many questions about his work and giving Jason updates on the news in Mississippi and the family business. Mr. Green told Jason that Uncle Harold Lin, his Hong Kong business partner, was ill with pancreatic cancer and would likely not live much longer, bringing tears to Jason's eyes. During the dinner, Jason and Philip played their customary and not-so-subtle game of pushing each other's legs under the table and frequently laughing together. Jason's father smiled at them both and tears rose to his eyes.

"What's wrong, Dad?" Jason asked with a worried expression.

"Nothing at all. You two just remind me of your mother and me."

Philip smiled. "Now I know where Jason's frequent tears come from."

Jason spent the night with Philip, and they made love for almost two hours. Even though they had been together for almost four months, they made love a minimum of four times weekly, and Jason fantasized about Philip on the other days. He wondered if Philip did the same.

The next morning they picked Jason's father up in the Jetta and drove to Wilton. Jason's father was welcomed with hugs from Mr. and Mrs. Olsen, and Jason was received with hugs and kisses. Philip's younger sister Anna bounced down the stairs as everyone entered the foyer. She was twenty-five years old and, like her mother, was stunning, with a beautiful, classic face, long blonde hair, and a perfect figure. She was doing graduate studies in hospital administration at the University of Pennsylvania and according to Philip was the smartest one in the family.

She ran to Jason, looked at him, and gave him a big kiss on the cheek. Then she made a dour face at Philip. "I don't know how you got such a gorgeous guy. It's not fair." She gave Philip a kiss and hugged Jason's father.

Philip's younger brother, Paul, who was twenty-four and a second-year law student at Yale, ran down the stairs after her, skipping two steps at a time. He was extraordinarily handsome, with long blond hair and a beautiful, square face, like Philip's. He gave his brother a bear hug and went to Jason and gave him a big hug. "I have no idea what you see in that bum, but I'm glad you do."

Everyone laughed. Paul shook Jonathan's hand and welcomed him to Wilton.

The house was warm, with large fires burning in the living room and den. As they sat in the living room, drinking wine and engaged in lively conversation, Jason opened his backpack and took out three wrapped presents, one for Philip's parents and one each for his brother and sister. Jason had taken scores of pictures at the hospital of Philip in his scrubs. His favorite was Philip sitting at a table with his chin resting on one hand. Philip was wearing a faint, impish smile and looking directly into the camera.

The picture would have been suitable for any magazine sporting the most handsome male models, and Jason had spent most of his first lab paycheck having them professionally framed. Jason's mother walked over and kissed Jason as Anna hugged the picture. Philip had not seen the picture. He went to Jason and whispered in his ear, "You're amazing. I love you."

Philip's brother caused everyone to laugh when he said, "Hey, Jason, I love the frame. Thanks very much.

But would you mind if I substituted a picture of my favorite *Playboy* model?"

The day was perfect for Jason, and he sensed his father
was not only comfortable with the Olsen family but also
thoroughly enjoying himself. His father was a staunch
Democrat but had always been a fiscal conservative, so
although Philip's father and his father had opposite political affiliations, they had similar attitudes regarding the
economy and social issues. Philip's parents had been very
interested in the Green family background and questioned
Jonathan about his family and his wife's family in a lively discussion at the dining room table. Jason and Philip
pressed their arms and legs against each other as they
usually did, laughing together on occasion, and not mind-
ing in the least that everybody noticed.

"You both are like two grade-school kids. It's nauseating," Paul finally said after the two laughed aloud after a
particularly strong push by Philip. Jason knew he was
blushing bright red. Philip got up to take his plate into the
kitchen for a second helping, and Jason followed him.
They grabbed each other and kissed deeply. Had his mother been present, Jason thought, the day would have been
perfection.

After the midafternoon Thanksgiving dinner, Jason
went for a seven-mile run, Philip and his brother threw a
football in the backyard, and the parents talked in the living room, mostly about Jason and Philip. After Jason returned, showered, and dressed, all returned to the living
room and the rest of the afternoon was spent in conversation about politics, social issues, and questions to all four
children about their studies and training.

During one of the economic discussions, Mr. Olsen ex-
pressed the view that China and the United States were
headed toward an economic war and mentioned that his
firm had just filed a legal claim on behalf of a defense con-

tractor against the Chinese government. Apparently, the firm's computer system had been broken into and top-secret information had been stolen. The breach had been traced to a group in China that was linked to the Chinese government, which in turn had ignored inquiries from both the corporation and the State Department.

Jason was curious and asked questions about the types of computers and programs that were involved, details that Mr. Olsen didn't know or understand. "Has it been documented that the Chinese government has been involved in any other computer attacks?"

"Well, I'm not the primary attorney on this case, but from what I understand, it is public knowledge that in 2003 and last year, hackers from mainland China breached several government computer systems in Taiwan as well as a number of private industry computers in Taiwan. And we know that these same hackers have attacked multiple unclassified military computer systems in the US. I'm not privy to details, but I know the state department is taking these attacks very seriously."

Jason frowned. "Do you know if there have been any cases of Chinese nationals caught spying in US industry or at universities?"

"I don't have any such knowledge, Jason. Why do you ask?" Mr. Olsen looked at him, his eyebrows rising slightly.

"It's just that there are so many Chinese nationals at almost every university in the US. A lot of valuable information in research labs could be easily stolen, particularly research into new pharmaceuticals. That could very profitable."

"Well, I haven't heard of any such thing. But it does seem surprising that we allow Chinese nationals into our government-funded research labs without more security measures being taken. By the way, Harvey tells me that you are doing amazing things in his lab. He thinks you might be trying to take over his position," Mr. Olsen said with a laugh.

"Dr. Glassman has nothing to worry about." Jason rolled his eyes. "I understand why he won a Nobel Prize. As I told Dr. Glassman, I'm taking a lot more from the lab than I'm giving." He looked at his father. "Dad, we should get back to the city before it gets too late. Philip is staying here for the rest of the weekend, and I want to get up early and show you some of the sights."

"Jason, come with me. I want to show you something before you leave." Philip stood up and Jason followed him upstairs to his bedroom. "I don't want to be without you this weekend. Can't you and your father stay?"

"It's best you spend some time with your brother and sister, and your folks have had enough of us."

Philip pushed Jason onto the bed, and they began kissing, passionately, desperately. Jason pushed him away. "Philip, not now. I'll be waiting for you at your place Sunday evening, undressed, in bed. My daddy leaves in the early afternoon."

❧❧❧

The traffic back to the city was light and the drive fast. "You know, I think Philip is wonderful." His father looked over at him, smiling mischievously. "He didn't take his eyes off you the entire time we were together. And you looked at him the way your mother used to look at me. I'm so happy for you."

"I never dreamed that I would ever be in a relationship as perfect and happy as yours and Mom's. I can't imagine my life without Philip, and it makes me all the more sad that you don't have Mom anymore. I don't know how you handle it."

"I have you and your sister, and the business keeps me busy."

"You know, Mom would want you to have companionship. It's been over two years. Have you thought of going out?"

His father sighed. "There is not a large market in our little town."

"Why don't you sell the business and move here or to New Orleans to be near Susie?"

"Jason, this business has been in our family for seventy years. It would be hard to give it up."

"There is no one in our family to take it over once you retire. It's just a business, it's not family. And there *is* a huge market of single women in New York and New Orleans."

His dad smiled. "That is thoughtful, Jason. I love you. We'll see."

The next morning, Jason showed his father the hospital, and then they walked to Dr. Glassman's lab. Dr. Glassman was busy at his desk. Jason knocked lightly on his door. "I'm sorry to interrupt, Dr. Glassman. I just wanted my father to meet you."

Dr. Glassman got up and came around the desk to shake Jonathan's hand. "It is certainly an honor to meet the father of this remarkable young man. You did good, Mr. Green."

Jason blushed, shocked by what Dr. Glassman had just said.

Jonathan chuckled. "I guess my bias is well-founded after hearing that accolade. I've talked with Jason literally every day since he has arrived here, and there has never been a conversation that he hasn't talked about you and your accomplishments. Thank you for taking him in the way you have. I'm grateful."

Dr. Glassman smiled at Jason. "Isn't there some work

you can do in your office for a few minutes?"

The rest of the lab was empty, and Jason went into his office. He was determined to take the weekend off from the lab and spend the entire time with his father. He frowned. A sixty-four-gigabyte memory stick was lying on the desk behind one of Dr. Fang's computer screens. It looked like one of the two he'd found in the desk drawer. He inserted the stick into one of the USB slots and a file appeared. He opened it, and his frown deepened. He recognized those numbers. It was the raw data from one of the other postdoc fellow's experiments from August through October. What possible reason could Dr. Fang have for downloading these results onto a memory stick?

His conversation about spying with Philip's father came back to him. *Not Dr. Fang.* Jason shook his head. Dr. Fang cared too much about what they were doing, particularly about the success of the project they were developing. He put the memory stick into the drawer. He'd ask him about it after the weekend.

His father and Dr. Glassman appeared at the door. "I wasn't serious when I said you had work to do. Get out of here and show your father a little bit of New York. See you next week."

Jason and his father spent the rest of the weekend going to the usual tourist spots—the Empire State Building, the World Trade Center site, and the Statue of Liberty. They went to the art museums, visited the Natural History Museum, and saw *Les Miserables* on Saturday night, Jason for the second time. Jason took him to his favorite restaurant in Chinatown, where he told his father about the night he'd taken Philip there for the first time.

Jason's father looked around with approval. "How did you find this place?"

"Uncle Harold told me about it. I had written to him that I was going to New York City last May, and he sent me the address of this place. I called Uncle Harold this morning, by the way." He smiled and thanked the waiter as he placed the next course in front of them. "He sounded weak, but he was happy to hear from me. I'll miss him."

"You were a good nephew to him." His father touched his hand. "And your Mandarin impressed us both—I could never learn even the easy tones. Harold gave up on me!"

They both chuckled over that.

Jason and his father had brunch at the Carnegie Deli on Sunday morning, and then Jason drove him to LaGuardia. Memories of growing up with his father and mother—sitting with his father listening to classical music on Sundays, discussing esoteric economic theories, discussing the classic books—remained vivid in his mind. He thought about how lucky he was as he hugged his father tightly and wouldn't let go.

His father was crying. "I'll be back soon. I'm proud of you, Jason. I'll talk to you tomorrow."

"I love you, Dad. Safe travels."

Jason drove slowly back to the hospital and parked his car. He walked to his apartment, put his running clothes on, and ran to Philip's apartment, which was only about two miles away. He decided to continue running and did the six-mile run around Central Park in a light mist, thinking about his father, his mother, and Philip and how lucky he was. He had always been tormented by all the evil in the world, the poverty, stupidity, racism, bigotry, and hate. He felt guilty because a loving family had always surrounded him, he had never wanted for material things, and he now had a loving partner. He had been associated with brilliant people, all with good intentions.

The thought that there must be a God had crossed his mind before, but Jason immediately remembered the masses that had to contend with evil, hate, and poverty on a daily basis. As always, he concluded that the explanation for his good fortune was simple: luck.

Jason undressed, showered, and was in bed when Philip arrived. Philip stood at the bedroom door. Both men looked at each other for a long moment without saying a word—Jason with a serious expression, Philip with that exquisite sly grin. Jason pulled the covers away to expose his body, already aroused. Philip undressed, and they made love for the next two hours, finally falling asleep in each other's arms.

CHAPTER 10

Jason finished his rotation on the oncology service at the end of November. Interns were allowed a month of elective during the academic year, and December was Jason's designated elective month. Most interns picked an easy rotation, such as a subspecialty consultation service like dermatology, allowing for relatively short hours and a good night's sleep. Jason had received reluctant permission to spend his elective month in Dr. Glassman's laboratory. The chief residents had initially not approved the request, since it was understood that the intern year was strictly for clinical experience. However, Dr. Stern had interceded after Jason asked Dr. Glassman to talk with the chief residents.

Jason arrived in the lab by six every morning and usually didn't leave until ten at night, almost always the last to depart. Philip had wanted Jason to move in with him, at least during his elective month, but Jason continued to insist on staying in his apartment because of the long hours. He continued to have lunch with Philip, except on days that Philip couldn't leave the operating room, but Jason spent every weekend at Philip's apartment.

Philip's parents came to the city the second weekend in December to have dinner with Philip and Jason, and Jason made a point of calling Philip's parents on occasion to say hello. Once or twice during the weekdays, Jason would leave the lab at seven or eight, put on his running clothes, and run to Philip's apartment, surprising him. They would make love and then, reluctantly, he would run back to his apartment to sleep.

Jason's work in the lab continued to be extraordinarily productive. He continued to work well with Dr. Fang, and the amount of information that they processed and analyzed astounded even Dr. Glassman. Jason had asked Dr. Fang about the sixty-four-gigabyte memory stick, and Dr. Fang casually stated that he frequently downloaded raw data to his personal computer to evaluate at his leisure at home.

The data that Jason and Dr. Fang analyzed resulted in notable discoveries in tumor genetics. Jason also started using their new computer program to make models of various proteins that resulted from genetic mutations and which helped to explain the disease process that resulted from the mutation. He had also developed a computer program that was able to make theoretical protein models that might help explain abnormalities in various disorders. These protein models would allow scientists to work backward to look for specific genetic mutations. Even Dr. Glassman had shown excitement about this novel computer program, exclaiming in one Friday afternoon conference that it was pioneering research.

Philip had been very busy in the operating room during December, and Jason ate lunch alone two or three days each week. One such day in mid-December, Jason looked up to see Seth Goldberg, whom he had not seen in over a month, standing over him.

Jason jumped up and hugged him. "How've you been? I miss seeing you."

"You spoiled me. I've been working my ass off trying to keep interns in line." Seth sat down to eat his lunch with Jason. "I hear you're doing your elective in Glassman's lab. I've never heard of an intern doing such a thing."

Jason laughed. "I'm actually working harder now than I did seeing patients, and I'm learning a lot. I'll get back to patients. I love doing clinical work. But it's been such a productive time in the lab, I just wanted to spend full time in the lab for the month."

"I'm not worried about you. How goes it with Philip?"

"I cannot believe how lucky I am." Jason grinned at him. "Anything new in your social life?" He raised one eyebrow, knowing what his answer would be.

"As a matter of fact, your friend Sheri finally agreed to go out with me. I'm sure you know we've been dating for the past three months." He chuckled. "And come to find out, you were responsible for her agreeing to go out with me."

Jason laughed. "How's that?"

"She told me that you two became good friends, and you told her that I was some godlike person who would be the catch of the century. Well, that's what did it. Of course, when she got to know me, she fell head over heels for me."

"Hey, Seth, if you were gay, I would have gone after you. I wasn't lying to her."

They both laughed.

☙❧

The following day Jason went to the cafeteria and waited ten minutes for Philip to arrive. *He must be in surgery again.* He bought a sandwich and decided to make the quick walk to his own apartment to get a CD of Chopin piano pieces he had made for Dr. Glassman. He had learned from one of the other postdoc fellows that Chopin was Dr. Glassman's favorite composer, and he'd forgotten to pack the CD that morning. It was a crisp, clear, beautiful winter day in New York City, and although Jason was usually bothered by the cold, he didn't feel the freeze that day as he walked home. He'd been with Philip the night before and thought of him on the entire walk, how much he loved him, how lucky he was. He didn't notice the ice forming on the sandwich as he ate it. He didn't notice the people he passed in the street.

Jason opened the door to his apartment. The lights were on and standing in the middle of the room, naked with a towel, was Lucas Franklin, the anesthesiology resident he had met at lunch several weeks ago. Jason stood frozen, confused, as Lucas gasped.

"Did you say something?" Philip walked out of the bathroom with a towel around his waist.

All three men stood, paralyzed. The only sound was the outside traffic. Jason's heart began pounding, hard and slow. He felt light-headed and vomited his sandwich onto the floor as a wave of nausea overwhelmed him. He slowly walked into the kitchen, opened a roll of paper towels, lowered himself to his knees, and slowly wiped up the vomit. Lucas disappeared into the bathroom, and Philip stood motionless at the bathroom door, pale and silent, watching Jason.

Jason finished cleaning, got unsteadily to his feet, put the soiled towels into a plastic bag, slowly walked to his bedside drawer, and retrieved the CD he had made for Dr. Glassman. He walked to the door, still light-headed, tears burning his face, and turned briefly to look at Philip. Then he walked out of the apartment.

He sat down on the stairs outside his apartment, continuing to feel nauseated and light-headed, afraid that he would faint if he stood up. He knew that his blood pressure had fallen very low as a result of the nausea and emotional trauma. He sat for several minutes, trying to understand what had just happened, tears running down his cheeks. Aside from the death of his mother, he had never felt such an unbearable emptiness and sadness. He wished he could go to sleep and wake up from this nightmare to realize it was just another vivid dream.

Questions flowed through Jason's mind: Did Philip love this other man? What had Jason done wrong? What could he have done differently to prevent this? Did Philip not love him anymore? How could such a profound love, which Philip seemed to have for him, evaporate so quickly? Jason finally stood up and walked back to the lab, tears flowing, unaware of the stares from other pedestrians.

Jason remained in the lab, trying to concentrate on his work and analyzing data they had received from a genome lab in San Diego. During the afternoon, visions of Lucas and Philip standing in his apartment brought on waves of nausea, causing him to turn pale and feel faint. The acid from his stomach had burned his tongue, and the taste of his own bile lingered.

Dr. Fang had told him several times that he looked ill and should go home, but Jason didn't move from his desk. He sat alone in the lab at nine o'clock, reliving what had happened, and began sobbing uncontrollably. The only other time he had ever sobbed was at his mother's funeral. He heard a soft knock at his door and looked up to see Dr. Glassman looking down at him.

Dr. Glassman's expression was almost desperate. "Jason, what can I do to help?"

"It's nothing, Dr. Glassman. Thanks for asking." Jason could not wipe the tears fast enough to dry his cheeks. "Dr. Glassman, I made this for you. I hope you enjoy it." He handed him the Chopin CD.

Dr. Glassman stood Jason up and hugged him tightly, not letting go for several minutes. Even in his anguish,

Jason was shocked at Dr. Glassman's demonstration of sympathy. Dr. Glassman finally let go and looked at Jason. "I'm a pretty good scientist but not so good in counseling about love. But whatever happened between you and Phil, it can be repaired." His voice sounded hoarse with emotion. "There are no perfect relationships, and I suspect you just discovered the first imperfection in yours. There will be other imperfections." He paused, and held Jason's shoulders. "You are strong, Jason, stronger than you'll ever know. Don't give up on Phil. He's not perfect, and you're not perfect either." Another pause. "Thanks for the CD."

Dr. Glassman turned and quietly left Jason, still in shock at Philip's betrayal but equally stunned at Dr. Glassman's compassion.

Jason sat catatonic for another twenty minutes, his mind blank and drained of emotion. He walked back to his apartment, opened the door and there sat Philip at the small dining table, eyes red, looking at Jason with a sadness that Jason had never seen. Jason stood frozen at the door, the two staring at each other in silence. Philip finally got up, walked to the door, and put his arms around Jason, hugging him tightly, not letting go for minutes. "Jason, I am so sorry, I'm so sorry. Please forgive me. I'm so sorry."

Jason tried to break away so that he could sit as Philip repeated the words. He had once again become nauseated and light-headed, and he thought he might faint but Philip would not let him go.

"Jason, please forgive me. I am so sorry."

Jason finally pulled away and sat on the couch. Philip took one of the chairs from the dining room table and sat in front of Jason. Both looked down at the floor, a resounding silence dominating the ambiance.

"Do you love him?" Jason finally broke the silence.

"No, no, no, no! It's not like that." Philip's voice rose and broke. "I have no feelings for him. For what it's worth, he's a Mormon, married with two children. It was sex, not even good sex. There was no meaning in it." He paused running his fingers through his hair. "It was something *he* needed—*he* wanted. I've been sitting here all afternoon trying to understand why I did it. There are no excuses. I've always been in control, all my life, and I have a control over him that I don't have over you. I've lost all control as far as my feelings for you. Sexually, I was always the one in control. Not with you. None of this makes sense, and there are no excuses. I know I can't live without you. Please give me a chance?"

"You still want to be with me?" Jason started sobbing again.

Philip's voice skated higher. "I meant it when I said I would not want to live if I lost you. I'm deeply in love with you. I don't know why I did it. I can't believe I've hurt you like this. Please get mad at me, hit me, do something."

Jason said nothing, couldn't look at him.

"Don't you want to know about what happened with Lucas? I know what I say has no credibility, but this was the first time with him since I met you. We used to hook up before I met you, but it was never emotional."

"I don't want to know anything about you and Lucas. I just need some time. Right now my only emotion is deep sadness. I've done something wrong to make you need that. I thought I had given you my body and soul." He couldn't look at Philip and kept his eyes on the floor.

"You did nothing wrong. Please forgive me."

Jason was silent for several minutes, looking away from Philip, gathering his thoughts. He finally turned to Philip. "What makes me so deeply sad is that our relationship has lost its perfection." He fixed his eyes on the floor once more. "I couldn't have imagined a more perfect relationship than the one we had, and now we've lost that forever, and that gives me a tremendous feeling of emptiness." Tears burned their way down his cheeks again. "Since I met you, I've often thought of what Tolstoy said in *Anna Karenina*: 'If you look for perfection, you'll never be content.' I never had to look for perfection with you. It was just there, and I had never been so content in my life. I—I'll miss that feeling of contentment."

Philip held Jason in his arms for a long time, saying nothing. Jason knew that Philip was in pain, maybe as much pain as he was feeling. But what he had done with Lucas did have some meaning. It had to.

"Can I stay with you tonight?"

"Not tonight." Those words hurt. "I'm exhausted and I have to get up very early. Maybe I'll come over on Friday, if it's okay with you, and we can meet for lunch tomorrow if you're available." The words were mechanical. Jason thought that he might have to move to another apartment. He was afraid that visions of Philip and Lucas would appear every time he opened his door. He would give it some time.

"I understand. I'll see you tomorrow at lunch. I love you, Jason."

The "I love you" sounded like a question.

"I love you too," Jason answered softly. And he meant it.

Philip left Jason alone. Sad, emotionally spent, he pulled his bed out, set his alarm, and without washing or taking his clothes off, got into bed, and fell asleep.

Jason awoke after a restless sleep to the alarm, put on his running clothes, and went for his run. He had a runner's high usually at the two-mile mark, and he looked forward to that feeling.

Maybe it would lessen the sadness that was overwhelming him.

෨෨෨

He was nearing the end of his elective month in Dr. Glassman's lab, it was already the twentieth of December, and the amount of data that was coming in from other institutions as well as their own laboratory was overwhelming but exciting. He would focus on the lab. He was, after all, privy to raw data from research labs across the country—he was literally at the forefront of genomic and bioinformatics research.

The next morning, Dr. Glassman stopped at Jason's office, something that he had never before done. "Jason, thank you again for the CD. That was very thoughtful. Are you feeling better today?"

Jason gave him the best smile he could manage. "Yes, thank you very much."

"Good. Get back to work."

Jason immersed himself in the data analysis. At noon, he walked to the cafeteria and saw Philip sitting with Seth Goldberg. Jason grabbed a sandwich—he had not eaten in twenty-four hours—and walked to the table. Seth immediately got up and gave Jason a longer than usual hug and then walked away without saying a word.

Jason smiled at Philip. "Hey."

"I can't believe you're talking to me."

Jason had never seen Philip with swollen eyes. He had obviously been in distress.

Jason started unwrapping his sandwich. "What's with Seth? He's acting weird."

"I told him what happened."

"Philip—" Jason jerked his head up, shocked. "—please don't tell anyone else. It's no one's business." To change the subject, he started asking Philip about his day, telling him about the CD he had given to Dr. Glassman and asking Philip about his family.

When they had finished eating, Philip put his hand on Jason's forearm. "I have a departmental lunch meeting tomorrow so I can't have lunch with you. And I'm telling you the truth. Will I see you tomorrow evening?"

"Of course. I'll be there when I'm finished in the lab." Jason said it automatically and without conviction. "See you then."

Everything had changed. He was profoundly saddened, but anger had entered his emotional basket. He was angry because of what had happened—in his own apartment, no less—and what that betrayal had done to what was, for him, a perfect relationship. Sadness was his overwhelming emotion, but his anger was increasing. And anger was an emotion that he was unwilling to live with for more than a brief time.

He was startled when Philip brought up the control issue in trying to explain his actions. The thought of him controlling Philip, or Philip controlling him, sexually or otherwise, had never entered Jason's mind. Their sexual relationship had been passionate, and they had openly explored each other's likes and dislikes. Jason was never domineering nor had Philip ever tried to dominate him. Jason would have to think about that explanation, and if Philip needed to be in control, sexually or otherwise...well, it wasn't in Jason's nature to be submissive.

He frowned. If Philip needed that sort of control, particularly sexually, then in order to continue their relationship, Jason would have to ignore future indiscretions because they would surely occur. Otherwise, their relationship would have to end.

His first angry thought had been, in fact, to end the relationship immediately since he doubted that this kind of need and behavior would ever change. But he decided to give it time.

He still loved Philip. Perhaps there would be a way.

CHAPTER 11

Jason and Philip had long planned to go to Wilton on Christmas Eve, which was the coming Saturday, and stay until Sunday night. Jason's enthusiasm for the visit had waned, and he was apprehensive. He didn't want Philip's family to know what had happened, and he was not sure if he would be able to disguise his anger. But Philip had told Jason several weeks ago that his parents were particularly looking forward to their visit, because this year Hanukkah started at sunset on Christmas day, and they had wanted to celebrate the Jewish holiday with Jason.

He continued to talk to his father daily and was fairly certain that he had been successful at not revealing his sadness, although he knew that his father was extraordinarily keen at sensing Jason's emotions.

Jason finished in the lab on Friday night at nine, walked home, and put on his running clothes. He ran to Philip's apartment and decided to run another six miles around the park before going in. He walked into Philip's apartment to find Philip sitting in the unlit living room, staring out the window.

"Hey, Philip," Jason said softly. He was sweating even though it was freezing outside.

Philip turned to Jason, eyes red and swollen. He got up and went to him, holding him without saying a word.

Jason pulled away after a few minutes. "Philip, I stink. I'm going to shower."

"I need to talk to you. I need to try and explain, both to you and myself, why I did this."

"I think you told me." Jason couldn't meet Philip's eyes. "That it is a control thing with you. And you had that with Lucas but not with me."

"I guess that's it. I've always been the dominant person in sexual relationships, and with you...well, we are equal or maybe you are even the dominant one. It's new for me. You don't really need me. Lucas needed me and wanted me to be dominant. He begged me—he was desperate—and I just succumbed. I'm not a psychotherapist, but it's the best I can do. It was just sex, and my ego."

Jason continued to stare at the floor. There was a chill in the apartment, and the evaporating sweat made him shiver.

"I never thought I was good enough for you. I couldn't understand why you wanted to be with me." Jason spoke slowly and deliberately and then looked directly at Philip. "But I'm not a submissive person, sexually or otherwise. I couldn't be happy in a relationship in which I had to play a submissive role. It's just not me. Nor is it in my nature to be dominant. I would never be attracted to a submissive person." He paused and again looked down at the floor. "I'm not judging you. If you have that need, then it's just the way you're wired. But I'm wired differently. It may be—" Jason paused as tears welled up in his eyes. "—it may be that we just aren't meant to be."

Jason tried to turn around to go into the bathroom, but Philip held him back.

"Jason, please don't say or think that." Philip's voice tightened. "Just give me a chance. I'll show you." He paused. "Do you think you'll ever be able to forget this?"

Jason looked at Philip and tears started to trickle down

his cheeks. "I don't forget things, Philip, even things that I want to forget. It's part of my...craziness." His voice caught on the word. "The shock on Lucas's face is just as vivid to me now as when I walked into my apartment. I see that hourglass shaped birthmark on his left thigh, the blank stare on your face, and your partially erect penis showing through the towel. I can even smell the soap on your bodies, and then I become nauseated. I can't get it out of my mind. It's—it's an affliction." Jason wiped the tears from his cheeks.

"It will never happen again. Never. I know you can't believe that now." Philip was pleading. "But give me a chance, give *us* a chance."

"I'm not going anywhere. I don't know what's going to happen with us, but I know I love you, and I'm willing to give it a try. You'll just have to be patient with me." Jason turned and walked into the bathroom, leaving Philip in the darkened living room. Jason was angry, and he didn't want it to show. After showering he got into bed, and Philip followed shortly after. That night Jason had a night terror, and Philip held him until he fell back to sleep. He didn't tell Philip that his vivid dream was about Philip and Lucas.

The following morning, Jason and Philip drove to Wilton in the Porsche. Jason made an effort to talk most of the way. He asked Philip about his work and persisted in getting answers, although Philip was unusually quiet. Jason talked about his research, the progress that he and Dr. Fang had been making, and how much he had come to like and respect Dr. Glassman. There were stretches of silence, and Jason took Philip's right hand into his for the last half of the trip.

They pulled up to the mansion and the front door immediately opened. Mr. Olsen came out and opened Jason's door. "Jason, it's good to see you again." He gave

Jason an unusually long hug. "How are you doing?"

"I'm well, Mr. Olsen. It's great to see you."

Mr. Olsen put his arm around Jason and led him into the house without saying hello to Philip, and Jason suddenly realized that Philip must have told his father what had happened. "Mr. Olsen, let me go help Philip get the bag. We'll be right in."

Jason walked outside to find Philip leaning against the car with tears in his eyes. "Philip, I asked you not to tell anyone what happened. You obviously told your daddy."

"I tell him everything. He's furious with me."

"If you tell anyone else, *I'll* be furious with you. Now come in." Jason's anger had become overt, and Philip appeared startled.

The two walked into the house. Paul came running down the stairs and gave Philip and Jason hugs without saying anything, which was most unusual for Philip's loquacious brother. Mrs. Olsen and Anna came in from the kitchen, both kissing Jason and Philip and forcing smiles. It was clear that the mood was far from festive, and Jason was determined to change that immediately.

"I can tell that y'all know Philip and I have had a minor glitch in our relationship. It is minor, and we are going to be fine." He held their gazes, one at a time. "We both love each other very much. This is a happy time, so let's all be happy." Jason opened his backpack, pulled out five packages, went over to the Christmas tree, and set them down next to the other presents. Mr. Olsen turned to Philip and embraced him. Jason ran up the stairs to Philip's room, remarking that he wanted to unpack the remainder of his bag.

Jason sat on Philip's bed, paralyzed. He shouldn't have made this trip. He should have made an excuse and let Philip and his family celebrate their Christmas. He closed his eyes briefly. He adored Philip's family, and he didn't want to be the source of tension. But he wasn't good at hiding his feelings, and Philip's parents were clearly upset. He would need to put on a good act, as if nothing had happened.

He drew a ragged breath. If he didn't, the weekend would be tense for everyone.

"Jason, what's wrong?" Philip stood at the door, his expression sad and concerned.

Jason shook his head. "I shouldn't have come. I can cut the tension downstairs with a knife. I adore your family, and I'm going to completely ruin their Christmas. That's the last thing I want to do. I think it would be best for y'all if I go back to the city."

"Phil, let me talk to Jason alone."

Jason startled at Mr. Olsen's voice. He hadn't seen him standing outside the door. Philip turned around and walked away.

Mr. Olsen came into the room, shutting the door behind him. He sat next to Jason on the bed. "Jason, our Christmas will be miserable if you leave. I know that you two are going through a difficult time. Phil told me what he did, and I know it must have been like a knife stabbing you in the heart. My wife, Paul, Anna, and I have all become very fond of you, and we hurt for you. And it would make us doubly sad if you left."

"Mr. Olsen—" Jason drew a deep breath. "—I don't want to ruin your family's Christmas. It's very hard for me to act happy when I'm sad, and I can't bear the thought of being responsible for any hurt to you and your family."

"Phil is the one responsible, not you, and we'll deal with it. In the meantime, you will make our Christmas much happier if you stay. Besides, your friend Seth is on his way up here and is going to stay until tomorrow as well."

Jason felt the tears begin. "Okay, Mr. Olsen. I just don't want to make the weekend unpleasant for your family. Maybe if I go for a run I'll feel better."

"That's a great idea. Paul is getting ready to go for a run. Why don't you go with him?" Mr. Olsen wiped Jason's tears with his hands. "The hurt lessens with time, Jason. Most of us have gone through this, and it gets better."

Mr. Olsen stood up and left. Jason slowly put on his running suit and tennis shoes and walked downstairs, feeling almost lethargic. Paul was waiting for him in the foyer.

"Come on, old man. See if you can keep up with me." Paul smiled and opened the door. Jason followed him out. "I have a three-mile route or a seven-mile route. Your call," Paul said.

"Let's do seven." Jason grinned. "I'll do my best to keep up."

Jason ran next to Paul for about five minutes and then left him behind. After a half mile, Jason stopped and ran in place, waiting for Paul to catch up. Jason repeated the sequence until they had completed the seven miles in front of the mansion. Paul was breathing hard as he finished.

Paul grinned as he tried to catch his breath. "Damn, you are a machine. Where did you learn to run like that?"

"Paul, I'm a gay Jew who grew up in Mississippi." Jason smirked. "Gay Jews in Mississippi learn to run fast."

Paul burst out laughing. Mr. Olsen and Philip came out the front door. "What's so funny out here?" Mr. Olsen asked.

"Don't get into a running match with Jason. This guy is a fucking machine." Paul was still leaning over with both hands on his thighs, trying to catch his breath. As the four stood out front, Seth Goldberg drove up in his

Ford Fiesta and quickly got out of his car.

"Hi, Mr. Olsen," Seth said as he got out of the car and shook his hand. "Thanks so much for having me here. Jews have nowhere to eat on Christmas, and as you can see, that is a very serious problem for me." Seth placed his hands over his somewhat prominent midsection and everyone laughed. "Paul, it's been a long time." Seth gave Paul a hug and then hugged Philip and put his hand softly on Philip's face after the hug. "And *you*," Seth said forcefully, turning to Jason. "You tricked Paul into running with you. You have no shame." Seth gave Jason a big hug, and, although he was smiling, Jason could tell that Seth had noticed his sadness.

They went inside, and Anna and Mrs. Olsen came from the kitchen to greet Seth. Everyone sat in the living room, and the chat was lively. Everyone talked, and Jason found himself feeling more at ease. Philip was less talkative than usual, but he related some amusing hospital stories that made everyone laugh, including Jason. Paul was his usual chatty self, and he surprised everyone by announcing that he had a new girlfriend.

"Okay, everyone hold on to your seats," he said, grinning widely. Her name is Amy Edelstein. She is beautiful, Jewish, and smart. She has dark, curly hair. In short, she is Jason Green without the penis."

Everyone broke into laughter.

Jason laughed with everyone else and looked at Paul's parents. "Mr. and Mrs. Olsen, my deepest condolences. No wonderful gentile family such as yours should have to suffer their children bringing home two curly-haired Jews." More laughter. "Please excuse me. I'm going to go shower before my odor ruins everyone's appetite." He got up and went upstairs.

Philip walked in as he was getting dressed and leaned against the doorframe. "Are you feeling better?"

"Yes, thanks. The run did me good, and I've settled down. I just get these waves of sadness. Be patient with me." Jason reached for his shirt. "I just don't want to ruin your family's Christmas."

"If anyone has ruined it, I did." Philip stood still. "Can I kiss you before we go down?"

Jason smiled and walked to Philip. "Of course."

They kissed lightly, not the passionate kisses that they had been used to. It wasn't the same. Jason took Philip's arm and they walked downstairs.

Mrs. Olsen had gone out of her way to cook a traditional Jewish meal of brisket and potato latkes. Everyone seemed jovial and happy, and Jason was greatly relieved that the tension had eased. Jason and Philip sat next to each other, but Philip didn't try to press his leg and arm against Jason's, both to Jason's relief and sadness.

Jason and Philip slept together as usual. Philip put his arm around Jason when they were both in bed and kissed him on the cheek, and Jason smiled for him. They were both exhausted from sleepless nights the past week and both fell quickly to sleep. Jason woke with a night terror and, as usual, Philip held him tightly, and they both fell quickly back into a comfortable sleep.

Jason woke to an empty bed at eight a.m. He couldn't remember the last time that he had slept that late. He hopped out of bed and dressed quickly. Everyone was already downstairs in the den, sitting around the fireplace and Christmas tree, and they all teased him for sleeping late. Philip got up and kissed him on the cheek.

Mr. Olsen clapped his hands. "Now, we can all open presents."

Philip's parents gave Jason a beautiful blue cashmere sweater, and Paul and Anna each gave him classical CDs. Jason gave Paul an antique law book from the late 1700s by Sir William Blackstone. He had made a unique montage of family pictures that Philip had loaned him, digitizing them and arranging them artfully on his computer. He'd had the montage printed and beautifully framed, and gave one each to Mrs. Olsen and Anna. For Mr. Olsen, Jason had found a first-edition copy of Winston Churchill's *The Gathering Storm.* He knew that Mr. Olsen was a devotee of Winston Churchill and a member of the Churchill Society.

Jason had gotten Philip's present weeks ago. He had been asking Jason for a picture of himself for months. Jason already had a picture of Philip, which he kept at his bedside with his own family's pictures. It was the same picture that he had given to Philip's parents at Thanksgiving, and he had wondered whether Philip had looked at it while having sex with Lucas. Jason had a picture of himself, standing in casual clothes in Central Park, taken by a professional photographer. The silver frame was inscribed: *Love always, Jason.* Philip stared at the picture in silence, got up, and walked slowly up the stairs.

Everyone watched Philip as he sadly left the room. Philip had given Jason a DVD of Vladimir Horowitz's Moscow piano concert—the one that he had given on his first return to Russia after sixty years of absence. His card said: *Nothing can make up for what I have done to us. I'll love you always. Philip.* Philip returned, eyes reddened, his running clothes on.

"Hold on, brother. I'll run with you." Paul got up. "I know I won't have any problems keeping up with *you.*"

"Well, as you can see, I don't run." Seth stood up. "But Jason, why don't you take a walk with me?" He grinned. "I need a little exercise and won't do it unless I have someone to push me."

"Sure." Jason got up. "Mr. and Mrs. Olsen, Anna, thank you so much for the gifts. We'll be back soon if Seth doesn't keel over."

The two put on their coats and walked out of the house, tracking the three-mile course that Jason knew well. They walked in silence for a few minutes. "So, Jason," Seth finally said. "I know it's not my business, but what's going on with you and Phil?"

"It's so hard. This is the first serious relationship I've ever had, and I'm devastated. I can't get the memory of me walking in on them out of my head. And I can't believe he did it in my own apartment. It's like he wanted me to catch him. It's driving me crazy."

"It didn't mean anything to Phil."

"You know, Philip said the same thing, and I guess that's the usual excuse when someone catches his partner." He let his breath out, more than a little surprised by his own sudden surge of anger. "But that's bullshit. It does mean something. It *does*. Saying it means nothing is a cop-out." His voice rose, despite himself. "It means that what we had wasn't enough for Philip, sexually or otherwise." When Seth did not respond, Jason bit his lip and went on. "I know this may be too much information for you, but we've had sex four or five times a week since we met, and I don't mean wham-bam-thank-you-ma'am sex. We made love for hours every time. His excuse is that he has always been the dominator in his sexual relationships, and that with me he isn't. And that this guy Lucas needed Philip to dominate him. I don't get it. But I am smart enough to know this: Whatever his needs are that I can't give him, those needs aren't going to go away and neither will his behavior."

They walked several minutes in silence.

"So you're not the perfect match for Philip. I doubt that Philip has a perfect match. And I can guarantee you that you don't have a perfect match." Seth stopped and looked at Jason.

"Philip was the perfect match," Jason said softly.

"You just thought he was the perfect match. Obviously, he isn't." Seth shrugged. "Jason, there's no such thing as perfection in a relationship."

Jason looked at the ground. "I know, I know. Those who seek perfection are never content."

"Oh, I should have known you've read Tolstoy." Seth shook his head. "Neither of you is perfect for the other."

"I can handle imperfection, but isn't this betrayal?" Jason clenched his teeth briefly. "This is on a different plane from my inability to be submissive."

"What Philip did is in the ballpark. It's within two standard deviations of normal. It's not something that needs to destroy a relationship."

"You don't understand something about me." Jason took a quick breath, fists clenching, despite his attempts to control his emotion. "I'm a little, or maybe a lot, crazy. I can't forget even the smallest detail of what I saw when I walked in on them. I've already had vivid nightmares about it. I can tell you everything about Lucas's naked body. He has a birthmark shaped like an hourglass on his left thigh. He's missing his right fourth toe. He has a disgusting, uncircumcised penis." Seth laughed and shook his head, but Jason went on without pausing. "He has a hairy chest that has a silver dollar-sized patch of missing hair just to the right of his sternum. One eye is hazel and the other blue. He has a mole just above his navel that looks like a melanoma. I know I sound crazy to you. But I have this crazy memory, and I don't—I can't forget." His voice was rising, but he got it under control with some effort. "Maybe electric shock therapy would erase it." He paused and lowered his voice. "I'm sorry, Seth. I'm rambling. By the way, in all honesty, someone needs to tell Lucas to get that mole looked at."

Seth laughed softly, shook his head, and put his arm around Jason as they continued their walk.

Jason managed a smile. "Thanks for talking with me, Seth. I've no one else to talk with about this. I couldn't tell my daddy. He would worry himself to death."

"Well, my advice is to go slow. Don't make any rash decisions. You two have something special. Don't give it up for something like this." The remainder of their walk was in silence.

The rest of the day, the Olsen family, Jason, and Seth sat in the living room, talking nonstop. At sunset, Mrs. Olsen brought in a menorah with the eight candles, lit one candle, and said the Hebrew prayer for Hanukkah.

Seth applauded. "Mrs. Olsen, I hereby declare you an honorary Jew."

"Seth, you probably don't know this, but my maternal great-grandmother was Jewish, so I'm already an honorary Jew."

Shortly after the candle lighting, Seth left, and Jason and Philip said their good-byes. Jason embraced Mr. Olsen and thanked him for talking to him and making him stay. The whole Olsen family was planning to come to the city for a New Year's Eve dinner, and reservations at Trattoria Del'Arte had already been made.

They didn't talk much on the drive back to the city. The silence was not uncomfortable for Jason. It was actually welcome. Halfway to the city, Philip said, "Your picture is beautiful. I'll treasure it. Did you really want to give it to me?"

"Of course, and I will always love you, no matter what happens to us."

The remainder of the drive was in silence.

CHAPTER 12

Only five days remained for Jason to work full-time in Dr. Glassman's lab with Dr. Fang before his transition back to clinical medicine. He was to start back on a general medicine floor with a new resident, Craig Thomason, a first-year resident who had graduated from Stanford University Medical School. Jason had met him briefly a few months earlier at an internal medicine gathering.

Jason was very anxious to make the most of his last full week with Dr. Fang. He worked in the lab from six a.m. to ten p.m. every day during the next week, analyzing huge amounts of data from various labs with Dr. Fang, making further corrections in existing software programs, and further developing their own project.

Using their novel computer program, Jason and Dr. Fang had designed three proteins that should have a high affinity to unique cell surface proteins found on human breast cancer cells, human melanoma cells, and mouse sarcoma cells.

Dr. Glassman had made an agreement with a lab at Washington University in St. Louis to synthesize the proteins and another lab at the University of Michigan to perform in vitro studies to determine whether their proteins had the predicted high affinity for those cancer cells.

Jason was completely immersed in his work, and he

was thankful that he could forget about Philip and Lucas at least for brief periods of time.

He ate lunch every day with Philip and tension eased between them. Philip had asked Jason to spend the weekday nights with him for the week before New Year's, but Jason told him that he needed to be in the lab by six every morning and preferred to stay in his apartment because of the close proximity. He promised he would stay New Year's weekend with him. At lunch they talked about their work and family, and occasionally Philip tried to engage Jason in conversation about what he did with Lucas, but Jason would not respond and became silent.

His anger had intensified rather than moderated over time. He seemed to have little control over his growing fury, even though he intellectually believed that Philip loved him and that he was suffering greatly because of his indiscretion. They had not made love since the Lucas incident, and Jason was apprehensive about having sex with Philip.

On the Wednesday before New Year's, Jason finished his morning run and walked to the Starbucks on his way to the lab. He was exhausted. He had been awakened twice by night terrors, both vivid dreams of Lucas and Philip having sex. It was six a.m., and he was surprised to see Dr. Fang sitting at a table with an older Chinese man dressed in a navy pinstriped suit. They both had Tumi leather briefcases at their sides, and the older Chinese man was talking quietly in animated Mandarin, obviously unhappy about something. Jason smiled and walked up to Dr. Fang.

"Good morning, Dr. Fang. I've never seen you here."

They both looked up, surprised, and the older Chinese man quickly got up, picked up the Tumi briefcase at his side, and left the coffee shop without saying a word to either Dr. Fang or Jason.

"I'm sorry I interrupted your meeting, Dr. Fang. Please forgive me."

Dr. Fang's smile seemed strained. "No problem. He my old professor at MIT. We meet sometimes. He likes to keep up on what I doing."

Jason wondered what Dr. Fang had done to make his mentor so angry. He gave a mental shrug. It wasn't his business, and they weren't close enough for him to ask.

"Can I buy you some coffee, Dr. Fang?" Jason changed the subject, feeling sorry for the researcher. Whatever had passed between him and his former professor had clearly upset him.

"No," Dr. Fang answered. "I'll go back to my apartment and get some things. I will be in the lab as usual at seven."

Jason smiled, got in line to get his coffee, and walked to the lab. But something about that encounter kept nagging at him. Halfway there, he realized what it was. The briefcase the professor had carried away had been Dr. Fang's. At least the initials were the same. Jason made a mental note to tell Fang as soon as he arrived.

❦❦❦

Friday night was New Year's Eve, and Mr. and Mrs. Olsen, Paul, and Anna were to arrive at Philip's apartment by seven. Jason left the lab early so that he would be ready in plenty of time. He walked into Philip's apartment and found Philip in the shower. Jason undressed silently and got into the shower with him. Without saying a word, they began kissing, at first hesitantly but then passionately. It had been over a week.

They both had simultaneous orgasms in the shower after only a few minutes. It was completely different from their previous lovemaking, but Jason thought it was a start, and he saw some relief in Philip's expression.

"I love you so much, Jason." Philip's voice was hoarse with emotion.

"I love you, too," Jason said, drying his hair.

He had startled several times while in the shower, as a vision of Philip with Lucas had entered his mind. He knew that Philip had noticed how he had briefly pulled away. Jason had tried to ignore it, but he was unable to prevent the flashbacks. A wave of sadness, and anger, briefly overcame him, but he hid it from Philip as he finished drying off.

The Olsens arrived at seven. They sat down to wine and cheese and a lively chat, and everything seemed normal. At one point, Mr. Olsen and Philip disappeared into Philip's bedroom, and Philip appeared mildly upset when they came back into the living room. They arrived at Trattoria Del'Arte at nine to a fixed menu of antipasto, Caesar salad, veal fettuccini, and tiramisu. A variety of cheeses and port wine topped off the meal. Jason drank too much of the Italian red wine. This restaurant had special meaning to him, and he wanted no sadness to intrude on this evening. The wine helped.

Saturday was New Year's Day, and he stayed with Philip the entire day. It was their first full day alone, and Jason wasn't at all sure about how it would go. Philip had seemed nervous as well. Jason woke up late with the headache that he always got when he drank too much red wine. After a few ibuprofens and a light breakfast, Jason took Philip by the arm and led him into the bedroom. They made love for almost an hour. It was not their usual passionate lovemaking, and Jason pulled back several times, hyperventilating as the all-too-familiar images popped into his head. It was still good, but that intangible closeness and bonding seemed absent. A wave of sadness overwhelmed him once more. Philip knew and held Jason tight. He wouldn't let go, and Jason told himself he was content to lie in his lover's arms. Later, they ran their six-mile route around Central Park, and the rest of the day they read to a background of music and the beautiful view of the park.

On Sunday, Philip and Jason both went to the hospital—Philip to make certain that all was in order with his residents and interns, and Jason to go over the charts of the patients he would be inheriting on Monday. Monday would be his first day with his new team on the tenth-floor general medicine unit, where he would spend the next eight weeks taking care of general medical patients. As he got off the elevator, he spotted his new resident, Craig Thomason, coming out of a patient room.

"Dr. Thomason!" Jason quickly walked to him and offered his hand. "Hi, I'm Jason Green, your new intern."

"I know who you are, and my name is Craig." His handshake was wary. "What are you doing here today?"

Dr. Thomason's tone sent a chill through Jason. He gave Craig an easy smile. "I just wanted to go over the charts so I would have a running start tomorrow."

"Well, I understand you're not likely to have any problems. I also understand you're from Mississippi, Jewish, and gay." His tone turned into a challenge.

Jason started laughing. "My, my. I guess my daddy was right when he told me there was no correlation between intelligence and preconception. Yes, I *am* from Mississippi, I *am* Jewish, and I *am* gay." He met Craig's gaze. "Do any, or perhaps all three of those things, bother you?"

"Well, being from Mississippi is all right, although that accent is annoying." His smile was stiff during a brief pause. "I do have several Jewish friends, whom I like and respect, but they're all raving liberals, and I'm very conservative. So we don't talk politics. And the gay thing…well, I just don't get it. Honestly, I've never really interacted with any gay people." The stiff smile came and went again.

Jason chuckled. "Well, you have lived a sheltered life. First, I'm not very political, and frankly I'm not fond of either political party. I'll talk music with you, but I promise not to talk politics. Second, I promise you that I won't try to convert you to my religion if you promise not to talk to me about Jesus. I know all about him, and he sounds like a nice fellow, but I'm really not interested. I'm actually an atheist. And the gay thing—if you're worried that I might try to make advances toward you, it won't happen. I'm in a relationship, and besides—don't be offended—you're a handsome guy and all, but you're not my type. So, now that we've settled your three concerns, how 'bout letting me get started with the charts? Let's have a great eight weeks together."

His own words surprised him. Although he kept an easy smile on his face, he had never been so impertinent with anyone, except perhaps with Philip when he had first seen Mrs. Shapiro.

His surprise didn't lessen as Craig started laughing. "I think we'll get along swell, then."

As they slowly walked to the nursing station, Jason learned that Craig was from a middle-class family south of Los Angeles, had worked his way through Stanford University as an undergraduate, and attended Stanford University Medical School. His father was a policeman, and he had grown up in a very conservative and religious family. Although he had been exposed to liberal ideas during his time in college, he remained a staunch conservative and was president of the Young Republicans at Stanford during his undergraduate years. Craig had relaxed considerably by the time they parted.

Over the next three hours, Jason reviewed the fourteen

charts of patients he would be inheriting the next day, and then he met Philip for lunch. During the afternoon, they ran around Central Park, returned to the apartment, and made love for the third time since the Lucas incident. Again Jason was reticent, not as passionate as he had been, and he knew that Philip sensed his reluctance and the occasional startled pullback as the unwanted images intruded. Jason had listened to Seth, and he was trying. But the anger still churned in his belly, and he was afraid it would never entirely go away.

Jason arrived on his unit at six a.m. to find two new patients who had been admitted to his service. He finished reviewing them just as Craig and two new students walked into the nursing station.

"I'm Jason Green." Jason shook the hand of the first student, Kate Schmidt. She was a third-year student from Tennessee who had attended Hendrix College, a fine, small liberal arts college in Arkansas. She was outgoing and attractive and had a firm handshake that Jason liked. "Kate, it's nice to meet someone else around here with a familiar accent."

She chuckled.

The other student, Todd Jacobs, had attended Columbia University and was from Westchester, New York. He was slight of build with a nice face and a firm handshake. "Dr. Green, we've heard so much about you. It's great to be able to be on your team."

Jason blushed, and Craig looked at Todd. "Hey, I'm the one who will be determining your grade." He raised an eyebrow. "I'm the one you should be sucking up to, not him."

Both students grinned and Jason laughed.

"You've all been through this before, and I'm sure you're familiar with the routine." Craig looked from one to the other. "We round at seven o'clock Monday through

Friday morning and eight o'clock on Saturday and Sunday. We have attending rounds with Dr. Berk at ten o'clock Monday through Friday. He's told me that he would like to round on patients the first hour with all of us and then spend the second hour with the students. You'll present the patients you work up to him. I don't know if you know, Jason, that in the second half of the year on Saturdays, all the interns meet with Dr. Stern in the conference room next to his office at ten o'clock. One of the chief residents will present a case, and then the interns discuss it with Dr. Stern. It's his way of getting to know the interns during the second half of the year. So if we happen to be admitting that day, I'll stay on the floor while you're there. Have you met Dr. Stern?"

"Yes, briefly. He seems nice." Jason remembered his one unpleasant encounter with the chairman of internal medicine on his first day of internship when he reported about the Code Blue situation. He had not seen him since.

"I don't think nice is the word." Craig gave him a crooked smile. "His name is appropriate to his personality, and he won't hesitate to embarrass you if you say something stupid. God knows he embarrassed me last year a number of times."

"Thanks for the warning. I'll try to keep my mouth shut, then."

"Anyway, Dr. Berk is an endocrinologist who has been around a long time. Quiet-spoken and a very nice man. His research interests have been in growth factors. He's a clinical genius, and we're lucky to have him. He still believes the physical examination is important, so don't start talking about diagnostic tests unless you have described a detailed physical examination."

Jason was excited that he would have an attending professor who was actually interested in the physical examination. He had observed both in medical school and the first six months of his internship that almost everyone relied on blood tests, X-rays, and MRI scans to make diagnoses and treat patients. Taking histories and performing physical examinations no longer seemed to be important.

Jason had started reading textbooks on the physical examination long before he'd entered medical school, books dating from the late 1800s to current textbooks, and had always been amazed at the subtleties that could be detected by careful physical examination.

Jason suddenly recalled a case that had occurred during his fourth year of medical school while on an endocrinology elective. A middle-aged man had been admitted to the hospital in a coma. His only past medical problem had been a pituitary tumor that had been surgically removed five years previously. Numerous doctors, including neurologists, had examined him, and virtually every relevant laboratory test and imaging procedure had not revealed a reason for the coma. The endocrine division was consulted because of his prior history of pituitary tumor, and Jason had taken a visiting professor from Australia, an endocrinologist, to see the patient.

The visiting professor proceeded to do the most extensive neurological examination Jason had ever observed. Jason couldn't believe it—an endocrinologist doing a more detailed neurological examination than any neurologist that he had ever witnessed.

When he finished, the visiting professor turned to Jason and said in his beautiful Australian accent, "This man has a left frontal lobe lesion, probably an infection resulting from disturbed anatomy from his prior pituitary surgery."

Jason was stunned. "Sir," he told the professor, "We did a CT scan, and it was normal."

"Young man, I give you guarantees that this patient has a left frontal lobe lesion. In Australia, we still value the physical examination. I have noticed in America the physical examination is not a high priority," he said in a non-condescending manner.

He proceeded to show Jason all of the subtle abnormalities on the physical examination. Jason recalled reading about many of the maneuvers that the professor performed but had never seen taught in medical school. It turned out that the patient had developed a fungal infection of his left frontal lobe that was drained by neurosurgery, and, after treatment with antibiotics, he fully recovered. Jason had vowed that from that time forward, he would perform a complete history and physical examination on all his patients.

"Jason, are you with us?" Craig's crisp comment brought him back to reality.

"Sorry." Jason grabbed the fourteen charts, and they started their first rounds together. They entered their first patient's room.

"Mrs. Gregory, let me introduce you to the new intern, Dr. Green, and our two new students, Ms. Schmidt and Mr. Jacobs."

Jason stepped forward, took Mrs. Gregory's hand, and sat next to her. "Mrs. Gregory, it's a pleasure to meet you. We're going to continue to give you the good care you've gotten and get you better and out of here as quickly as possible. If it's okay with you, I've read about your case, and I will just share your history with the students. You correct me if I say anything wrong. Is that all right?"

Mrs. Gregory nodded.

Jason proceeded to give a detailed history of this sixty-eight-year-old lady who had been admitted three days before after experiencing severe shortness of breath and a fever.

She had been on a trip to Europe and had returned feeling well. She developed a fever three days before admission, and on the day of admission, she became very short of breath.

Jason gave a complete history of her past problems, all obtained from his review of her chart, citing details that Craig, to judge by his bemused expression, had long forgotten.

They had done cultures, X-rays, and MRI scans and had thus far made a diagnosis of urinary tract infection complicated by a hemolytic anemia.

Jason then stood up and proceeded to examine Mrs. Gregory rapidly but thoroughly. After looking into her eyes with his ophthalmoscope and listening to her heart and lungs, Jason said, "Mrs. Gregory, I see you have nail polish remover here. I'm an expert at applying fingernail polish. If I promise to come back later and polish your nails, would you mind if I removed your nail polish?"

He proceeded to remove her nail polish and examine her nails, finishing the examination to the stunned silence of the three observers.

He turned to Craig. "Dr. Thomason, would you mind looking in her eyes? Here's my ophthalmoscope. Then show the students. Also please listen to her heart and then look at her fingernails." Each took turns and when they finished, Jason asked, "Mrs. Gregory, do you have any history of heart problems in the past?"

"No, Doctor, I've been in good health." She hesitated. "Well, I was told by a doctor some time ago that I had mitral valve prolapse."

"Have you had any dental appointments or any minor surgeries in the past few months that you forgot to tell us about?" Jason asked.

"Yes." She brightened. "Before I left for Europe, I had a root canal done."

"Mrs. Gregory, it's been a pleasure meeting you." Jason took her hand. "I'll be back a little later and talk to you about what we need to do to get you up and running again."

The encounter had taken only twenty-two minutes. The group left the room and closed the door. Craig smiled. "Well, Dr. Green, that was certainly a stunning demonstration, but you're making me look very bad."

Jason felt himself flushing. "Dr. Thomason, the last thing I want to do is make you or anyone look bad. I'm so sorry."

"First, as I told you yesterday, my name is Craig. Second, that was an amazing demonstration of how to do a history and physical." He looked at the students. "Never forget what you just saw." He went over with the students the retinal hemorrhages that Jason had discovered, the splinter hemorrhages of the nail beds, and the heart murmur that was subtle but clearly present.

"Jason, what made you think something else was going on?"

"I didn't. I just did a physical exam and found those abnormalities. And then it dawned on me that the bacteria that grew out of her urine is an unusual urinary pathogen, and how often do you see a hemolytic anemia as a result of a urinary tract infection? That's as rare as hen's teeth. And as you just explained to Kate and Todd, one should always look for a single cause for a clinical syndrome, and an infected heart valve would explain everything."

"Okay, so after rounds, you can take care of what needs to be done to establish the diagnosis. C'mon, we have to finish rounds before Berk arrives at ten."

Over the next two and a half hours, Jason performed in similar fashion, taking each patient's hand, telling the history to the team, and then performing a physical examination. On a few of the other patients, he discovered significant physical findings that resulted in a clear diagnosis, changing the course of their hospitalization. He also asked Craig thought-provoking questions about several of the patients, resulting in new directions for diagnosis and treatment.

The team finished rounding just before ten. As they finished, Jason saw Seth Goldberg approaching them.

Jason walked quickly to Seth and hugged him. "Hey, Seth!"

"Well, Seth, that was some hug." Craig snickered. "I didn't know you were gay too."

"I'm not, Craig. Jason is a hugger. If you manage to teach him something during the next eight weeks, you might get a hug as well." Seth smirked. "And in the unlikely event that happens, don't let your little conservative mind get all bothered that Jason is coming on to you. He has a partner, and, besides, you're not good enough for him anyway."

Jason blushed, and the students laughed.

Jason was writing orders on Mrs. Gregory for an echocardiogram and a change in antibiotics when Dr. Berk arrived on the floor. He was shaking hands with Craig and the two students as he finished writing the orders.

"Dr. Berk." Jason stood and offered his hand. "I'm Jason Green, Dr. Thomason's intern. It's an honor to meet you, sir."

Edward Berk was tall, with a full head of salt-and-pepper hair and with a reserved expression. He had recently stepped down as head of the endocrinology division and was now spending his time doing research and teaching. He had gained fame decades ago for his discovery of various growth factors, and he had been the first to complete amino acid sequencing of several unique proteins. He had also edited several textbooks of endocrinology, all of which Jason had read.

Jason grabbed the charts and placed them on a rolling

cart. They went into Mrs. Gregory's room. Jason had already briefly explained to her what had been found, reassuring her that antibiotic treatment would cure her. Craig introduced Dr. Berk to Mrs. Gregory and turned to Jason. "Dr. Green, why don't you give Dr. Berk a summary of Mrs. Gregory's problems?"

Jason proceeded to concisely give a history and a summary of the physical findings. He asked Kate to demonstrate the pertinent physical findings to Dr. Berk. Jason then discussed diagnostic and therapeutic plans, frequently asking Craig to give his opinions. They went from room to room, with Jason repeating a concise history and physical for each patient, then asking the students to demonstrate pertinent physical findings to Dr. Berk, and finally discussing diagnostic and therapeutic plans, always asking Craig to comment. Jason noticed that Craig wore a faint smile for the entire two hours of rounding with Dr. Berk, although Dr. Berk remained expressionless. Jason wondered whether all the older attending physicians were like Dr. Glassman and Dr. Berk, completely without emotion, at least in the hospital environment.

Philip had called Jason to ask if he was meeting him for lunch, but Jason had explained that there was too much work, this being his first day on the new service, and told Philip he would call him after work. One of the students brought him a sandwich from the cafeteria, and for the rest of the afternoon, Jason spent time with each patient, explaining their medical problems and plans. He admitted three patients, performing complete histories and physical examinations, and, with Craig's permission, assigned one patient to each student.

By six p.m., the team had completed their work. Jason was required to remain in the hospital until seven p.m. on his admitting days until the night float resident arrived, but Craig approached him and said, "Jason, go home. We have everything under control and I'm meeting a friend in the cafeteria and will be here anyway. There's no reason for you to stay until seven."

"Well, I'd like to go over to the lab." Jason looked up with a smile. "So I'll be close if we get an admission. Just give me a call and I can be here in two minutes."

"I heard you were doing some research." Craig shook his head. "That is the most cockamamie thing I've ever heard of."

Jason smiled. "Thanks, Craig. It was a good first day."

Jason went to the lab and found Dr. Fang hard at work. He noticed that Dr. Fang had the Tumi bag with his initials, so he had recovered it from his professor. Dr. Fang had worked every day over the holidays. He told Jason that Christmas and New Year's meant nothing to him, and he had made considerable progress in catching up on data analysis and statistics. They had worked together for an hour when Dr. Glassman surprised them both.

"I just got word from our collaborators at the University of Michigan. Your protein had exquisite affinity for the melanoma protein, and they're working on designing some in vivo studies. Pretty exciting." He smiled. "You two should be proud."

Dr. Fang had a wide grin after Dr. Glassman's pronouncement, and it was Dr. Fang's grin, not Dr. Glassman's accolade, that made Jason smile.

"Thanks, Dr. Glassman," Jason looked at him. "I think Dr. Fang will have plenty more for you over the next few months."

"How are you doing, Jason?" Dr. Glassman turned serious. "How was your holiday at Phil's house?"

"It was fine, thanks. They are truly a wonderful family."

"And I know it's none of my business. But Phil?"

Jason paused. "Everything is going to be fine, sir. Philip is amazing."

Dr. Glassman smiled, turned around, and walked away. Dr. Fang wore a persistent smile after Dr. Glassman's visit, and Jason excused himself, telling Dr. Fang that he would return the next evening. It was nice to see the man smile. He always seemed so serious and stressed. Jason walked back to his apartment, wondering what Philip was doing. He opened the door and there was Philip, sitting in a chair facing the door.

Jason blinked at him. "Hey, what are you doing here?"

"Just wanted to see if you would stay at my place tonight or let me stay here."

"Philip, it's not a good idea." Jason frowned. "I have a routine. I'm up at four-thirty, and you don't need to be up that early. I go for my run, eat breakfast, and go right to the hospital. It's just easier to do that from here. We've been through this before. You know I'll stay the weekends with you."

"Move in with me." Philip's eyes fixed on Jason. "Get rid of this apartment."

Jason looked down at the floor. "I'm not ready for that yet, Philip," he finally said. "Hopefully, one day."

Philip stood up and pulled Jason close. He held him tightly and then kissed him lightly on the lips. "I understand. I'll be patient."

Without saying another word, he walked out the door, leaving Jason alone. Jason heated a can of chicken noodle soup and ate two protein bars. After his meal, he went to bed and slept soundly until the alarm rang at four-thirty a.m.

CHAPTER 13

Jason arrived on his unit at six a.m. after his usual morning run. Results from the echocardiogram confirmed that Mrs. Gregory had an infected heart valve, and the infectious disease consultant confirmed that Jason had ordered the proper antibiotics. Jason reviewed the results of tests from the other patients, making mental notes of further tests and orders that needed to be done. Craig and the students arrived at seven, and Jason once again took control of rounds. Craig had found some esoteric papers on heart valve infections, which Jason eagerly absorbed, and he could see that Craig was quite pleased with himself.

On the previous day of rounds, Dr. Berk had been virtually silent, only listening to the presentations of each patient. On the second day, he was full of questions, and Jason could see immediately that, like Dr. Glassman, Dr. Berk knew exactly the right questions to ask. He would ask the students a question about a particular aspect of a patient's problem, and if they were unable to answer, he would look at Craig and Jason for an answer. Jason always let Craig answer, but on the unusual occasions that he couldn't, Dr. Berk and Craig would turn to Jason, who readily answered the question, complete with article, journal, and author, always blushing bright red, no matter how much he tried not to.

Jason invited Craig to have lunch with him and Philip the second day. Jason could see the surprise on Philip's face as they walked up to the table.

"Philip, this is Craig Thomason, my resident."

Philip shook hands with Craig. "Nice to meet you, Craig. Jason speaks highly of you."

"That's surprising. I gave him a pretty hard time for being gay and Jewish, not to mention his awful accent."

Philip laughed.

"I hear you are one tough chief resident," Craig continued. "I have a friend who is one of your residents. He's scared to death of you."

"Well, I hope that isn't the case. It's certainly not my intent." Philip was serious.

"Seth tells me you were an all-state quarterback in high school. You know, we have an intramural team, and we need a quarterback. Any interest?"

"No, my football days are over." Philip smiled and shook his head. "I've been threatened by my professors about playing football. They don't want me to injure my hands. So I just run with Jason."

"You're a runner, Jason?" Craig asked.

"Somewhat." Jason shrugged. "It's exercise."

Philip laughed. "Craig, Jason was an All American track star at the University of Mississippi. He runs backward faster than I can run forward."

Craig looked surprised. "Geez, I think I'm going to have to change my beliefs about gay people. You two certainly don't fit the stereotype."

"Philip, Craig is still a Young Republican, and I am the only gay person he has apparently met." Jason smirked. "You'll have to give him a little latitude."

He joined in as Craig and Philip laughed.

⟡⟡⟡

On Saturday, the fourteen interns had their first conference with Dr. Stern, who had been Chairman of the
Department of Internal Medicine for seventeen years.
Prior to becoming chairman, he had been a successful
researcher in insulin and muscle metabolism. But his
greatest success had been in raising money for the medical school, and in that role his abilities were legendary.
Seth had told Jason about a National Institutes of Health
site visit to their clinical research center, a facility that
had received more than twenty million dollars a year in
research grants. The visitors from NIH had challenged
the director of the center about the monies requested and
were about to officially reduce the grants to less than
half. At just the right moment, Dr. Stern walked into the
conference room. Thirty minutes later everyone emerged,
smiling, and the NIH group had decided to increase the
grant monies from twenty million to over thirty million
dollars.

Dr. Stern had a reputation among the interns and residents of being very tough, and he didn't hesitate to embarrass a doctor who said or did something that Stern re-
garded as less than intelligent. On the other hand, he was
also known as a brilliant thinker, and it was rare to leave
one of his conferences without taking some wisdom away
from the encounter. The fourteen interns sat around a
huge conference table, nervous, with Dr. Stern at one end
and one of the chief residents at the other end. The only
sound in the room was a rapid foot tapping by one of the
nervous interns.

"I hope everyone has settled in for the second half of
internship," Dr. Stern began, without a smile.

Jason wondered whether he would grow into a staid
old professor like Glassman, Berk, and Stern. He tried to
suppress a smile but saw that the chief resident caught his
subtle smirk.

"These conferences are informal and just a chance for me to get to know you better. Dr. Ryan is going to present a case, and he'll give you enough information that could allow you to at least discuss how you would approach making a diagnosis. We know what the diagnosis is, but I want to hear you discuss the case—see if you have developed good reasoning skills. Frankly, it's unlikely that anyone will make the correct diagnosis. That isn't the point. The point is to help you develop good reasoning and a rational approach."

The chief resident proceeded to present a case of a fifty-eight-year-old man, a longtime smoker with a history of hypertension and diabetes, who presented with florid Cushing's syndrome, a condition that results from an overproduction of cortisol by the adrenal glands. This overproduction is almost always caused by either a benign adrenal tumor that produces the excess cortisol or by a benign pituitary tumor that produces excessive ACTH, the pituitary hormone that stimulates the adrenal gland to make cortisol. The patient had normal laboratory studies, except for those related to the Cushing's syndrome and diabetes, a normal EKG, and a normal chest X-ray. A CT scan of his adrenal glands did not reveal any tumors, but an MRI scan of his pituitary gland revealed a tiny pituitary tumor. The patient elected to have his adrenal glands removed rather than undergo brain surgery. His Cushing's syndrome had resolved following the surgery, but his ACTH levels skyrocketed to ten thousand within a month after removal of the adrenal glands. Normal levels were less than a hundred. A repeat MRI of the pituitary three months later showed no change in the tiny pituitary tumor.

After the presentation, the interns took turns discussing the case, concluding that this was a classic case of Nelson's syndrome following removal of the adrenal glands. The discussion took no longer than ten minutes because the answer seemed obvious to everyone.

Alex Groh, an intern from the University of Michigan, with whom Jason had become very friendly, looked at Dr. Stern. "Dr. Stern, I don't know why you said we would not get this diagnosis. It's very clear to anyone who knows basic endocrinology."

Dr. Stern looked around the table. It seemed that all were holding their collective breath. Dr. Stern then fixed his gaze on Jason. "Dr. Green, you haven't contributed to this discussion. Do you have any comments?"

"No, sir," Jason answered.

"Dr. Green, I don't believe you. I watched you during the discussion." Dr. Stern frowned. "I think you do have something to contribute, and we'll just sit here until you talk."

Jason looked around and everyone was staring at him. He felt his face getting warm. "Well, the question I have is the same one Dr. Groh has. Why would y'all have presented a case that, on the surface, has such an obvious diagnosis, when you told us up front that you doubted we would make the correct diagnosis?"

"Okay, so go on," Dr. Stern demanded.

Jason remained silent.

"Dr. Green," Dr. Stern prodded Jason.

After a pause, Jason proceeded to give a literature review of tumor size and ACTH levels in ACTH-secreting pituitary tumors, citing specific papers and authors, and concluding that it was impossible for this tiny tumor to be responsible for such elevated levels of ACTH so soon after surgery. "On the other hand," he continued, "carcinoid tumors, which are rare tumors that can occur in the lungs or gastrointestinal system and which may also produce ACTH, can secrete large amounts of ACTH after cortisol suppression by the adrenal glands has been removed, as was the case with this patient. Furthermore, most ACTH-producing carcinoid tumors usually occur in the lungs. So I suspect," he concluded, "that this man had a carcinoid tumor in his lung."

"But the chest X-ray was normal, and he did have a pituitary tumor," one of the other interns interjected.

"Nonfunctioning pituitary tumors are very common, and chest X-rays are crude and may not show a small tumor." Jason shrugged. "I suspect a CT scan of his chest was done at some point and revealed the tumor."

There was a long silence.

Dr. Ryan looked at Jason. "Dr. Green is correct. A CT scan of the chest was performed four months after the surgery, when the patient presented with blood in his sputum. A tumor was detected in the lower lobe of his right lung, and it was removed. It was found to be a carcinoid tumor, and his ACTH levels returned to normal immediately after removal of the tumor."

Dr. Stern looked at all the interns. "Dr. Green and Dr. Groh asked the proper question: why would we give you an obvious case when we told you that you would likely not be able to make a correct diagnosis? To get the correct answer, you have to ask the right question. It is fundamental to being a good doctor."

There was complete silence, and Jason saw that all the other interns were staring at him. His face was burning, and he wished that he had kept his mouth shut.

"Okay, ladies and gentlemen, good discussion. Coffee and donuts over there, and we'll meet next week."

Everyone stood as Dr. Ryan and Dr. Stern left the conference room. Some of the interns turned away without speaking to Jason, but several came up to him and slapped him on the back.

Alex Groh cornered him as he started to leave. "Jason, that was pretty amazing. I think you shocked the hell out of Stern." He laughed a bit nervously. "If you ever want to go out for dinner sometime or get together, let me know."

Jason wondered whether Alex asking him out on a date.

"Sure, I'd love to have dinner sometime. Give me a call and let's figure something out." He made his voice casual but still felt himself blushing once again. Alex was thin, with short curly hair. He was very smart, and he was Jewish as well, but Jason was not interested in going out with anyone other than Philip, at least for now.

As everyone was leaving, Dr. Stern stepped out of his office. "Dr. Green, come here please."

"Yes, sir."

Dr. Stern smiled slightly. "That was quite a show you put on in there."

"Sir, that was embarrassing for me, and I'm sure it did not endear me to the other interns."

"Dr. Green," Stern said severely, "you should never be embarrassed to teach your fellow physicians. It's your duty."

"Yes, sir."

Jason walked slowly back to his unit, still embarrassed by the conference. He knew at a young age that his intellectual abilities were unusual, at least in his small world. By the time he was in kindergarten, he was teaching the other children how to read, and by the time he reached eight years of age, he was reading books from his father's library and helping his sister, who was four years older, with her math problems. By ten years of age, he had taught himself calculus and started reading the great books with his father. Math concepts and basic science, particularly physics, were rational and exciting for him, and he had read all the biographies about Einstein.

By ten years of age, he had also started questioning his

parents about religion and God, and at twelve years he proclaimed to his parents that religion was just a fairy tale. He smiled as he remembered his father's words: '*Jason, you taught me that it is a fundamental law of physics that matter can only come from other matter, so if that is the case, where did the first matter come from? It had to come from God.*'

Jason understood the fundamental nature of that question, and he still didn't have an answer to it. But he was certain that religion was a fairy tale and that, if there were a God, it was likely that God would excuse him for his skepticism, as long as he was a good person.

Jason's parents had resisted sending him to special schools for gifted children. They were more concerned that he should develop into a happy human being and insisted that he have a normal social and family life. The only time they had to reprimand him was when he became condescending toward his classmates or teachers. His parents had taught him early on that he had a unique gift and insisted that he should never use that gift to make others feel bad. As a result, he'd always gone out of his way to hide his intelligence. Clearly, Dr. Stern wasn't going to let him do that here.

Jason's eight weeks with Craig, Dr. Berk, and the two students were exciting for him in many ways. He learned to become even more efficient in his patient care, completing tasks in half the time that it took most interns and residents to do them. That gave him time to spend with the students, teaching them physical examinations and history taking. But his greatest satisfaction came from developing relationships with his patients and their families, and he became very close to many of them. Jason sensed that Dr. Berk and Craig were pleased with his contributions, although when possible he continued to give Craig credit for all the team's work.

Many of his patients deeply affected him. One forty-four-year-old woman was admitted to his service in mid-February because of severe mid-back pain of sudden onset. The emergency room staff discovered she had a severe compression fracture of a thoracic vertebra that appeared to have been caused by a tumor. On physical examination, Jason found a breast mass and enlarged axillary lymph nodes, as well as an abnormal neurological examination. A chest X-ray showed many tumors in both lungs, and her liver enzymes were markedly abnormal. The woman was beautiful, like his mother, and she had a loving husband who never left her side, much like his father.

After examining her and reviewing her initial tests, Jason sat next to her on the bed, tears in his eyes, and held her hand. He looked at her husband, who was standing next to them, and then at her. "Mrs. Grayson, you have breast cancer that has spread to your bones, lungs, liver, and probably your brain. It is a terrible situation."

Mr. Grayson began crying quietly.

"Dr. Green, I'm in such pain." Her voice was quiet and determined. "I hurt everywhere, and the back pain is intolerable. I cannot live with this, and I do not want to put my husband and children through hopeless torment. What are my options?"

"I will have the oncologist consult. They'll be able to offer you chemotherapy, which may delay the progression for some time, and we can give you radiation to the areas in your bones that are particularly painful. In the meantime, we will increase your pain medications to ease the pain."

"Dr. Green, you have been so nice." She smiled at him, her head high. "My husband and I have discussed this sort of thing in the past, and I refuse to prolong this.

Please don't call the oncologist. I'm intelligent, I'm of sound mind, and I'm ordering you to please give me pain medications and let me go home to be with my family."

Jason touched her cheek, and Mr. Grayson followed Jason out of the room, tears now running down his cheeks.

"Dr. Green, please give me plenty of pain medications to give her. We have two teenage children who will have a difficult time watching her suffer."

Jason held him as he began sobbing. Dr. Berk, Craig, and students were looking on, as attending rounds were set to begin.

"Mr. Grayson, if you want to take her home today, I'll arrange it as soon as I finish rounding with my team. We will give you plenty of pain medications. We'll also arrange for hospice nurses to come in daily to help out."

Mr. Grayson nodded and returned to his wife.

Jason joined his team to begin rounds, his eyes moist with emotion.

"What was that all about, Dr. Green?" Dr. Berk asked.

Jason presented the case to his team and explained the wishes of the patient and husband.

"Dr. Green, you have no imaging studies of her brain. How do you know that she has tumors in her brain?"

Jason detailed the findings on her neurological examination. "Sir, I'm certain that she has lesions in her right frontal lobe and left parietal lobe just on the basis of my examination. She has multiple tumors in her lungs on her chest X-ray, and she has multiple lesions in her thoracic and lumbar spine and most of her ribs. If you'd like me to speak with them about getting a brain scan," he said quietly, "I'm sure they would be amenable to that, but I'm as certain as anything that the scan will show at least what I have described. I'll demonstrate to you when we go and see her."

"You don't have a biopsy to prove she has breast cancer, Dr. Green?" Dr. Berk persisted.

"Dr. Berk, I will have you feel her breast when we go into her room."

"Let's go and see her now," Craig suggested.

The team went into the room. "Mrs. Grayson, this is Dr. Berk, our attending physician; and this is Dr. Thomason, my resident; and Ms. Schmidt and Mr. Jacobs, the two medical students working with us. As I told you and your husband, Dr. Berk and Dr. Thomason are my bosses and they, along with you and your husband, make the final decision regarding your treatment. Dr. Berk and Craig shook her hand and proceeded to ask her questions as Mr. Grayson looked on.

"Dr. Green, could you show us what you found on physical examination?" Dr. Berk ordered.

Jason proceeded to have everyone feel the rock hard walnut-sized right breast mass and the enlarged, hard, axillary lymph nodes. He then showed the subtle abnormalities on neurological examination that showed that she did indeed have the brain lesions that Jason had previously described.

Dr. Berk looked at Mr. and Mrs. Grayson. "Are you certain that you do not want to try chemotherapy? Your life could be prolonged."

"Dr. Berk, we understand." Mr. Grayson spoke firmly. "We have watched other family members and friends go through chemotherapy. Life was miserable for everyone. We are content with our decision."

"Dr. Green will arrange everything for you, then." Dr. Berk led the team out of the room and then looked at Craig and Jason. "It is highly unusual that in a situation like this we would not start chemotherapy or at least document the extent of the tumor. On the other hand, of all the attending physicians, I suppose I have the reputation of depending on a physical examination more than any of the others, and your physical examination is compelling, Dr. Green."

"Dr. Berk, I saw my mother suffer through chemotherapy. I've read most of the studies of stage-four breast cancer treatment. I've even been privy to some unpublished data on genetically directed treatment through Dr. Glassman's lab." Jason spoke clearly and firmly. "Her life expectancy is a few months at best with chemotherapy, and she will be in unbearable pain for the entire time. If there was ever a case to be made for euthanasia, Mrs. Grayson would be that case."

"Dr. Thomason, what are your thoughts?" Dr. Berk asked.

"I feel a little uncomfortable not having a tissue diagnosis. But we deal in probabilities, and I would say with ninety-nine-point-nine percent confidence that Dr. Green's diagnosis is correct and that the humane decision would be to let the Graysons go home with plenty of pain medication. I would sleep better at night with that decision than with any other decision we could make."

Over the next two weeks, Jason visited the Grayson family every evening before he went to the lab. They lived near Philip on the other side of Central Park in a beautiful penthouse that overlooked the park. Mr. Grayson was a successful hedge fund investor and was obviously of considerable means. Jason made certain that Mr. Grayson had plenty of pain medication to administer and had arranged for hospice nurses to bathe Mrs. Grayson daily and make certain that she was not in pain.

He sat daily with Mrs. Grayson, holding her hand and talking with her. He told her that he saw much of her in her children, and that she would live on in them, which made her smile. Jason was present fourteen days after Mrs. Grayson left the hospital, when she passed away. He cried with Mr. Grayson and his children, stayed with them until the funeral home removed the body, and attended the funeral two days later. Jason could not take his eyes off the two teenage Grayson children, remembering the suffering he had endured when his own mother had passed away of the same disease. A month later, Jason received a letter from the medical center's research foundation, notifying him that Mr. Grayson had donated one hundred thousand dollars in Jason's honor to be used for breast cancer research.

The last week of his rotation with Craig, Jason admitted a patient whom he had taken care of previously while working with Seth and with whom, despite her severe psychiatric disorders, he had developed a close relationship, occasionally visiting her at her nearby nursing home. Dorothy was fifty-five years old, had had poorly controlled insulin-dependent diabetes for the previous forty-five years, and now suffered from all the complications that occurred when a diabetic individual did not take proper care. In particular, she had had both eyes removed ten years previously because of painful neovascular glaucoma that had blinded her, and she now wore beautiful blue glass eyes in both eye sockets. She was under the care of a psychotherapist for depression and hysteria with conversion reactions. Her conversion reactions were characterized by the sudden onset, for no apparent reason, of catatonia. She would suddenly become stiff as a board, with no movement whatsoever. Even respirations were not visible without close examination.

When this condition occurred, the personnel at her high-end nursing home, where she had lived since becoming blind, would worry that she was dying and usually call nine-one-one. The emergency room personnel had learned over the years that when Dorothy was brought in by nine-one-one, the diagnosis was likely a conversion reaction and, after confirming that she was medically stable, would let her lie quietly in an examining room until she decided to wake up. Then she would be sent back to the nursing home.

This admission was for diabetic ketoacidosis, the extreme of uncontrolled blood sugars, and a condition that could lead to coma and death if not properly and promptly treated. On the third day after her admission, Jason sent her to the radiology department for an ultrasound of her kidneys because of the presence of blood in her urine. He was on his unit writing a progress note when he heard a Code Blue called for the ultrasound floor of the radiology department. Usually Jason would not react to a Code Blue, since a Code Blue team had been established to react twenty-four hours a day, seven days a week—largely as a result of Jason's talk with Dr. Stern and the medical chief residents the first week of his internship. However, Dorothy was on the ultrasound floor, and he wanted to be certain she was not the source of the Code Blue.

He hurried down to the ultrasound suite to find the Code Blue team surrounding Dorothy. A third-year medical student was on top of her, pumping her chest, and a resident was about to insert a large catheter into her internal jugular vein. One of the residents had already placed a tube into her trachea and was breathing for her with an Ambu bag. The electric cardioversion paddles were being charged for use.

"Everybody stop," Jason said loudly. "Stop now."

The three residents and the medical student appeared stunned, and the medical student resumed pumping Dorothy's chest.

Jason went to the medical student and gently pulled his hands away. "Stop it now," Jason repeated softly.

The medical student glared at him. "Her pupils are fixed and dilated. I can't stop this."

"Just stop it," Jason repeated.

Jason felt the carotid artery, which was pulsating normally. Everyone stood back as Jason deflated the balloon on the endotracheal tube and removed it. He then stroked Dorothy on the head and whispered into her ear, "It's Jason, sweetheart. Everything is okay now. You can wake up."

Dorothy immediately sat up in bed, and everyone gasped. The medical student turned beet red. "But her eyes—I don't understand."

"Your observation was correct. Her pupils are fixed and dilated." Jason looked at all the residents and students. "Y'all did the right thing. There's no way you could have known that her eyes are glass prostheses."

The Code Blue team quietly gathered their supplies, looked at Jason, and shuffled out of the room, obviously stunned and speechless. Jason would later learn that everyone in the hospital was repeating the story of Dorothy, the Code Blue team, and Jason.

Friday, February twenty-fourth, was the last day of Jason's rotation with Dr. Berk. Jason stayed the entire two hours, listening to the students' final presentations to Dr. Berk, smiling because he could see in their presentations the influence that he and Craig had on their delivery and thought processes. Craig was smiling as well.

When the students had finished, Dr. Berk looked at them. "Very good. Both of you have come a long way in the past eight weeks. I'm proud of you. I enjoyed these eight weeks very much. Good luck to you all." Dr. Berk stood up, shook Craig's hand and then Jason's, and quickly walked out. Jason quickly opened his backpack, took out a CD he had made for Dr. Berk, and went running after him.

"Dr. Berk, wait, sir." Dr. Berk stopped in the hallway, and Jason caught up. "Dr. Berk, I wanted to thank you so much for these past eight weeks. You've been an amazing attending, and I've learned so much from you. I made this CD for you as my way of saying thank you. I have no idea what your tastes are in music, but I know from being with you these eight weeks that you love music. So thank you, sir, for everything."

Dr. Berk's eyebrows rose. "Jason, how would you know that I love music?"

"Sir, I just know."

"Jason, I know I'll be seeing a lot more of you. It's been a pleasure being with you these past eight weeks."

Jason hugged him, which, he thought with amusement, to judge by Dr. Berk's expression, might be the first time that had happened in Dr. Berk's forty years as an attending physician. Smiling, Jason turned around and quickly walked away.

Saturday was Jason's last day with Craig. Craig had been a wonderful resident for him and, like Seth, had taught him a considerable amount about taking care of patients. He enjoyed watching Craig's interactions with patients, joking and being lighthearted with patients and families when it was appropriate. He'd learned that such an approach eased tensions and made patients more comfortable, and he often incorporated Craig's approach into his own interactions. Craig had also worked hard to bring him and the students the latest published studies that related to their patients' problems. Jason could not have asked for a better resident. He rivaled Seth.

After rounds and writing notes, Jason approached Craig. "Craig, I don't know if Republicans listen to music, but I made a two-volume CD for you. It is a compilation of my favorite musical pieces. But I warn you, if you listen to it enough, you may become a Democrat." Craig laughed as he took them. "Seriously, I want you to know how grateful I am to you." Jason gave him a big hug. "You've been an awesome resident, and I'll miss being with you."

"You know, Seth said you might hug me at the end of the eight weeks." Craig winked. "You sure you're not coming on to me?"

"No, Craig, I'm not coming on to you." Jason smiled. "I'm taken. I just wanted you to know how grateful I am to you. You should know that not all my residents have gotten hugs."

Craig laughed again. "Well, I have to say that being your resident has been a unique and an amazing experience. And I'll greatly miss working with you." He put his hand on Jason's shoulder. "You've not only taught me a lot of medicine but also changed my attitude about a lot of things. I'm grateful to you."

❧❧❧

During the eight weeks with Craig, Jason continued going to Dr. Glassman's lab at least three days during the week, every Saturday, and some Sundays. He continued to work closely with Dr. Fang and attended most of the Friday afternoon conferences that Dr. Glassman held with his postdoc fellows.

By mid-February, Jason learned that the protein he and Dr. Fang had developed on the computer that would attach to the mouse sarcoma antigen had been synthesized and used to treat advanced sarcoma in mice, and that in all cases the mice had become tumor-free after ten days of treatment. Jason had never seen Dr. Glassman or Dr. Fang so animated as when they told him the news of those experiments.

Dr. Fang continued to get phone calls every evening at

precisely eight p.m., and he always returned to the computer room visibly disturbed. Jason convinced himself that Fang was in trouble with a woman and was sending her all his money.

Jason was most disturbed with his relationship with Philip. He continued to spend weekends with Philip, and they continued to have lunch most days during the week. They talked about their days as usual, and Jason continued to ignore the business with Lucas when Philip tried to discuss it. Philip kept saying that time would heal and that Jason would forget. But Jason knew better. The memory was as vivid as if it had happened an hour ago. He still seethed with anger and continued to have vivid nightmares. They had sex frequently, but it was just sex. It was not the passionate lovemaking that had previously characterized their sexual relationship.

Jason loved Philip deeply. He knew that he did, because Philip was his first thought when he woke in the morning and his last thought before he fell asleep at night. Sure, infidelity and betrayal were in the ballpark of some enduring relationships, just as Seth had told him at Philip's house at Christmas. And it wasn't so much the betrayal that bothered him, but rather Philip's need to control, which Jason rationalized must be an intense need for him to risk what had been a perfect relationship. Jason concluded that unless the two could come to some sort of resolution about the control issue, and unless Jason could rid himself of his anger, their relationship would not endure.

On the last day of his rotation with Dr. Berk, Philip and Jason were invited to Dr. Glassman's home for Friday night dinner. Jason remembered that it was his twenty-seventh birthday only after talking with his father in the early afternoon.

Birthdays had never been important to him. No one

knew it was his birthday. He doubted that even Philip knew.

Jason and Philip were greeted with a kiss from Mrs. Glassman, and as they entered the living room, a raucous "Surprise" erupted from a group of approximately thirty people. Jason looked baffled, not realizing at first that the surprise was for him. Then it dawned on him that it was his birthday. He shrugged and glanced over at Philip, who was smiling. Then he saw his father standing at the front of the group with his sister, and emotion overwhelmed him. He kissed his father and hugged him tightly and then hugged his sister.

"I'd forgotten it was my birthday." He looked at his father. "No one could have known. I'm so embarrassed. Who arranged this?"

"Philip did," his father said.

Jason went to Philip. He kissed him lightly on the lips and then hugged him tightly. "I wish you hadn't done this. I'm completely embarrassed."

Everyone important to Jason was there. In addition to his father and sister, Mr. and Mrs. Olsen, Paul and Anna, Seth and Sheri, Dr. and Mrs. Berk, Craig, the Glassman family, and even Dr. Fang were present. Jason figured that Dr. Glassman had not given Dr. Fang a choice, and he smiled to himself.

After Jason greeted everyone, Mrs. Glassman asked everyone to sit down at the several tables that had been arranged in the dining room. "Jason, you are the guest of honor, and you are required to light the candles tonight," she ordered with a smile.

Jason stood up and went around to the buffet to light the candles. "First, I want to tell y'all how embarrassed I am that I'm the object of this party."

"Shut up and light the candles, Green," Dr. Glassman interrupted.

"Dr. Glassman, with all due respect, sir, you are out of order."

Everyone laughed and applauded. They all knew it was highly unlikely that anyone else could have told Dr. Glassman that he was out of order.

Jason smiled. "As I was saying, I did nothing to deserve this attention. I must be the luckiest man in the world. I'm surrounded by those that I love and hold most dear and by the greatest scientific and medical minds anywhere. Who could be luckier than that?"

He lit the candles and sang the prayers and felt happiness for the first time in several months. He knew Philip loved him and that he loved Philip. But the chasm between them had not yet been filled. The playful under-the-table gestures were gone. That intangible closeness was not there. Jason looked at his father and saw sadness in his expression. He knew.

CHAPTER 14

Jason skipped intern conference with Dr. Stern and spent Saturday morning with his father and sister. He took them to Carnegie Deli and then to the Museum of Modern Art. Jason had always amazed his father at art museums by recognizing the artists and knowing their backgrounds, and he didn't disappoint his father that day—it was like a private professional tour. Jason's visual skills and memory were so fine-tuned that he would usually recognize the artist long before they were close enough to read the placard.

When his sister left to use the restroom, Jason's father looked at him, appearing sad and concerned. "Jason, I know something is not right between you and Philip. I could sense it in your voice these past couple of months and now, after seeing you, I know. Can I do anything to help?"

"Everything is going to be fine." Jason's eyes moistened. "I'm growing up, I suppose. We've had some problems. It's as much my problem as Philip's. Everything will be fine. We love each other very much, and things will work out. It will be much worse for me if I know you are worrying. So please, just know that professionally things could not be better. I'm having an amazing experience. And as far as Philip goes, as I said, it will work out, one way or the other. Okay?"

His father put his hand on Jason's face and forced a smile. "Okay, I won't worry. Just take care of yourself."

Jason took his father and sister to LaGuardia Saturday afternoon, and he spent the rest of the weekend in the lab and with Philip. Dr. Fang told Jason that he had enjoyed meeting his father and sister and that he had even enjoyed the party. It was the first time that Dr. Fang had talked about personal matters in an animated manner, and Jason thought maybe he was seeing a minor crack in the cultural barrier.

⸙⸙⸙

On Wednesday, the first day of March of 2006, Jason started a four-week rotation in the cardiac intensive care unit. He was required to be present, along with a resident, from six a.m. to six p.m., Monday through Friday and every other Saturday. The unit was staffed twenty-four/seven by cardiology fellows who had completed their internships and two years of residency in internal medicine. They were planning a cardiology career, either in clinical practice or in academics and research.

The director of the unit was Morris Frankel who rounded with the fellows, resident, and intern on a daily basis. He came from Duke and had made his fame as one of the pioneers in coronary artery stenting. Dr. Frankel was in his mid-fifties and was jovial and outgoing, a marked contrast, Jason thought, from his prior attending physicians. Jason learned quickly, however, that Frankel was a perfectionist and had high expectations of his fellows as well as the resident and intern. Several different cardiology fellows, all of whom seemed dedicated and very bright, covered the unit in different shifts. The assigned resident, Jason had learned, was a graduate from Northwestern and had had problems with a severe depression after a breakup with his longtime girlfriend. His interns had been complaining for months that he did not perform well in the resident role.

Jason spent four hours on Sunday reviewing the eighteen charts of the patients who were in the intensive care unit. He introduced himself to each of the patients who were conscious and not on ventilators. Almost all the patients were critically ill, most having had heart attacks with complications such as heart failure or recurrent life-threatening arrhythmias.

Jason had played with models of the heart since childhood, and his understanding of heart anatomy and physiology was profound. By the time he had graduated high school, his understanding of the cellular and electrical changes that resulted in heart muscle fiber contraction was near the level of a cardiology fellow. He had taught himself echocardiography in medical school. It had actually been easy for him because of his understanding of heart anatomy. He was excited to use his knowledge now in patient care.

On Monday morning, Jason arrived at five forty-five a.m., anxious to meet the fellow and resident. He was disappointed that there were no medical students during this rotation. He would miss his teaching role.

The cardiology fellow arrived at six a.m., and Jason approached him. "Dr. Bollinger, I'm Jason Green, your new intern."

"Nice to meet you." Bollinger gave Jason a thin-lipped smile. "You said Green was your last name?"

"Yes, sir."

"I was thrown by your accent. Well, it's nice to meet you. Unfortunately, there won't be a resident this rotation. He apparently has an illness and will be out for the next month. So it will just be me and the other fellows with you." Stress edged his voice. "The intern and the resident usually do the daily dirty work, but we'll be here to help you, since you won't have a resident. It'll all work out, so don't worry."

"I'll do my best, sir."

"We'd better get going. This is my first day, too, and I'm not familiar with these patients. So we have two hours to get ready for Dr. Frankel."

Jason grabbed the charts and placed them on the rolling cart, and the two went into the first room. Dr. Bollinger opened the chart. Jason went to the patient and shook his hand. "Mr. Noonan, this is my boss, the man I told you about yesterday, Dr. Bollinger. Dr. Bollinger, Dr. Frankel, who will be with us in a few hours, and I will all be working hard to get you better and out of this hospital."

Mr. Noonan smiled at Jason and nodded to Dr. Bollinger.

Jason then proceeded to give a detailed history of Mr. Noonan's problems, his past history, and his hospital course with details of all the labs and tests that had been performed. Mr. Noonan had been admitted on Saturday evening with crushing substernal chest pain and was found to be in the process of having a heart attack. He had been given thrombolytic therapy, medications that break up blood clots, and he had immediate relief of the chest pain. After presenting the history to Dr. Bollinger, Jason proceeded to perform a detailed although rapid examination as Dr. Bollinger looked on with a puzzled expression.

As Jason listened to the patient's heart, he asked Mr. Noonan to squeeze his hand and then asked Dr. Bollinger to listen to his heart as Mr. Noonan squeezed Jason's hand.

"Mr. Noonan," Jason said with a smile, "Dr. Bollinger and I will be back in a while to talk further with you. But you're going to be just fine. Do you have any questions right now?"

Mr. Noonan shook his head, and Jason patted him gently on his arm. The two doctors walked out of the room.

Dr. Bollinger was slightly shorter than Jason and was pleasant looking, but Jason wasn't certain he had a sense of humor. He seemed very serious. His Bulgari cologne was a welcome relief from the smell of feces coming from one of the other rooms.

Dr. Bollinger looked at Jason. "I thought this was your first day on the service as well."

"It is. I came in yesterday afternoon to learn about the patients."

"So what were you showing me on that exam? I've not seen that before."

"Well, I'm concerned, because he has continued to be short of breath and has had some intermittent chest pains. I talked to him yesterday, and he was reluctant to admit that he was having more chest pains. But he is. When he squeezes my hand, he increases his peripheral resistance slightly, and I'm sure you heard the S3 gallop that he developed when he did that. So I think either he has reclotted after the thrombolytic therapy or at least he has a critical lesion that needs to be opened."

"So what do you think we should do?"

"I would suggest he be taken back to the cath lab as soon as possible."

"I agree. We'll present him to Dr. Frankel when he gets here, and if he agrees, we'll arrange it for later this morning."

"Sir?" Jason frowned and hesitated. "I would feel more comfortable if we got him back down sooner rather than later."

Dr. Bollinger looked at Jason for a long moment. He

then took his cell phone out and called the catheterization lab.

Jason then followed Dr. Bollinger into Mr. Noonan's room and listened as the fellow gently explained what they had found. Within fifteen minutes, Mr. Noonan was carted down to the cath lab, and Jason and Dr. Bollinger continued their rounds. In each room, Jason introduced the patient to Dr. Bollinger, and, while Dr. Bollinger looked at the chart, Jason gave a concise history, detailed the hospital course, and performed a physical examination.

Midway through rounds, Dr. Bollinger received a call from the cath lab. "Well, Dr. Green, that was a great call." His eyebrows rose. "Our patient had a critical lesion in his left main, and the fellow said he would not have lasted very long without the stent. You probably just saved his life."

Jason blushed but smiled. "Dr. Bollinger, it was your decision, not mine."

They finished rounds just as Dr. Frankel approached them. "Good morning, Dr. Frankel," Dr. Bollinger said, greeting him with a handshake. "This is Jason Green, our new intern."

Jason shook Dr. Frankel's hand. "Dr. Frankel, it's a pleasure to meet you, sir."

"So you're the famous Dr. Green who did the shakedown on the Code Blue team a few weeks ago." Dr. Frankel started laughing uncontrollably. "That was classic. Good work, son."

Dr. Bollinger looked completely confused as Jason felt his face turn warm.

"Dr. Frankel, what are you talking about?" Dr. Bollinger asked.

Dr. Frankel proceeded to tell an embellished version of the Code Blue called on Jason's patient with the glass eyes. He was laughing so hard that tears were running down his cheeks. He took a handkerchief out of his pocket and wiped the tears away. "So, do you boys need more time before rounding? I know it's the first day for both of you."

"We're ready, Dr. Frankel." Dr. Bollinger smiled. "Dr. Green will present all the patients as we go along."

Over the next two hours, Jason presented each of the patients, demonstrating new physical findings and frequently asking Dr. Bollinger for his opinions. Jason noticed that Todd Bollinger had a fixed smile on his face, and Dr. Frankel listened intently, occasionally questioning Dr. Bollinger about specific published articles. After examining a patient who had prior stenting of a major coronary artery with a non-medicated stent several years previously, Dr. Frankel asked Dr. Bollinger what the statistics were for failure of that particular type of stent.

"Dr. Frankel, I really am not familiar with that particular stent. I don't know the answer to that."

"Dr. Green, do you know?" Dr. Frankel looked at Jason, who felt himself blushing yet again.

"No, sir," Jason answered.

"Dr. Green, I don't believe you. Answer the question." Dr. Frankel's smile disappeared for the first time that morning.

Jason looked at Dr. Bollinger, almost apologetically, and after a pause he said, "Sir, you published the definitive answer to that question three years ago in the *New England Journal of Medicine*. There is a sixty percent five-year failure rate."

Dr. Frankel started laughing again. "See there? I could tell you knew the answer." They finished rounds and Dr. Frankel turned to face them in the hall. "Good rounds, boys. Todd, you and the other fellows try and teach

Green something over the next four weeks." He walked away, laughing.

Over the next two weeks, Jason became an equal member of the cardiac intensive care unit team. He was so efficient in retrieving labs, writing orders, and talking to families that the cardiology fellows didn't have to help with any of the busywork usually reserved for the intern and resident. Jason knew that all four fellows went out of their way to teach him sophisticated cardiology. He learned echocardiography on a higher level, and he became proficient in performing all the invasive procedures routinely performed in the ICU. On rounds, Dr. Frankel made a game of trying to stump the cardiology fellow with esoteric questions. Jason dreaded that part of rounds. When the fellow couldn't answer the question, Dr. Frankel would stare at Jason and wait for him to answer. If Jason remained quiet, Dr. Frankel would say sternly, "Dr. Green, we're not moving until you answer the question."

Jason would then almost always know the answer, and Dr. Frankel would break into laughter. Eventually the fellows started laughing as well, while Jason tried to smile, his face burning.

Jason's final two weeks in the ICU were extraordinary for him. The cardiology fellows had made it their mission to teach Jason. In turn, they recognized that Jason had an extraordinary knowledge of the cardiac physical examination, and so the fellows insisted that Jason teach them everything he knew about the cardiac examination. Jason did so, eagerly.

During the four weeks in the ICU, Jason also continued his work in Dr. Glassman's lab. He was able to go most weekday evenings for a couple of hours and every Saturday for several hours. The progress being made on the computer program that Dr. Fang and he had developed was most exciting. Several additional proteins that attached to various tumor antigens had already been synthesized and were being tested in animals with good results.

Dr. Glassman had stopped on his way out one evening after Dr. Fang had already gone home. "Jason, the program that you developed has huge potential, not only in cancer treatments but also in all sorts of autoimmune processes. When did you get your computer training?"

"Sir, Dr. Fang was instrumental in developing the program. He is really very dedicated and amazingly talented."

"Enough with this modesty." Glassman stared at him. "Just tell me where you got your training."

"I just picked it up in Dr. Osserman's lab. I'm very visual, and, when it came to studying protein structure, it just came to me."

"Well, I think this could be the basis of significant research. I don't say that lightly. What would you think about delaying clinical training for a few years and pursuing this in greater depth? You could have your PhD in a couple of years, much quicker than usual."

Jason shook his head. "Dr. Glassman, I'm grateful for your offer and confidence, and for letting me spend time in your lab. But I want to finish my clinical training before I start research." He smiled to take any sting out of his refusal. "Dr. Fang will run with this, and of course, I would be grateful if I could continue coming to your lab during my residency."

Dr. Glassman paused then chuckled. "Hmmm. Well, this is the first time that anyone has ever turned down my offer of a research position. I guess you've put me in my place."

Jason felt his face heat. "Sir, please don't take offense. To receive a PhD under you is a dream of mine. I hope your offer is still good when I finish my clinical training."

"Good night, Jason." Dr. Glassman smiled and walked out of the lab, leaving Jason stunned at what Dr. Glassman had just offered him.

Jason continued to spend Saturday nights and Sundays with Philip during his four weeks in the ICU. He could sense that Philip was becoming impatient with him and had started to pull away. There had even been several nights when they didn't have sex. Even though their sex was not the passionate lovemaking that had characterized their sexual relationship prior to the Lucas affair, the complete lack of sex, even for a night, was a shock to Jason. He wondered whether it was as much a shock to Philip. The chasm between them was widening, and he was helpless to resolve what was really his own problem. Philip had done all he could, and yet Jason couldn't shed the anger. The vivid dreams continued, and he was frequently startled with visions of Lucas and Philip when having sex with Philip. As he lay awake in the wee hours of the morning, he knew he had to do something to resolve his issues, or the relationship with Philip was likely doomed.

The last Friday of Jason's rotation, Dr. Frankel invited the cardiology fellows and Jason, with spouses, to his apartment for dinner. Philip actually looked forward to the dinner, since two of the four fellows had been Harvard Medical School classmates, and Philip was eager to see them. Mrs. Frankel welcomed everyone at the door, and Dr. Frankel served everyone champagne as they came into the living room, as jovial and outgoing as he had always been on hospital rounds. Two of the cardiac fellows were single, and two brought their wives.

"Dr. Frankel, this is my partner, Philip Olsen," Jason said as he shook Dr. Frankel's hand.

The rotund cardiologist broke out in a huge smile. "Jason Green, you are full of surprises. I had no idea you were gay. I've known your partner for years." He turned to Philip and gave him a big hug. "He actually operated on my son."

Philip smiled. "Dr. Frankel, it's so good to see you again."

"Well, both of you did good, and what a handsome couple. Jason, your partner has the reputation of being the most talented orthopedic surgeon anywhere, and I'll be forever grateful to him. My son was struck by an automobile and fractured his leg. His femoral artery was severed. Your partner here, when he was a first-year resident no less, happened to be in the emergency room when he arrived, took him right up to the operating room himself, within fifteen minutes had repaired the artery, and then put his leg back together before any of his bosses had a chance to even get there. His attending was perturbed at the audacity of this young resident, but had he waited, my son would be without a leg."

"Philip is modest. He never told me about that." Jason smiled at Philip, who was actually looking uncharacteristically flushed. "Getting him to tell me anything about his work is like pulling teeth."

"And, Philip, I guess you're tired of hearing about Jason. But I'll tell you that we've never had so much fun in the intensive care unit as we have had this past month with Jason." Dr. Frankel laughed. "Those fellows over there, and I, for that matter, have never been more challenged trying to teach an intern or resident something they didn't already know."

Jason quickly changed the subject. "Dr. Frankel, my month in the ICU was awesome. I made this CD for you. It's music that I love and that I thought fitted your personality as my way of saying thanks."

The CD had lively pieces on it such as Stravinsky's *The Firebird* and Tchaikovsky's *1812 Overture*, as well as several other less serious pieces.

"Thanks very much. But you know my favorite pieces are funeral dirges by Bach and Beethoven." Dr. Frankel stared at the CD with a serious expression on his face.

Jason felt himself going pale—he'd misjudged that badly?

And then Dr. Frankel started laughing boisterously. "Relax, Jason, just playing with you. These pieces are perfect."

CHAPTER 15

A t Dr. Frankel's dinner, Jason had been struck by the absence of frequent glances that Philip had routinely given him at past social events. On the way home, Philip talked about his friendship with the cardiology fellows while they were together at Harvard. When Jason asked Philip why he had seemed to ignore him at the party, Philip shrugged his shoulders and continued to talk about his friends. There was no sex that night, and Jason realized that their relationship was likely entering the final inning. He stared into the darkness, feeling sad and helpless.

On Monday he would be starting a month rotation on a combined neurology/neurosurgery service. Hopefully, immersing himself in learning neurology would lessen his pain.

The following morning, Jason went to the Saturday morning intern conference with Dr. Stern and the chief residents. He had been attending the conferences almost every Saturday, and after his embarrassment at the first conference, he quickly found a way to ensure that he would not be the object of attention should the other interns not make the diagnosis. He discovered that if he asked the right questions during the discussion, he could redirect the other interns into discussing issues that led them to the proper diagnosis. Virtually every Saturday, one of the other interns made the correct diagnosis, which, according to Dr. Stern, had never before happened. He was pretty sure that the chief residents and Dr. Stern knew what he was doing. Every time he asked a question, Dr. Stern would give Jason a look as if warning him to be silent, or one of the chief residents would smile and shake his head. None of the other interns noticed, which relieved Jason.

On Saturday his favorite chief resident, Dr. Santiago, presented a difficult case of a woman who had recurrent fainting spells from sudden profound drops in her blood pressure. She could be sitting or standing anywhere, and suddenly she would become light-headed and lose consciousness. She had actually been admitted after falling and striking her head, resulting in a minor subarachnoid hemorrhage, a bleed between the skull and the brain. The chief residents and Dr. Stern probed the interns about how they would approach the diagnostic workup, resulting in a lively discussion.

Jason asked Dr. Santiago several questions, which should have redirected the interns' discussion. But this time Jason's strategy was not successful—the diagnosis was too obscure. After thirty minutes of lively discussion, none of the interns had been able to offer a rational plan for diagnosing the problem. The chief residents prodded the interns, telling them in a lighthearted manner that they were "not thinking smart."

Jason's friend Alex Crohn, who had been a leader among the interns and was considered brilliant by the residents and attending physicians cleared his throat.. "Okay, Jason, prove to Dr. Santiago and Dr. Stern that we're not as stupid as they think."

Jason frowned at him, startled. The other interns then started to encourage Jason to talk. As usual, he felt his face getting red hot as he began a seven-minute discussion of the differential diagnosis of episodic hypotension, discussed the laboratory results of the patient, and explained the reasons why she certainly had an epinephrine-secreting pheochromocytoma, a tumor of the adrenal gland that rarely produced pure epinephrine, a hormone that would result in a profound lowering of blood pressure. Usually the tumor would produce norepinephrine, which would actually cause marked elevations in blood pressure.

The room was silent. Alex looked at the chief resident. "Well?"

Dr. Santiago looked at Dr. Stern. "Dr. Green is correct. I don't have anything to add to his discussion. Dr. Stern?"

Dr. Stern shook his head.

As the interns were drinking the coffee and devouring the donuts, Alex pulled Jason aside. "I could tell you knew. You had that sly grin on your face."

"Alex, you embarrassed me. I'm sure you knew the diagnosis."

"Jason, I had no idea what the diagnosis was. You're a hoot."

Jason and Alex had become good friends.

Alex had made it clear to Jason over the previous months that he was gay and interested in him. Alex was not in the least coy. "I would still like to get together with you sometime."

"Alex, I find you attractive and I like you a lot, but I'm still with Philip. Things are not going well and that may change. So be patient with me."

Alex smiled. "I'm here for the next three years."

∽∾∽

On Monday, April third, Jason started a four-week rotation on the combined neurology/neurosurgery service. Although Dr. Glassman's research had been the main reason he had wanted to come to New York City for his internship, he was particularly excited that internal medicine interns were required to do a neurology rotation. Jason had been fascinated by the nuances of the neurological examination and had read many old and new textbooks describing the physical findings related to brain abnormalities. He thought often of that Australian professor whom he had met during his endocrinology elective his fourth year of medical school and who had been a major influence on him. He was also relieved that he didn't have primary responsibility for patient care on this service and would be able to leave every day by five o'clock, allowing him to spend more time in the lab.

In addition, he had weekends off, and he was determined to spend more time with Philip, hoping to reignite their sexual relationship. It was his fault, but he couldn't help it. The anger continued, the vivid memories persisted, and Philip knew it. Jason had even been approaching Philip more, but Philip would make excuses half the time.

Jason guessed that he might be saying yes to dinner with Alex before too long.

Jason arrived on the neurology service unit at five-thirty a.m. Unlike his previous rotations, he had not reviewed patient charts prior to starting this rotation. Rounds started very early each day because the residents had to be in the operating room by seven. He had been assigned to a team consisting of a neurology resident who was training to become a nonsurgical neurologist, a neurosurgery resident who was training to become a brain and spinal cord surgeon, and an attending neurosurgeon. This neuro service was very unusual, almost unique, because the neurology and neurosurgery services had been integrated into one service. At most institutions the two were completely separate, but the integration resulted in the neurology residents having a much greater appreciation for neurosurgical interventions and the neurosurgery residents having superior training in general neurology.

Jason knew that neuro residents considered the internal medicine interns a nuisance for the most part. They were primarily observers and rarely contributed to patient care. The neurology resident, Carl Strauss, was a Duke graduate, and the neurosurgery resident, Kevin Gray, was a second-year resident from Yale. The attending physician was Sanford Cox, a famous neurosurgeon who had made his name by pioneering new techniques in pituitary surgery.

Jason shook both of their hands. "Dr. Strauss, Dr. Gray, I'm Jason Green, your intern for the next month."

They both nodded. "You can just attach yourself to one or both of us," the neurosurgery resident said in a disinterested tone, "and watch us work up patients. If you want, you can work a patient up, and then one of us will go see the patient with you and show you the proper neurological examination. You don't have to work patients up if you'd rather not. It's up to you. You can come into the operating room if there is a particular case you'd like to observe. You won't be able to scrub in, but you can stand behind and watch. You don't have to be here on weekends. You're really more of an observer than anything." His tone was cool and his speech one that he had obviously given many times. "You're welcome to ask us questions, but try to not get in our way."

Jason smiled. "Yes, sir, I promise not to be a nuisance to you."

The three rounded on their twelve patients over the next forty-five minutes. The residents offered very little information about each patient and performed cursory examinations. Jason was disturbed and surprised at how aloof the two residents were with their patients.

"We're off to the operating room. There's a patient coming up from the emergency room with new seizures. Why don't you stay and work the patient up?" the neurology resident suggested. "Just do a medical workup and get her settled in. We'll be back after the first surgery and go over the patient with you."

"Happy to do it, Dr. Strauss. See you in a few hours then."

The patient arrived from the emergency room, and Jason spent the next hour and fifteen minutes with her taking a history and performing a physical examination. He recorded his history and physical into the chart, wrote admitting orders, and went back to spend more time with the patient. Dr. Strauss and Dr. Gray returned at ten, wearing their surgical scrubs, discussing the case that they had just assisted on. "So, Dr. Green," Dr. Strauss said, "give us the bottom line on the seizure patient."

Jason proceeded to give them a concise history and then described a detailed neurological examination. "She demonstrates echopraxia, she fails the applause test, and she neglects the left side. She also demonstrates limb apraxia and buccofacial apraxia, and she has an impaired, wide-based gait with a short, hesitant stride. She also demonstrates poor insight and anosmia."

Dr. Strauss and Dr. Gray looked at each other, wide-eyed, as Jason described the neurological examination.

"On the non-neurological examination, she has localized wheezing centrally on the right side and one enlarged right supraclavicular lymph node."

"So what is your assessment?" Dr. Strauss asked intently.

"She most likely has lung cancer with a right frontal lobe metastasis, which is likely causing her seizures. She could have other central nervous system metastases that are silent. But her neurological examination suggests only a frontal lobe lesion."

"So where did you learn how to do these neurological examinations?" Kevin Gray asked, obviously surprised by Jason's presentation.

"Just reading and practicing, sir."

"Come show us your neuro exam," Dr. Strauss said shortly.

Jason led the two residents into the patient's room and took her hand. "Mrs. Allen, these are the two doctors I told you about, Dr. Strauss and Dr. Gray. They are the residents who will be caring for you. If it's okay with you, I would like to show them a few things that we did a little while ago. Do you remember me examining you a few minutes ago?"

She smiled hesitantly at him. "Of course, Dr. Green."

Jason proceeded to perform a comprehensive neurological examination, pointing out the abnormalities to the two doctors. He then had them listen to the wheezing and feel the lymph node. "Mrs. Allen, I'll be back in a few minutes and talk to you about what we need to do and make certain you understand everything."

The three men walked out. "That was impressive, Dr. Green," Dr. Strauss said. "I'm a little embarrassed. A medicine intern knowing more about a neurological exam than a neurology resident. Would you mind writing up your history and physical, and then we'll write some orders?"

"Dr. Strauss, I've already written the history and physical into the chart, and I took the liberty of writing some orders. You just need to review them and cosign them if you agree."

Jason returned to Mrs. Allen's room and sat with her, holding her hand. "Mrs. Allen," he said gently, "you probably have a tumor in your lung that has spread to your brain, and that is why you are having these seizures. But we have good medication that will help you." He held her while she cried.

The two residents returned to the operating room. Over the next several hours, Jason admitted two more patients and reviewed the charts of the old patients on the service. The residents returned at four p.m. to make rounds with Dr. Cox. The neurosurgery professors always made their rounds in the late afternoon because of the early morning surgery schedule. Jason had read many of Dr. Cox's research papers and was anxious to meet him. He was elderly, tall, and distinguished looking. Jason could tell that, in his younger years, he must have been very handsome.

"Dr. Cox, it's a pleasure to meet you." Jason offered his hand. "I'm Jason Green, the new intern on service."

"I've heard a lot about you from my good friend, Harvey Glassman."

The two residents looked at each other with a blank stare.

They began rounds, and Jason could immediately see that Dr. Cox was from the same school as Dr. Glassman. He asked pertinent questions and challenged the residents with every patient, forcing them to think about diagnosis and treatment in different directions. The first patient they visited was a forty-year-old man with a pituitary tumor that secreted the hormone prolactin. The tumor was pressing on the optic nerve, causing loss of vision. The endocrine consultant had suggested starting the medication, bromocriptine, which would reduce the size of the tumor, but Dr. Cox was concerned about the vision loss and favored surgical removal. He asked the residents for literature that would support either medication or surgical intervention in such a specific case, but neither resident could cite any articles.

Dr. Cox looked at Jason expectantly. "Dr. Green, do you have anything to add?"

Jason tried unsuccessfully not to blush. "Well, sir, you published the definitive study in the *New England Journal of Medicine* in 1998." He went on to explain the statistics in the article and that patients who had optic nerve involvement had a better outcome in terms of visual loss with surgical intervention than with treatment with bromocriptine alone.

"Well, Dr. Green, what would you do in this situation? The endocrine consultant wants to treat with bromocriptine and avoid surgery."

"Sir, I would thank the endocrine consultant for his opinion and take the patient to the operating room. These tumors tend to be aggressive in men and more resistant to bromocriptine treatment. In my mind it's a no-brainer, no pun intended."

Dr. Cox smiled. "Okay, let's move on."

After each patient, Dr. Cox asked questions, challenging the residents, and when they were unable to answer, as Jason feared, Dr. Cox turned to him. Jason would cite the articles with journals and authors, blushing each time, hoping that his two residents didn't completely resent him. But after that round, both residents had clearly changed their attitude toward him. They didn't seem to resent him, and instead made him an integral part of their team. They made efforts to teach him, and in turn, Jason showed them all he knew about the neurological examination.

Two weeks into the rotation, Dr. Gray told Jason on morning rounds that he was scrubbing in on a laminectomy, a type of spinal surgery, and that the spinal surgeon who had developed a new technique that would benefit this particular patient had specifically asked that Jason come and observe. "I was a bit surprised by the request. He must know you."

"Is it Dr. Olsen?" Jason asked.

"Yes, you know him?" Dr. Gray asked, surprised.

Jason laughed. "I should say I do. I've slept in the same bed with him for the past nine months."

Dr. Gray looked shocked, and blushed.

Jason went to the operating room with the residents. Dr. Gray scrubbed in and assisted Philip, who had already started the procedure with another attending neurosurgeon. Philip looked up at Jason and then continued his work, explaining to the two neurosurgeons what he was doing. He held out his hand to the nurse. "Give me the Green retractor."

Jason was startled, realizing that Philip had named one of the instruments that he had invented after him. No one noticed the moisture that came to Jason's eyes, except for Philip, who looked at him after the nurse handed him the instrument. Waves of guilt came over Jason for being so unforgiving. He wished that he could help himself. He continued to watch Philip operate. He was confident and in control in the operating room, teaching and correcting the neurosurgeons during the procedure, and Jason thought that perhaps he could understand Philip's need to dominate his lover. Jason also saw that Lucas was the anesthesiologist on the case.

When they finished, the attending neurosurgeon looked at Philip. "Dr. Olsen, that surgery was very impressive. You should have been a neurosurgeon and not an orthopedic surgeon."

"Thank you, Dr. Clayman, but I prefer bones over brains."

They both laughed.

Jason followed Philip into the doctors' lounge to change clothing. After the other doctors had left, Jason went to Philip and put his arms around him, hugging him tightly.

"I just wanted you to know that no matter what happens to us," Philip murmured in his ear, "I named that instrument after you because I love you so much, and it will always be there to remind me of you."

Jason choked out a "thank you" and left, shocked by the reality that Philip also saw their relationship nearing an end.

He was writing orders one morning during the third week of his neurology rotation when he felt a tap on his arm. He turned to see Kevin Gray looking over his shoulder. "Hey, Kevin, I thought you were in surgery."

"Oh, I've assisted on those laminectomies many times, so I let Carl assist this morning." Kevin paused, and Jason continued look at him. "I wanted to talk to you about something," Kevin said. "I've never approached anyone like this before, but I've gotten up the courage to say something to you."

"Sure, what is it? Did I do something wrong?"

"You didn't do anything wrong." He paused briefly but then casually said, "I would like to have sex with you."

Jason sat stunned and speechless, blushing. He knew that Kevin had a girlfriend. "It's just sex," Kevin continued. "I would never do anything to interfere with your relationship. I have a girlfriend, but I've had sex with a few guys in the past, and I've fantasized about you since the day I met you."

There was another lengthy pause. Jason sat silently, not knowing what to say.

Kevin persisted. "Don't worry. I'm not in love with you, but you are very attractive and I'd like it. I understand if you say no." He smiled crookedly. "But I had to try before you left the service. By the way, you've made quite an impression with everyone in neurology and neurosurgery. The impression you've made with me is just a little different." His smile was a bit embarrassed now.

Jason sat silent, thinking for several moments, and then said, "I tell you what. Do you mind if I talk with Philip about this? Would you be interested in having sex with the two of us at the same time?" He surprised himself with the question.

Kevin nodded immediately. "Definitely."

Jason sat in thought for some time after Kevin walked away. He had not had previous relationships and had little sexual experience. Maybe it was normal for gay couples to have sexual liaisons on the side. If that were the case, perhaps he was overreacting—just being naïve. Perhaps Seth was right. Maybe Philip's betrayal was still in the ballpark for enduring relationships. Jason understood all of that intellectually. He shook his head as a headache nibbled behind his eyes. He just could not get over the emotional impact, and the vivid dreams and memories continued to haunt him. Maybe having a threesome with Kevin would allow him to separate sex from making love. He laughed silently to himself and thought he must be incredibly immature about sexual matters.

Saturday afternoon, on the way to Wilton to visit Philip's parents and, after driving in silence for fifteen minutes, Jason finally turned to Philip. "I'm worried that we are both giving up on our relationship, and it's because of me. I'm sorry. I want to change. I know you love me. I know the affair with Lucas was just sex. I know I should be able to forgive and forget. But I've failed. I've tried."

Philip's knuckles had turned white on the wheel. "Are you trying to tell me it's over?"

"No, no. But I want to try something."

Philip remained silent, not taking his eyes off the road.

"I was approached by Kevin Gray, the neurosurgery resident who assisted you on that laminectomy." Jason paused. "He propositioned me. He's apparently bisexual, and out of the blue, he told me he wanted to have sex with me."

Philip turned pale. "And?"

"I was stunned at first. I didn't know what to say. And then the thought occurred to me that if we had a threesome, maybe that would let me separate sex from making love, and maybe it would help me forget, and maybe it would give you something that you need at the same time."

Philip scowled at the road ahead. "I don't need to have sex with anyone else."

"Philip, you have needs that I've not been able to meet." Jason's voice rose despite himself. "That's what happened, plain and simple. Those needs don't go away."

"I don't understand how having a threesome is going to help you get over what I did. What I did was a betrayal. I can't deny that."

"I don't know either, but I think maybe I will look at sex differently. I don't know. I'm grasping. I'm desperate. So let's try it."

"I don't know," Philip said after a pause. "Let me think about it."

Jason and Philip spent Saturday afternoon and Sunday morning with Mr. and Mrs. Olsen before returning to the city on Sunday afternoon. They had sex Saturday night, but it still felt…flat.

It was a beautiful early April spring afternoon, and Jason was enjoying the countryside on their way home when Philip suddenly spoke up. "I've thought about our conversation. I'm worried about doing this. But I'm more worried about what is happening to us. So if you think this can help us, then let's do it."

The following Saturday, the day after Jason finished his neurology rotation, Kevin arrived at Philip's apartment for dinner. He was tall and handsome, visibly nervous but friendly and loquacious. The conversation during dinner was limited to medicine and the hospital, and both Jason and Philip had more wine than usual. When they had finished eating, there was an uncomfortable silence.

"You two go on into the bedroom while I clean up," Jason said. "I know this is awkward, but you two start while I'm cleaning, and I'll join in."

Philip looked at Jason as Kevin turned around, and Jason nodded to him. Jason cleaned the dishes, and after ten minutes went into the bedroom, not knowing what to expect. Both Philip and Kevin were naked. Kevin was on his knees, giving Philip oral pleasure. Jason undressed and went to Philip. He kissed him more passionately than he had been able to do for several months. Philip then became very aggressive with Kevin, and Jason watched as Philip had his way with him. Jason saw that Philip was plainly not in control of himself as he completely dominated Kevin, verbally and physically, and Kevin completely submitted to Philip. Jason had an orgasm just watching them, and soon after, both Philip and Kevin climaxed, both sweating and breathing heavily.

Jason got up from the bed, almost in a daze, and went into the shower. He was numb. He didn't know how he felt about what had just happened. A few minutes later, Kevin stood at the shower door, fully clothed. "Jason, thanks. I'll see you around the hospital." And he disappeared.

Philip got into the shower with Jason and they washed each other off. Jason was silent.

"Are you okay?" Philip asked.

"I'm not sure. You were just like you were in the operating room, dominant, in charge. I'm a failure."

"Jason, that isn't what I want with you."

Jason hugged Philip, and they got into bed, saying nothing more of what had happened. Jason was shaking inside, confused, wondering whether this had been a good idea after all. It was clear that Philip could not be happy without being dominant. How could their relationship endure? He had no answer to that question, and he fell into a restless sleep.

CHAPTER 16

Jason awoke at four a.m., feeling very tired. He quietly put on his running clothes and went for a run around the park. It was a beautiful spring morning, the last day of April, and he looked forward to the coming warmth. He had never adapted to the cold New York temperatures.

He had planned on going to the hospital to review the charts of patients on the general medical service where he would spend the final eight weeks of his internship. He was paired with a senior resident, Mark Fuller, who had gone to medical school at Johns Hopkins but about whom all his interns and medical students had bitterly complained. Jason heard that he did little to no teaching, had an unpleasant personality, and would not allow his interns or students any independence. However, his attending physician was to be Franklin Skor, a famous oncologist who had made his name in bone marrow transplantation research.

Jason returned from his run to find Philip cooking breakfast. "You should have waited for me. I wanted to go running with you."

"I'm sorry. I woke up early. And I have a busy day planned."

"Today is Sunday," Philip protested.

"I know, but I need to go to the lab, and I want to review charts for my new rotation. So I'll be gone most of the day."

Philip didn't say anything and put breakfast on the table. The tension between the two was palpable.

Jason arrived at the lab by nine a.m., and found Dr. Fang busy at the computer. Dr. Fang seemed surprised to see Jason, probably because he had not been coming in on Sundays for the past few months. They spent two hours going over data from other labs and then went over the status of their own project. They had configured several more proteins, which would attach to several other known cancer antigens, and laboratories at Washington University in Saint Louis and the University of Michigan were in the process of synthesizing the proteins.

Dr. Fang seemed quite animated and smiled easily. Jason noticed two sixty-four-gigabyte memory sticks sitting next to one of the computer screens and also noticed the Tumi briefcase without his initials was open. In the briefcase were several more of the memory sticks in a plastic bag.

"What do you use all those memory sticks for?" Jason asked, keeping his tone casual.

Dr. Fang's expression stiffened. He explained that they were backups of previous work that he had collected over the years and just kept them in his briefcase. It was a plausible explanation, but it nagged at Jason for the rest of the morning.

A little after noon, Jason said good-bye and walked over to the hospital to review charts. He spent four hours going over the charts and briefly introduced himself to each of the patients. He had arranged to meet Philip in the cafeteria for an early dinner. Jason wanted to sleep at his own apartment so that he could arrive early on the floor Monday morning to meet his new team. The dinner with Philip was strained. Neither said anything about Saturday night, and the conversation was superficial and sparse.

It was over. That bleak thought haunted Jason as he dumped his half-eaten meal and headed back to the floor.

The following morning, Jason went for his run and arrived on the floor at six-thirty a.m. A half an hour later, he saw Dr. Fuller and the two new students approaching. "Dr. Fuller, I'm Jason Green, your new intern."

Dr. Fuller shook Jason's hand but didn't answer. He was about five feet ten inches tall and had disheveled brown hair. It was apparent he had not shaved for several days. Jason thought, from his body odor, he probably hadn't showered for several days as well. Jason introduced himself to the new students.

"Dr. Green, we're excited to work with you," Gerald Shenkman, a third-year student, said with a smile.

"Grab the charts," Dr. Fuller interrupted, "and let's make rounds. Here's how it works on my service. We make quick rounds at seven. I'll ask the patients if they have any complaints, we'll do a brief exam on each, and then the students are to go down and retrieve any X-rays that were taken the day before. You and I will sit down and write orders together and finish by nine. From nine to ten, the students will present their patients to me, and you can finish writing orders and retrieving test results. Then Dr. Skor will make walking rounds with us on each of the patients from ten to eleven. I'll present the patients to him on rounds." He glanced at Jason. "I would rather you leave the patient presentations entirely to me. The second hour will be spent in the conference room with the students presenting their patients. After rounds, you and the students can go to lunch, and then in the afternoon you can complete any of the work that wasn't finished and work up new admissions on our admitting day. The students are here to help you. I'll go over everything with you around four to make certain that you've written appropriate orders and that no mistakes were made." Dr. Fuller turned around and walked into the first patient's room. Jason and the students followed him, stunned at Fuller's aloofness.

"Good morning, Mrs. Grassi," Fuller said in a monotone.

Mrs. Grassi had been admitted with pneumonia in both lungs, which was diagnosed as a complication of influenza. Without introducing Jason or the students, he asked her a few questions and listened to her lungs, with Jason and the students looking on. After he finished, he turned to walk out.

"Mrs. Grassi, good morning. I'm Dr. Green. We met yesterday evening." Jason took her hand. "I want to introduce you to the two new medical students who are going to help take care of you. This is Gerald Shenkman, and this young woman is Erica Strickland."

Dr. Fuller glared at Jason as he introduced the students.

"Would you mind if the students took a quick listen to your lungs?" The students came over and listened with their stethoscopes, after which Jason explained the abnormal sounds. "I'll be back a little later to see how you're doing and to see if you need anything." He continued to hold her hand as he talked to her, and she smiled and thanked him.

The group walked out of the room. "Dr. Green, that was completely unnecessary," Dr. Fuller snapped. "The students can go back and introduce themselves and examine her later if they want to."

Jason looked directly at Dr. Fuller. "Dr. Fuller, it's rude not to introduce unfamiliar people to our patients. Our patients are stressed enough, and having strange people hover over them just increases their anxieties. I've already introduced myself to all of our patients. Either you introduce the students to them, or I will."

The students looked at Jason with disbelieving eyes. Dr. Fuller turned on his heel and walked into the second patient's room. Again, he questioned the patient briefly and then examined the patient. Jason was again forced to introduce the students to the patient and demonstrate a few physical findings, again receiving a piercing glare from Dr. Fuller. The same scenario was repeated for the remainder of the patients. When they finished, Dr. Fuller gave the students a list of X-rays to retrieve and bring to the nursing station.

After the students left, Dr. Fuller turned to Jason. "Dr. Green, it looks like we're going to have a problem getting along. I'm the leader of this team, and you're to follow my directions."

Jason did not blink and looked directly into Dr. Fuller's eyes. "Dr. Fuller, the last thing I want is to offend you or to have problems getting along with you," he said quietly. "But know this: I will not allow you or anyone else to be rude to our patients. They deserve to be treated with courtesy and respect. And if there are interesting physical findings, it takes an extra thirty seconds to demonstrate those findings to the students. It will make their experience with you much more meaningful. If you have a problem with any of that, then we should sit down with Dr. Skor and work this out, so that we can all have a positive experience for the next eight weeks."

Dr. Fuller looked at Jason with a blank stare. "I'm going to review charts and write orders. You can look at my orders as you wish."

He went to the nursing station and started reviewing charts, while Jason went back to each patient, questioned each in detail, and examined each carefully. The students returned with the X-rays and found Jason with the third patient. They followed him into each patient's room, observing as he questioned and examined. Jason pointed out interesting physical findings to them and discussed each patient after they left the room.

Jason and the two students finished their rounds just as Dr. Skor arrived. He appeared to be in his sixties and was physically fit, about five feet nine inches, and distinguished looking with a full head of gray hair. Dr. Fuller shook his hand as Jason and the two students approached.

"Dr. Skor, I'm Jason Green, the new intern on service. And these are the students, Gerald Shenkman and Erica Strickland." Jason shook Dr. Skor's hand. "It's a pleasure to meet you, sir."

"Well, it's a pleasure to meet you all. I'm looking forward to the next eight weeks. I expect to learn a lot from you young people." Dr. Skor was soft-spoken, but he had the reputation of being demanding. "I know it's the first day on service for all of us, except for you, Dr. Fuller. Why don't we go around and see our patients? You can present each of them, and we can discuss them."

They stood in front of Mrs. Grassi's room, and Dr. Fuller took her chart from the rolling cart. "Mrs. Grassi is a sixty-eight-year-old lady who was admitted three days ago with a bilateral lower lobe pneumonia. She has been in otherwise good health. I placed her on broad spectrum antibiotics, and she is slowly getting better." There was an uncomfortable pause. "Shall we go in and see her, Dr. Skor?" he asked.

Dr. Skor looked at Dr. Fuller with a puzzled expression. "Dr. Fuller, you're not setting a good example for Dr. Green and the students. I want a concise but *complete* history and physical, a report of her laboratory studies, and the assessment and plan."

Dr. Fuller frowned, clearly distressed, and opened her chart to find a copy of the patient's history and physical.

He fumbled through the chart, clearly confused and not prepared.

"Perhaps I can help," Jason said after an uncomfortable pause, his face heating and turning red.

He proceeded to give a complete history of her current medical problem and extensive past medical history, a description of her physical findings, a detailed accounting of her laboratory and X-ray findings, and the assessment and plans up to the present. Jason could feel Dr. Fuller's glare as Dr. Skor listened intently, with a hint of a smile on his face.

"Thank you, Dr. Green," Dr. Skor said as Jason finished. "So can any of you tell me what the salient question is regarding Mrs. Grassi? Dr. Fuller?"

"The question?" Dr. Fuller asked.

"Yes, the question. Anyone."

Jason's face was becoming even hotter. "Sir, the question is why this lady would have gotten a severe pneumonia. When an individual gets pneumonia, one should always question why. In this case, it was ascribed to influenza, but she did not have the symptoms of influenza, and her nasal swab was negative."

"So why did this lady get pneumonia?" No one answered. "Anyone. Dr. Green?"

Jason hesitated, looking at Dr. Fuller to answer. Clearly he wasn't about to. "Well, we've found that she has a mildly elevated calcium that did not correct with rehydration. She also has a mildly elevated total protein and a mildly depressed serum albumin level. We suspect that she has underlying multiple myeloma, and I believe that Dr. Fuller ordered the serum protein electrophoresis this morning."

"Very good, Dr. Green. If the protein electrophoresis confirms your suspicion, then a bone marrow biopsy will need to be done, of course. Usually a hematology fellow does this, but I'd be glad for you to do it under my super-vision, Dr. Green."

"Thank you, sir, but I've done plenty of bone marrow biopsies. I'm sure, however, that the students would love to participate."

"Then we'll plan on it." Dr. Skor smiled warmly at them. "Let's go meet this nice lady."

Dr. Fuller, completely subdued, was the last to enter the room. Clearly, his resident had completely dissociated himself from rounds and was not going to take control.

Jason stepped forward and took Mrs. Grassi's hand. "Mrs. Grassi, I want to introduce you to our boss, Dr. Skor, who will be helping us take care of you while you're here."

Dr. Skor proceeded to talk with the patient and then asked the students to demonstrate the physical findings.

When they had finished, Jason smiled at her. "Mrs. Grassi, Dr. Fuller and I will be back a little later to talk with you about some things we believe need to be done and make certain that you are being well taken care of."

The team proceeded to the next patient's room. Dr. Skor asked Dr. Fuller to present the patient, but Dr. Fuller merely turned to Jason. "Dr. Green, go ahead and present the cases if you don't mind. I'm a little under the weather this morning."

Over the next ninety minutes, Jason proceeded to present complete histories and physical examinations on the remaining thirteen patients, in addition to all the laboratory data, assessments, and plans, all without using the charts. He introduced Dr. Skor to each patient, and Dr. Skor interacted with the patient, usually inviting the students to demonstrate physical findings. The team would stand outside the room and discuss the assessment and plans. Jason frequently asked Dr. Fuller for his opinions, which he occasionally offered, and Jason gave credit to

Dr. Fuller whenever it seemed appropriate and not patronizing. Dr. Skor asked questions regarding each patient, wanting confirmation from the medical literature to support opinions or plans. Jason always deferred to Dr. Fuller, but when he hesitated or could not answer the question, Jason would cite articles with authors, dates, and medical journals to answer the questions, always flushed with embarrassment.

Following rounds, Jason asked the students to go eat lunch and bring him back a sandwich. He then approached Dr. Fuller. "Look, Dr. Fuller."

Dr. Fuller faced him, wearily. "Call me Mark."

Jason kept his voice deferential. "I'm not sure what happened this morning on rounds. You didn't seem engaged. The last thing I want is to usurp your role on this team, but you simply were not participating."

"Jason, I have problems, psychological problems, that I don't want to discuss." Mark looked away. "I'm just trying to get through this year. I don't know what I'm going to do next year. You're obviously a remarkable doctor, and I expect that the chief residents put you with me for a reason."

"Is there something I can do to help?" His flat affect worried Jason. "Have you gotten any psychiatric care?"

"I've tried to get counseling, but I'm not a good patient. Look," Mark said brusquely, "I want to get along and make the best of my time with you. You take care of the patients. I'll look over your shoulder and add where I can. I'll go to the library every day and try to bring you some information that is new for you. If you can take the students with you daily as you care for the patients, I'll prepare them for their presentations to Dr. Skor." He drew a deep breath. "The students will enjoy being with you. They are obviously completely in awe of you. Is that a reasonable plan for the next eight weeks?"

"I'm fine with all of that, Mark." Jason forced a smile. "But you have much more patient experience than I, and I'd welcome all input."

"Of course," Mark said impatiently. "I'll do my best with you."

Jason's team was the admitting team on the first day, and, that afternoon, he admitted and performed history and physical examinations on five new patients. He assigned a new patient to each of the medical students, and he watched and critiqued each student as they performed their history and physical examinations. He discussed the patients with the students and wrote orders with them. Jason asked them to watch him perform history and physical examinations on the other three patients. By five, Jason and the students had completed their work on the new patients and had finished completing work on the established patients, three of whom were discharged from the hospital. Dr. Fuller was on the floor at five o'clock, and Jason went over all of the new patients with him, as well as the established patients. It was apparent that Dr. Fuller had no interest in the patients. He seemed to be intellectually paralyzed.

Jason was very worried about him, and, after work was completed, he decided to see if the chief residents were still in their office. He walked over to the departmental offices, and the chief residents' door was open. Both chief residents were sitting on the couch, conversing with Dr. Stern.

Dr. Stern motioned Jason to sit in one of the side chairs. "Come in, Dr. Green."

"Sir, you must think I'm always coming over to complain about something." Jason smiled but didn't sit. "I wanted to discuss something with the chief residents, but I don't think you should be bothered with it. I'll come back another time."

"Nonsense. Come in." Dr. Stern waved him to sit down. "I can handle it."

Jason sat down. "My resident, Mark Fuller, has a serious psychiatric problem," he said after a pause. "I don't know what the problem is. He won't discuss it with me. But whatever it is, well, he is completely disabled. He is simply paralyzed. I feel like I am ratting on him, but he needs help. He appears very depressed, and I think it's possible he is suicidal—"

One of the chief residents interrupted. "We've known for some time that Dr. Fuller has problems, but we weren't aware they were as serious as you seem to say. Frankly, we've done you a disservice. We assigned you to him, knowing that you could fill in where he is deficient. And Dr. Skor, who is acutely aware of the problem, was frankly astonished at your performance today."

"Sir, I'm not here complaining about the work." Jason frowned. "I'm here because I'm worried about Dr. Fuller—"

"We understand," Dr. Stern interrupted. "I think we've overestimated Dr. Fuller's ability to continue until he gets the proper help. Dr. Green, do you think you can handle the service if Dr. Fuller leaves?"

"Yes, sir." Jason nodded. "I would feel more comfortable if Dr. Skor would agree to spend an extra thirty minutes with me every day after the student presentations to go over specific questions I might have, since I won't have a resident to run things by. But, sir—" He hesitated. "—if you are going to fire him because of what I've just told you, I don't know that *I* would be able to handle that, emotionally."

"Jason, don't give that any thought." Dr. Stern shook his head. "You've done a great service for Dr. Fuller. He's not going to be fired. We're going to get him the proper help, and we're going to make certain that he is competent before we certify that he has completed his residency. Boys, I'm going home. Jason, do you want a ride home?"

"No, thank you, sir, I'm off to the lab for a few hours. Thank you for listening to me." Jason got up, very upset, and left Dr. Stern and the two chief residents.

The following morning, Jason arrived on the floor by six, not knowing whether Dr. Fuller would come in. When Dr. Skor and the students approached, Jason looked at them, surprised. "Dr. Skor, it's seven o'clock on Tuesday. What are you doing here?"

"Jason, Dr. Fuller is taking a leave of absence for the next few months to work out his problems. It's you, the students, and me for the next eight weeks. Don't worry about Dr. Fuller." Dr. Skor put a hand on Jason's shoulder. "He's getting the proper help, he's continuing to get his usual salary, and the department is paying for his psychiatric care. So you should feel good about what you did." He turned to the other students. "Now let's get to work. I will round with you this early only today. Starting tomorrow, I'll be here at the usual ten in the morning, and, Dr. Green, I'll spend time with you after rounds going over patients."

Over the next ninety minutes, the four rounded on their sixteen patients. In each room, Jason related the events that occurred the prior day. For the new patients, he presented a complete history and performed a physical examination. He pointed out the pertinent physical findings, and on the students' assigned patients, he asked them to give updates and point out the physical findings to Dr. Skor. As they stood outside each patient's room discussing assessments and plans, Dr. Skor would ask questions, and Jason always let the students answer first. When one of them answered correctly, Jason would smile and give a slap on the back, eliciting a chuckle from Dr.

Skor. When they couldn't answer, Jason answered the question, citing articles from the medical literature, complete with author, journal, and date.

When they had finished, Dr. Skor took Jason aside. "Jason, I don't think you'll have any problems. By the way, I can't remember a time that I enjoyed rounds more than this morning." He smiled broadly. "Good job."

"Thank you, sir. I appreciate all the great questions that you asked us. I learned more from those questions than you can imagine."

"How's that?" Dr. Skor asked with a puzzled look. "You knew all the answers."

"I learn how you think. The questions are much more important than the answers."

Dr. Skor laughed. "Get busy. I'll go spend some time with the students. See you tomorrow at ten o'clock."

Jason had called Philip on Monday night and related what had happened with Mark Fuller. He told him that for the next several weeks he would be extremely busy because he and the students were taking care of all the patients without a resident. He would not be able to meet for lunch or supper but would see him Saturday afternoon and would spend Saturday night with him.

Philip's answer was simple and flat: "Okay, see you Saturday afternoon."

Jason was sad and, at the same time, relieved that he would not be seeing Philip for the rest of the week. It was probably time to put an end to this, he thought. He closed his eyes as a wave of sadness swept over him. This weekend would be a good time to do it. There was no way that Philip could live with him and be happy. Philip needed a more submissive person in his life. And the last thing that Jason wanted to do was to make Philip unhappy. He loved him too much. His pain was palpable, but he would focus on his patients.

On Thursday, Jason admitted a fifty-five-year-old man for recurrent chest pains. Jason immediately recognized him as Francis Lackland, the man whom he and Nurse Chapman had resuscitated alone during the early morning hours that first day of his internship. In reviewing his previous medical records, Jason read the note he had written that first day, ending with *Nurse Chapman saved this man's life.*

Jason hadn't followed up on him after that resuscitation and wasn't aware of his outcome, but he learned, after reviewing his records, that he had been taken back for a cardiac catheterization and that the stent, which had been placed the day prior to his cardiac arrest, had clotted. A new stent had been inserted, and he had been placed on a blood thinner following that procedure.

Jason also discovered that he was an appellate court judge for the Second Circuit, Southern District of New York, and realized that he had read a number of decisions that the man had made over the past several years. This judge had been nominated by President George H. W. Bush and was known for his conservative leanings.

Jason had become interested in him because he had upheld a controversial lower court decision that denied custody of a child to the child's mother who had partnered with another woman after her divorce. Judge Lackland's ruling had affirmed the lower court decision, which essentially said that it was in the best interest of a child to deny equal custody to a lesbian mother. Jason also noted in the chart that the judge was a heavy smoker.

Jason knocked on the door and went into his room. "Judge Lackland, my name is Jason Green. I'm the intern who will be caring for you while you are here. It's a pleasure to meet you, sir. How are you feeling now?"

"Jason Green? It's nice to meet the man who saved my life." The judge smiled at him. "I had meant to write you after I went home last year, but you know how time gets away."

"Certainly, sir. I'm just glad to see that you have been doing so well."

Jason proceeded to take a complete history and then perform a physical examination.

"Judge, based on your history and physical examination, I believe you have some significant blockages that will need to addressed. I'll call your cardiologist and have him see you immediately, but I'm certain that you will need to have another cardiac catheterization very quickly. Hopefully, the cardiologist will be able to take care of the blockages with one or more stents."

Judge Lackland scowled. "Why does this keep happening to me?"

"It's quite simple, Judge. It's your smoking." Jason faced him squarely. "Your cholesterol levels are excellent on your current medication, and your blood pressure is also excellent. You have to discontinue the tobacco use, or you're not going to get to enjoy watching your grandchildren grow up."

"You doctors are all the same. You really have no proof that cigarettes are related to my problem."

Jason sat on the bed next to the judge and put his hand on his shoulder, which seemed to take the judge by surprise.

"Judge Lackland, you're an intelligent man. I've read many of your opinions over the years, and I know that you are a logical person. I can cite thirty definitive studies showing the profound impact that cigarettes have on the development of coronary disease and peripheral vascular disease. That relationship is not in question."

The judge frowned. "You're a doctor. Why have you read my legal opinions?"

"That's not important." Jason shook his head. "What

is important now is that we get your cardiologist in and get those blocked arteries taken care of before you sustain any damage to your heart muscle. But after that is done, I will be relentless in trying to get you to stop smoking. And if necessary, I'll copy the thirty articles for you, and after reading those articles, if you're able to write a logical opinion that smoking and coronary disease are not related, well, then, I'll eat my hat, as we say in the South." He smiled and stood. "I'll be back in a few minutes. I'm going to call your cardiologist."

Jason went to the nursing station and called Dr. Mendenhall, the judge's cardiologist for the past decade and chief of the cardiology division. Jason described the history and physical examination. He did not ask for Dr. Mendenhall's opinion. Instead he ended by saying, "I think he needs to have a cardiac catheterization immediately."

"Dr. Green, it's already two o'clock. Why don't you see if you can get him in for a stress thallium test, and we'll see what that shows?" The chief of cardiology sounded impatient. "Then we can talk about a cardiac catheterization."

"Sir, I think he is hanging on a thread. Minimal isometric exercise during my physical examination resulted in his going into congestive heart failure. I don't think he would make it through a stress test, and I think there's a good chance he'll infarct before tomorrow without intervention."

"Let me speak with your resident." Dr. Mendenhall's tone turned angry.

"Sir, I'm both the intern and acting resident on this service. I can ask Dr. Skor, who is my attending, to call you. But, Dr. Mendenhall, Judge Lackland needs a cardiac catheterization now. I won't settle for anything less."

"How dare you talk to me that way!" Dr. Mendenhall

was clearly furious now. "You wait right there. I'm on my way over."

In five minutes Jason saw a short, middle-aged doctor walk into Judge Lackland's room. In ten minutes he marched out, spotted Jason, and walked to him. "Are you Dr. Green?"

"Yes, sir, I'm Jason Green. Dr. Mendenhall, it's a pleasure to meet you. Thank you for coming over."

Dr. Mendenhall stared at Jason. "Why do you think he is hanging on a thread, as you say?"

"Sir, he is very stoic, and I think his symptoms are worse than he is letting on. Also, as I said on the phone, he immediately goes into heart failure after squeezing my arm for just a few seconds."

"Okay, we'll see." Dr. Mendenhall took out his cell phone and made a phone call as he was walking toward the elevators. Within fifteen minutes, Judge Lackland was being taken down for a cardiac cath. Two hours later, he was brought back to his room. Jason read the cath report, which indicated that a stent had been placed in a ninety-nine percent blocked left main coronary artery. Jason knew that the cardiologists called that kind of blockage the widow maker. He also had a ninety-five percent blockage of his circumflex artery, which was also successfully stented.

Jason walked into his room after finishing the chart he was working on. "You look much better, Judge. How are you feeling?"

"Feeling much better." The judge gave Jason a measured look. "No more shortness of breath, and the chest pains have disappeared. This is the second time you've saved my life."

"Now, I want a promise from you that you're going to stop smoking. If you continue to smoke, Judge, you'll be back here soon. And one of these times you're not going to make it." Jason held the judge's stare. "So I want a promise you're going to stop. I'll disrupt your courtroom if I have to."

"Sit down here a minute, Dr. Green. I want to know why you have read my opinions. That's all I thought about while they were doing my catheterization. Was it because you resuscitated me last year?"

"Sir, until today I had no idea that Judge Lackland was the individual whom I helped resuscitate." Jason smiled. "And why I have read your opinions is unimportant. What is important is that you stop smoking cigarettes."

"I tell you what," the judge continued. "I promise you that I'll quit smoking if you tell me why you, a young doctor, have been interested in my court opinions."

"Sir, is that a real promise?" Jason raised an eyebrow. "Will you really quit smoking?"

"You have my word."

Jason nodded. "I read an article a few years back in *The Advocate*, which is a gay publication, regarding an opinion you rendered affirming a lower court ruling denying equal child custody to a lesbian mother following her divorce from the father. The writer obviously started from a biased position, so I read your original opinion. I was fascinated by your thought process, and the opinion was beautifully written, so I took it upon myself to read probably ten or fifteen other opinions you've written over the past five years. You've taught me a lot, and for that I thank you." He smiled. "So having said that, I believe we now have a binding agreement, and if you break your end of the agreement, I want you to know that I am very close friends with a high-powered litigator who will help me to legally force you to give up cigarettes."

The judge laughed. "And who might your high-powered litigator be?"

"His name is John Olsen, sir, and I know he will be

very aggressive in making you keep your end of the agreement."

"Dr. Green, you are funny. And how do you know my friend John Olsen?"

Jason blinked. "Oh, I didn't know he was your friend. Well, he won't be your friend if you break our agreement."

Both men laughed.

"And how *do* you know John?"

"Sir, if same-sex marriage were legal, he would likely be my father-in-law."

"I see." Judge Lackland's eyebrows rose, but his expression was enigmatic. "So I suppose that you disagree with my opinion in the child-custody case."

"Sir, I understood your logic and that your opinion was based on procedural grounds. However, I believe that our Constitution was left out of the discussion. So to be blunt, I disagreed with your opinion. But I want you to know that I think you write beautifully, and I agree with most of your other opinions. And I want you to know that I think no less of you because of that opinion. It's just an opinion, and I know you are a good person." Jason smiled. "Except for the cigarettes."

The judge laughed again. "Jason, if I can call you Jason, when gay marriage is legal, and it will one day soon be legal, I would be honored if you let me perform the marriage vows for you and Phil."

"I'd be honored, sir, but I would have to teach you a little Hebrew first."

They were both laughing as Dr. Mendenhall walked in.

Dr. Mendenhall smiled. "Well, I see you are doing much better, Francis."

"Excuse me, Judge, Dr. Mendenhall. I have to get back to work." Jason nodded to the judge. "I'll see you in the morning. If you want to go home tomorrow, you'll have to convince Dr. Mendenhall. He calls the shots."

Jason patted the judge on the shoulder, turned, and left the two men alone.

The next morning, Jason discharged Judge Lackland. The judge took an unused pack of cigarettes out of his pocket and gave it to Jason. "I keep my promises." He hugged Jason and was wheeled to the elevator by the nurse.

CHAPTER 17

The remainder of the week went smoothly for Jason and his two students. Jason stayed late every day, and his students stayed late with him. His students were in awe of and dedicated to Jason and helped him with a heavy patient load far beyond the usual student involvement.

Jason hadn't seen Philip all week and guessed that Philip was as relieved as he was. Philip continued to be in his thoughts day and night. But there was no way that Philip would ever be happy with him. He was more certain of that each day they were apart. When Saturday finally arrived, he ran to Philip's apartment after finishing at the hospital midafternoon. It was the first he had seen of him since the prior Sunday.

Philip was sitting in the living room reading when he let himself in. Jason walked to him and kissed him lightly on the cheek.

Philip smiled at him. "I know you've been terribly busy, but you could have called me."

"I'm sorry, Philip." Jason paused. "Do you mind if I shower? Then I'll take you for dinner. We need to talk."

Philip looked at him without saying anything. Jason showered and slowly dressed. They walked six blocks to a family Italian restaurant they had frequented. Philip asked Jason how things were going without a resident, and Jason gave a detailed description of his week without a resident and his interactions with Dr. Skor and the students.

Then Jason turned somber and looked at Philip. "Philip, the thing with Kevin Gray just reinforced what I had thought," he said without preamble. "You need someone who is submissive, and I don't think I could ever make you happy."

Philip looked away for a long moment without speaking. "You're wrong." He turned to him at last, moisture glimmering at the corners of his eyes. "I know I betrayed you. I can't take that back. But your idea that you can't make me happy is foolishness. And I can't make you hear that."

"I understand what you need in a partner. You told me, and I saw it with Kevin."

"That's just part of me, a tiny part of me." Philip shook his head and after a long pause looked into Jason's eyes. "I'm weary and depressed. Maybe it *is* best we stay away from each other for a while and see what happens."

There was silence as the waiter brought their entrees.

"Perhaps so." Jason tried to stop the tears but couldn't. "Philip, you are the first person I have ever loved. I love you deeply, still. You are my first thought in the morning and my last thought before I sleep. I'm so sorry it has turned out this way."

Philip said nothing.

Outside the restaurant, Jason held Philip tightly for several minutes. He turned and walked slowly back to his apartment. He dozed through the night and got up at four a.m. He was to admit that day but decided to go early to the lab to work on his computer program rather than run. He had been unable to go the lab the previous week because of the workload in the hospital and was anxious to work on his project. Jason slowly dressed, ate a protein bar, and walked to the Starbucks, where he bought a strong brew that would give him the needed buzz. He walked slowly to the Olsen Research Center, exhausted and deeply saddened. As he approached the entrance to the research center, Jason saw the same Chinese man whom Dr. Fang had introduced as his MIT professor exit the building with the Tumi leather briefcase. He wore the same pinstriped navy suit. *How odd*, Jason thought. *What an early hour for a visit*. It was just after five a.m. and on a Sunday morning. Jason stopped and watched him as he disappeared around the corner.

Jason stopped in front of the dedication plaque, and his eyes moistened once again. He entered the computer room, and there sat Dr. Fang with two external hard drives attached to the main computers. Each backup drive had "3 Terabyte Capacity" stamped on the top. Jason instantly realized that these huge-capacity backup drives could be used for only one purpose: to download all the information on the mainframe computer system.

"My God! Dr. Fang, what are you doing?" Jason screamed. He should have known, he should have realized. "Dr. Fang," he continued in Mandarin, his voice rising, "why are you stealing our work? That man who just left—are you working for him?"

Jason gasped for breath, hyperventilating. With unexpected force, Dr. Fang lunged at Jason, knocking him down. Jason's head struck the edge of the desk, and everything went dark.

✌ঌৎঌ

When Jason awoke, he sat up, dazed, his head throbbing. He looked at the clock. He had only been unconscious for a few minutes. He sat, trying to gather his thoughts. Fang and the hard drives were gone. The mainframe computer was still humming. The sixty-four-gigabyte memory sticks, the Tumi briefcases—but Dr. Fang had cared so much about their work. He was proud of it. He would never—

Only he had. He sold it to someone or gave it to a spy.

He took out his cell phone and dialed Dr. Glassman's number. No answer. He put the phone down and touched his head. It was bleeding, but he didn't think it was too bad. He dialed Philip's number. "Philip, I need help," he gasped.

"What's wrong?"

"I need to see your daddy right away."

"My father knows everything about us. He's in as much distress as I am."

"No, Philip, this is not about us. Please, come and take me to your daddy now. I need to tell him in person what has happened. A phone call won't do. Your daddy will know what to do. It's an emergency, a big one. I'll explain on our way. Please help me."

"Where are you?"

"I'm in the lab. Please, pick me up at front of the entrance."

"I'll be there in fifteen minutes." Philip hung up the phone.

Jason sat, still dazed. He wiped his left temple. There was blood all over his hand and on the floor. He stood up and walked slowly to the entrance, light-headed and nauseated. The labs and building were deserted since it was only five-forty on a Sunday morning. Philip drove up and reached over to open the door, talking to his father on the phone, looking at Jason with a stunned expression.

Jason got into the car, and Philip looked at the blood running down his face. "Jesus, Jason, what happened? That cut over your eye is bad!" He opened the glove compartment and took out some paper napkins, holding them over the cut. "Put pressure on this. I'll fix it when we get to my parents' house. What is this all about?" His voice was tight with stress. "Are you sure this isn't about us?"

Jason was still in a fog. He spoke slowly. "I caught Dr. Fang this morning stealing data from our mainframe computer. You're going to think I'm really crazy, but Fang is a spy." He leaned his head against the window and continued to talk slowly. "He's been stealing data all along. I should have put two and two together, but I liked him. And he cared—he cared about what we were doing."

"You sound a little crazy. Are you sure you're okay?"

"I promise you, I'm telling you the truth. You'll hear the whole story when I tell your daddy. I don't know whom else to talk to. I can't get Glassman on the phone. Maybe he's out of town. Your daddy will know what to do." Jason suddenly vomited his protein bar and coffee. "Philip, I'm sorry. I'll clean it up. I'm sorry."

He opened his window to get fresh air. It dawned on him that what happened to him this morning was the second major betrayal he had ever experienced. Each betrayal resulted in the same reaction: he vomited. He closed the window and saw the speedometer reading ninety-five miles per hour. "Be careful, Philip," he said, realizing he was slurring his words slightly.

Philip's father was standing in front as Jason and Philip drove up. It was not quite seven o'clock. "Jason, what happened to you?"

"Dad, can you get a first-aid kit?"

Philip helped Jason into the house and sat him next to the fireplace in the den. He got some water, and Mr. Olsen brought the first-aid kit. Philip cleaned the head laceration and taped it closed.

It would do, he said, until he could get some sutures to

close it properly. He gently cleaned the blood from Jason's face.

Philip and his father sat down. "So what happened to you? What's this all about?"

"Mr. Olsen, what I'm going to tell you will sound crazy." Jason took a deep breath and tried to gather his thoughts. "I've been working in Dr. Glassman's lab with Dr. Fang. You met him at the Glassmans' apartment at my birthday party. He's a Chinese national who is working in Dr. Glassman's lab under an NIH grant. He is brilliant and has been a great mentor to me and very productive for Dr. Glassman. Over the year, I noticed a few odd things that I didn't think much about. He had some sixty-four-gigabyte backup sticks that he carried, and he actually admitted to me that he occasionally downloaded raw data to look at on his home computer. So I didn't think too much about that. He also had two Tumi leather briefcases, one with his initials branded on it and another without initials. Otherwise, they were identical. They are expensive briefcases. Sometimes he would bring one in, at other times the other.

"One morning a month or two ago, I stopped at a Starbucks on my way to the hospital, and Fang was sitting with an older Chinese man. They both had Tumi leather briefcases. When I approached Dr. Fang, the older man immediately got up and left. Dr. Fang told me that he was his old MIT professor with whom he met occasionally. I realized on the way to the hospital that the professor had picked up Dr. Fang's briefcase, the one with the initials. I left him a message on his answering machine so that he could retrieve it. Dr. Fang thanked me later for noticing, and I didn't think any more about it. Also, for the entire year I've been in the lab, Fang would get a phone call every night at precisely eight o'clock. He would always go into the hall and speak in Mandarin. I could never hear the conversations, but he always came back very agitated. I tried to ask him if I could help, and he told me that his sister in California was having problems and that he had to send her all his extra money. Dr. Glassman later told me that he had no siblings, so I assumed that he might have gotten a woman pregnant and was having to send her money. In any case, all of these things by themselves were odd, but I didn't put them all together." Tears started forming in Jason's eyes.

"This morning I walked into the lab just after five. As I was entering the building, that same Chinese man that I saw Dr. Fang with at Starbucks was exiting the building. He was dressed in a navy pinstriped suit and was carrying Dr. Fang's Tumi briefcase. I couldn't understand what his old professor would be doing up at five on Sunday in New York City and how he could pick up the wrong briefcase twice. Anyway, I walked into the computer room, and Dr. Fang had two three terabyte backup drives connected to the mainframe computer. I—I yelled at him, and he jumped up and shoved me down. I guess my head hit the desk or something, and I passed out. When I woke up, the backup drives and Fang were gone. I know that he was copying everything we had on that computer, and I'm sure he was using the sixty-four-gigabyte sticks to steal information as well."

Jason paused. Mr. Olsen and Philip sat silently, staring at him, obviously stunned and speechless at these revelations.

Jason looked up, tears starting to trickle down his cheeks. "There's more. Last year when you were telling me about your lawsuit against the Chinese government, I was intrigued about the possibility that the Chinese could also be stealing from university research labs. Just for kicks, I went on the websites of six other important bioinformatics lab in the US, and all have Chinese researchers.

I just thought it was curious. I have no idea whether they are US citizens or Chinese nationals. But bioinformatics labs accumulate huge amounts of data from many different labs and would be a natural source to steal information. I am certain that Fang was stealing data, and I would suspect that it's happening elsewhere."

He looked away. "I should have suspected this earlier. He was just such a great mentor. I—I just can't believe it." He drew a shuddering breath. "All of the computer data is automatically backed up by EMC Corporation. There's a strict rule in Dr. Glassman's lab that no data be backed up to any external drives. I knew he had broken that rule with those sixty-four-gigabyte drives, but his explanation was plausible, and I didn't think too much about it."

"We should call Dr. Glassman," Mr. Olsen said, staring intently at Jason.

"I tried calling him before I called Philip. There was no answer. It was either too early or maybe he is out of town. Mr. Olsen, I figured you would know what to do. I'm sorry to bother you." Jason looked at his watch. "Mr. Olsen, Philip, I have to get back to the hospital. I have no resident. I'm the only one taking care of my hospital patients."

"Wait here, boys. Jason, don't worry about the hospital. Your patients will be taken care of."

Philip's father went into his study, and Mrs. Olsen, who had been standing behind Philip and Jason, came in and kissed Philip and Jason. She brought coffee and toast, and Jason and Philip sat silently, drinking the coffee. Mr. Olsen came out of his study twenty-five minutes later. "C'mon boys, the limo should be outside already. You won't need to bring anything. We'll be back tonight." Mr. Olsen kissed his wife. "See you this evening, honey."

They went out the front door where a limousine was waiting, doors opened.

ⱷↄⱸↄ

"Dad, where are we going?"

Mr. Olsen was deep in thought. "To see the president."

"The president of what?" Jason sounded frantic.

"The United States. Jason, the president and I are good friends, because I give him a lot of money for his campaigns, but we were also college buddies. We're going to Camp David."

Jason felt himself getting light-headed again and guessed he was looking pretty pale. "Mr. Olsen, what if I *am* crazy and this is all nothing?"

"You're not crazy. I called the president. He wants to see us now. I suspect this is not the first time he has heard about Chinese data theft. The FBI and CIA will be there as well. Harvey is meeting us at the Danbury airport." Mr. Olsen's law firm kept a corporate jet housed only twenty minutes away.

Jason sat stunned, doubting himself, wondering what he had gotten himself into. "How did you find Dr. Glassman?" he asked, his mouth dry.

"I have his cell number. I told him to not ask any questions. I sent a limo for him to take him to the Pier Six heliport. He should be there shortly after we arrive."

Jason shifted on the seat, running over everything he remembered of Dr. Fang. "Mr. Olsen, what if I am completely wrong about all of this?"

"I'm not a betting man. I deal in probabilities every day." Mr. Olsen gave Jason a grim glance. "But I'm betting that you have discovered part of a widespread espionage operation." He took a deep breath. "Now, this is none of my business, but how are you two doing?"

"Dad, don't—" Philip began.

"Mr. Olsen, I love your son. We're fine."

Philip looked at Jason, who briefly caught his eyes.

The remainder of the drive to the Danbury airport passed in silence. They were taken to the general aviation terminal, where two pilots were waiting for them.

"Good morning, Mr. Olsen." One of the pilots smiled and shook Mr. Olsen's hand. "We have already filed our flight plans to Frederick Municipal Airport. A limousine will meet you there for the twenty-minute trip to Camp David."

"Thanks, Jimmy," Mr. Olsen said to the pilot. "We're just waiting for one more passenger, Dr. Glassman."

The pilot chuckled. "He's already on the airplane. He didn't look very happy. Apparently, the helicopter ride was not to his liking."

The pilot led them to the Cessna Citation. They entered the airplane to find Dr. Glassman sitting in one of the four seats, which had been arranged so that all four faced each other.

Dr. Glassman appeared agitated as he looked up and saw Jason and Philip enter the cabin. "What in God's name is this all about?" he snapped.

The plane took off, and over the next thirty minutes, Jason recounted what he had told Mr. Olsen. Dr. Glassman's face went ashen as the import of the news sank in.

"Dr. Glassman, I'm so sorry I confronted Dr. Fang without talking to you first. I was just so overcome this morning when I saw those backups that it just came out. Am I mistaken? Was Dr. Fang copying all of this data at your request?"

"No, Jason," Dr. Glassman said heavily. "If I had asked him to do that, he certainly wouldn't have become violent with you. He was obviously stealing information.

And his professor at MIT was not Chinese. Where in God's name are we going?"

"We have a meeting with the president."

Dr. Glassman jerked around to stare at John Olsen. "Of the United States?"

"Yes, Harvey. And I know what you think of him. Just put your politics aside."

Jason looked at Dr. Glassman. "Sir, could you tell me something? How did Dr. Fang come to work for you? Did you receive any recommendations or calls, particularly from anyone in government?"

"As a matter of fact, I received a call, confirmed by letter, from a congressman." Dr. Glassman frowned. "I think his name was Harrison, from Georgia. His accent was worse than yours. He explained that he was a member of some House subcommittee that appropriated NIH monies to scientific laboratories. He said that he knew we had many applications for postdoc positions, and he also knew that funding was getting more and more difficult, but that he could guarantee generous funding if we would consider taking in Fang. He said the committee had developed good working relations with the Chinese scientific community and that taking Fang would help with those relations. I looked at the applicant pool, and Fang was at the top, so we took him. He has been a diligent worker, and I never suspected any hanky-panky. Why would you ask that?"

Jason took a deep breath. "Mr. Olsen told me last year about a lawsuit his firm was filing against the Chinese government regarding computer hacking and information theft. I figured that science labs would be easy targets for computer theft. The Chinese have a burgeoning pharmaceutical industrial program, and this kind of information would give them a running start. And there are Chinese nationals at almost every university. So I did some Internet searches after our conversation at Thanksgiving and found some interesting facts. First of all, I looked up the names of the various faculty and postdoc fellows at the major bioinformatics labs—you know, Harvard, Washington University in St. Louis, University of Washington, University of California at Berkeley, Stanford, and MIT. They all have Chinese faculty and postdoc fellows. I don't know if they are American or Chinese nationals, but I would be concerned. I wrote all their names down, and I've had the list in my wallet since then. I forgot about it, really."

He took out a piece of paper from his wallet and unfolded it to confirm that he still had the information. On it were ten Chinese names with their associated institution next to each name. He folded it and returned it to his wallet. "Almost all the postdoc fellows were funded by NIH grants. So just on a hunch, I also looked up the congressmen who are responsible for appropriating NIH monies. They publish committee meeting minutes on the Internet, and Franklin Harrison from Georgia seemed to be the one congressman who kept bringing up the necessity for improving relations with the Chinese scientific community, just as you said, Dr. Glassman."

"So what are you getting at?" Mr. Olsen asked with a frown.

"Well, I looked into his background. He is a fourth-term congressman from Georgia. He was from a poor family and had a small law practice in a suburb of Atlanta when he ran for Congress. He lived in a modest house in Georgia, and when he went to Washington, he shared an apartment with two other congressmen. Two years ago, he bought a two-point-four-million-dollar townhome in Georgetown and moved his family up from Georgia. I guess I'm naïve about politics and money, but that seemed odd to me. I didn't think much about it until today."

Dr. Glassman was staring at him, his eyebrows raised. "How in God's name did you find all of this out?"

"It's all available on government websites. And as far as real estate records, it's all public and available with a few clicks on the computer."

The flight was less than an hour, and a limousine was waiting for them at the tarmac. It was only eleven-thirty a.m., and the drive to Camp David was through beautiful country. They passed through three security checkpoints and arrived at the main house. Jason stared at the building, feeling numb. He was about to meet the president of the United States. Jason swallowed hard. What if he had overreacted? What if he were wrong?

Two marines standing guard at the entrance to the main lodge opened the doors of the limousine. The president came out the front entrance as the marines were about to electronically search the four men.

"Sergeant, that won't be necessary. John, great to see you again. Dr. Glassman, I haven't seen you since your Nobel Prize dinner at the White House. Hope you are well." The president shook both men's hands. "And this must be your son, Phil. The resemblance is clear. I hope I never need your services." He shook Philip's hand. "And this must be Dr. Green, the next head of the CIA." The president shook Jason's hand and patted him on the back. "How is your head feeling?"

"Fine sir." Not quite. Jason felt positively light-headed and hoped it didn't show on his face.

The president led them into the large living room, and they sat in a circle around the broad stone fireplace. A marine offered each drinks and small sandwiches. The president smiled. "I assumed you hadn't eaten anything since this all started this morning."

As they started to eat, a uniformed marine came in and spoke in rapid Mandarin. "Dr. Green, I am supposed to find out if you are really fluent in Chinese. The president wants to know."

Jason stood up, holding on to the chair, still feeling dizzy. After a pause, he answered in Mandarin. "Sir, you can tell the president that I am quite fluent in Mandarin. You can also tell him that one day I may want to marry another man, and his political support for marriage between two men could earn him my vote."

The men all looked at Jason and the sergeant, who was now bright red in the face.

The marine stared at Jason for a moment and then turned to the president. "Mr. President, Dr. Green is fluent in Chinese." The marine saluted, turned, and walked out of the room.

"Sorry, Dr. Green. After John told me about you, you sounded a little too good to be true. Just checking you out." The president smiled. "May I call you Jason?"

"Of course, Mr. President."

"I understand that you broke some records in track at Mississippi and some of them still stand."

"Sir, I would have no idea. I really don't covet any records I may have set. I always figured someone's stopwatch wasn't properly working."

Everyone laughed, except Jason who remained tense.

The president looked intently at Jason. "So fill me in."

Jason repeated what he had told Mr. Olsen and Dr. Glassman. Dr. Glassman had taken out a piece of paper and was writing as they were talking.

"Well, men, I think you have something here. The CIA and FBI have already uncovered a substantial program of computer hacking that has originated from Chinese government-sponsored groups. Some breaches have been leaked into the press. This is the first I've heard of a spy being planted in an academic center—"

"Mr. President," Jason interrupted, "I suspect this is

widespread. And I believe that a US congressman may be involved."

The president did not look pleased. "Jason, that's a serious accusation."

Jason went on to explain the names he had found associated with the top bioinformatics labs and the facts surrounding Congressman Harrison. The president pushed a buzzer, and the marine who had questioned Jason came into the room. "Sergeant, could you bring them in here and pull up another two chairs? The marine brought in two chairs and looked several times at Jason, causing Jason to blush.

The president introduced the heads of the FBI and CIA to all four men. "Gentlemen, they have listened to our conversation and are caught up. Do either of you have any questions for Jason or Dr. Glassman?"

The FBI director turned to Jason. "Do you know where Fang lives?"

Jason gave him the address and apartment number. He also gave a description of the older, well-dressed Chinese man that Fang had met with at least on two occasions. Jason saw the surprised look of the FBI director as he gave an incredibly detailed description of the Chinese man: height, weight, the color of his eyes and socks, a one-inch scar on the left side of his chin, a stripe of gray hair over his right temple, a half-centimeter growth on his right nostril, a gold ring on his left fourth finger, and his manicured, clear-polished fingernails.

"You said that you had a list of other Chinese researchers. Do you have that list with you?" the FBI director continued.

Jason took the list out of his wallet and handed him the list. "If you can find out whether any of these are Chinese nationals, I would suggest that there is a possibility they are involved."

"I should have that answer for you within ten minutes." The FBI director gave the list to the marine sergeant, who immediately left.

Dr. Glassman unfolded the piece of paper that he had been writing on. "This is a list of the chairmen of the bio-informatics programs at the six institutions on Jason's list. I know them all very well. If any of these people are Chinese nationals, I would like to talk to the relevant chairmen. If they were contacted by Congressman Harrison as I was, then I believe it would be strong evidence that the congressman was somehow involved and that the computers at those institutions have probably been breached as well."

"We'll have the answer in a few minutes." The president looked at Jason. "You should be proud of yourself for handling this in the way you have. I understand you are an intern in the medicine department. I didn't think interns had enough time to do research."

"Sir, Dr. Glassman has been very gracious in giving me the opportunity, and I've taken advantage of it."

"You must have no time for anything else. Don't you have any other interests besides medicine and research? I can see by your physique that you're still running."

"Sir, my only other interest has been Philip."

The President looked over at Philip. "What do you mean?"

"Sir, Philip and I are in love with each other. We've been together for the past ten months. He has been my only other interest. I'm living quite a full life."

"My FBI man told me you were homosexual, but I didn't know about your relationship. Well, good for you."

The president smiled without quite looking at anyone. Jason noticed that Dr. Glassman was unsuccessfully trying to suppress a smile.

The sergeant brought the piece of paper back to the

FBI chief. "Mr. President, of the eight people on the list, six are Chinese nationals here on green cards, and all six institutions are represented."

"Get the heads of their departments on the phone, one at a time. Bring a phone in here for Dr. Glassman," the President ordered.

Dr. Glassman spoke to the six chairmen individually, and the answer was the same each time. Congressman Harrison had called each chairman and guaranteed NIH funding in return for taking on a Chinese national post-doctoral fellow. None of them had had any reason to think that files were being copied or that their computer systems had been breached. After Dr. Glassman had talked to each one, the FBI director spoke to each chairman, instructing each to say nothing to anyone or act differently in any way until the FBI and CIA could investigate further. They were each told that national security was involved and that not even their spouses should be told.

"Well, gentlemen." The president stood up. "This is an important day. I think an important espionage program has been discovered, and it may just be the tip of the iceberg." The meeting had taken less than an hour. The president looked at the FBI and CIA directors. "Do what you have to do to get this cleared up. Obviously, get Fang and his contact, if you can. Send your experts to these other institutions and see what's up. Regarding Harrison, what do you think we should do?"

"Mr. President, we need a little more evidence before we go get him," the FBI director said. "I'll start working on it right away."

"We'll work with our contacts in Beijing and Shanghai and see if they can add anything," the CIA director added.

"Dr. Glassman, Jason, John, Phil, you've made an important contribution." The president put his arm around Jason's shoulders. "You deserve something. I'm not sure yet what, but at the least let's plan on dinner at the White House in the near future."

John Olsen shook the president's hand. "Mr. President, thank you for being so accommodating and believing in us. Not every leader would have listened."

The president led the four men to the limousine, shook their hands, and waved good-bye.

CHAPTER 18

The only sound in the limousine was the humming of the motor. All four men sat speechless and in shock. Jason and Philip looked at each other, expressionless. Philip had not said a word since leaving his house. Jason wondered what Philip had thought when he'd told the president he was in love with Philip. He wondered whether Philip had told his father that they were breaking off their relationship. Jason looked out of the window to hide the tears that were starting to form.

Dr. Glassman was sitting across from Jason and noticed. "Jason, are you okay?"

"Yes, sir, thanks." Jason quickly wiped his eyes. "Dr. Glassman, I'm sorry I didn't put this all together sooner."

"Nonsense." Dr. Glassman waved his hand. "I'm really interested, right now, in only one thing about this whole affair. What was the Chinese conversation between you and the sergeant? Whatever you told him embarrassed the hell out of him."

Jason remained silent.

"Come on, Jason," Dr. Glassman prodded, smiling. "Don't keep us in suspense."

"Oh, he told me the president wanted to know if I really spoke fluent Chinese, and I told him that he could assure the president that I did, and that he should also tell the president something to the effect that if he and Republicans ever wanted my vote, they were going have to stop being hypocrites about individual liberties." He wasn't about to repeat his actual words.

"Well, good for you." Dr. Glassman laughed and slapped John Olsen's thigh. Mr. Olsen chuckled and shook his head.

They arrived at the Frederick airport at two o'clock. The pilots were waiting for them in the general aviation terminal.

"Where to, Mr. Olsen?" the pilot asked.

"Harvey, how about if we drop you off at LaGuardia? You should be home in time for dinner. And then we can fly on to Danbury. Jason, you spend the night at our place," Mr. Olsen ordered.

Jason looked at Mr. Olsen with a sad smile. "Thank you very much. I would like that, but I have to go to the hospital. I haven't rounded on my patients, and my students probably think I've deserted them. In fact, I don't have a resident, and I'm responsible for these patients. I'm very concerned that no doctor has seen them today." He just hoped all was okay with his patients.

"Don't worry," Mr. Olsen interrupted. "I talked with Dr. Stern before we left. Dr. Skor rounded with the students this morning."

Jason should have called Dr. Skor. He stared down at his hands. He'd let Dr. Skor down.

Philip looked at Jason. "I'll drive back to the city this evening. I'll be there around seven or eight. Will you please come over? I'll bring some sutures and stitch up that laceration."

Jason hesitated. It really wasn't a good idea, now that they had decided to separate. But this really wasn't the time to upset Mr. Olsen. "Of course, I'll come over when I finish in the hospital. It'll take a few hours."

The plane touched down at LaGuardia at three-thirty

p.m., and a limousine took Dr. Glassman and Jason to the research center, where they arrived at four-fifteen. They entered the lab to find four men from the FBI in the bio-informatics lab searching the drawers, taking fingerprints, and shooting pictures.

"Dr. Glassman, we would like permission to have our computer people come tomorrow and go through your programs carefully," a tall, thin agent told him. "We will not alter any of the programs. We want to see if there was any remote access, e-mails, and so forth."

Jason clearly wasn't going to have computer access. Not that he had time for it right now.

"Dr. Glassman, if it's okay with you, I should go to the hospital and check on my patients. I'll come over tomorrow after rounds if you're available and make plans with you about how to continue here."

"Okay, Jason. I want you to know how grateful I am to you." Dr. Glassman nodded. "I'll see you tomorrow."

Jason walked slowly to the hospital. The students were still on the floor and told Jason that Dr. Skor had just left.

"Dr. Green, are you okay? What happened to your eye?" Gerald Shenkman sounded worried. "Dr. Skor said you had an emergency."

"Yes, everything's fine now." Jason smiled for them. "We'll continue as usual in the morning. You guys, thanks for being here all day. Go home and I'll see you early tomorrow."

Jason spent another hour going through the charts, catching up on events. Notes were written on every pa-tient, most by the students and cosigned by Dr. Skor. Ja-son was relieved that all was in order and made a mental note to apologize to Dr. Skor tomorrow for his absence.

Jason left the hospital at six. It was a beautiful late spring day. The air was particularly fresh, and the streets were quiet. He walked slowly back to his apartment, emotionally drained from the events. Everything still seemed surreal. And what about his relationship with Philip? It appeared to be at the end, at least for now, probably forever. A fresh wave of sadness rose inside him. As he approached his apartment building, his neighbor, Mrs. Holiman, with whom he had become friends, passed him with her standard poodle, saying a happy hello.

Jason forced a smile and was about to turn up the steps leading to the entrance of his apartment building when he heard a *Pop*. Suddenly feeling a stinging sensation on the right side of his chest, he looked down and saw blood staining his shirt. Then he heard Mrs. Holiman's scream. He began to feel light-headed, and his legs suddenly gave way. Jason collapsed to the ground and began feeling short of breath. Lying on the sidewalk, unable to move, he became aware of a nauseating, hissing sound each time he took a breath. He felt as if he were drowning— suffocating. He looked up at the blue sky, his vision blurred with tears. He could tell that Mrs. Holiman was kneeling next to him, and her poodle was barking. He heard a siren, and then everything turned black and quiet.

෨෴෨

Jason opened his eyes. Men had surrounded him and someone put a mask over his face, but he couldn't catch his breath. And then, again, everything became black and quiet.

Jason felt bumps and jolts as they moved him into an ambulance. He was going in and out of consciousness, aware and then unaware, jolted again as they removed the stretcher from the ambulance and rushed him in to the emergency room. He heard men and women yelling at each other and he felt helpless and frightened.

Someone was ripping his clothing off. He heard someone say "Jason Green," and another person say "Dr. Olsen."

He suddenly felt an excruciating stab on the right side of his chest, as an emergency room doctor inserted a tube through his chest wall so that his right lung would reinflate. Jason passed out from the pain.

And then he heard people yelling again.

"O negative blood now! Chest X-ray! Jason, I'm going to put a tube into your throat to breathe for you! Quit shaking your head, Jason. Give him Versed, now!"

And all was dark and quiet again, the pain thankfully gone.

ၑၝၑ

Jason opened his eyes. The lights were bright, and he couldn't see well. He felt as if he had paste in his eyes. His right chest ached terribly. He tried to grab the tube coming out of his throat—it was choking him and he wanted it out—but his hands were tied down, and he couldn't move. Looking to the right, he saw a head of blond hair lying on his bed next to him. Could it be Philip? Philip would help him get the tube out of his throat. Jason started shaking, and then he saw Philip's face. Philip put his hand on Jason's cheek, a nurse injected something into his IV, and everything was dark and quiet once again.

Jason woke up several times, but he had no concept of time. It looked as if he were in the same place, and Philip was always there. Philip kissed him on the forehead and talked to him, but Jason didn't understand him. He just wanted the tube out of his throat. He tried moving the tube with his tongue, but it wouldn't budge. Feeling tears coming out of his eyes, he couldn't make out Philip's face anymore because of his blurred vision.

And then again, everything was dark.

He woke up in a different room. The goop was out of his eyes, and he could see more clearly now. His chest hurt, and he had a terrible headache. The tube was choking him, and he wanted it out. Philip stood over him, tears rolling down his cheeks, kissing him again on the forehead. Jason thought he heard him say, "I love you. Everything is going to be fine." Then things got dark and peaceful again.

Jason woke up sometime later as someone was washing his body. Philip sat next to him, asleep in the chair. Jason told himself to remain calm. He didn't want the nurse to give him more sedation. If they untied his hand, he would grab the tube and take it out. His chest ached, but the headache was gone, and he was thinking more clearly now. The nurse untied his right hand to turn him onto his left side, and Jason quickly grabbed the endotracheal tube and pulled it out, causing him to cough violently. The coughing went on for several minutes. The nurse ran from the room, yelling for a doctor to come in.

Philip woke up, startled. "Jason, what have you done?" He sounded desperate.

"I'm fine," Jason said in a barely audible, raspy voice, still coughing. "Leave this goddamned tube out of my throat."

The nurse and resident ran into the room, and Jason turned to them. "If you put any more Versed into my veins, I will slap the shit out of you." His voice was already stronger, and he was furious. He glowered up at the surgical resident. "If you even think about putting that endotracheal tube back down, I'll make certain you never operate again."

Jason lay back down, breathing deeply, grateful to have the tube out of his throat. He was no longer short of breath, and although it hurt to take deep breaths, he welcomed the pain. Philip stood over him, bent over, and kissed his forehead, tears running down his cheeks. Jason heard the nurse tell the resident that his oxygen saturation was ninety-two percent.

"Okay," the resident said. "Let's see how he does on his own."

Jason fell back to sleep, holding Philip's hand, relieved that he was breathing on his own and wondering what had happened to him.

He woke up some time later and looked at the clock on the wall. Ten minutes after five. It was light outside so it must be afternoon, not morning. Frowning, he stared at the ceiling and tried to remember. He last remembered walking to his apartment around six in the afternoon. So that had been at least a day ago. He had an uncomfortable feeling it might be more than one day ago. He heard some noise and turned his head. Philip was hugging Jason's father, and Mr. Olsen was standing next to them.

"Dad!" Jason said as loudly as he could, his voice still raspy.

His father looked at him and started sobbing. He walked over, kissed Jason on the cheeks, and cupped his face between his palms.

"Hi, Dad," Jason rasped. "Quit crying. I'm fine."

Mr. Olsen came over. Jason could not imagine him ever crying, but there he stood, tears flowing. "Mr. Olsen, I'm fine. There is nothing to be upset about."

Mr. Olsen leaned over and kissed Jason on the forehead. Philip went to the other side of the bed and continued to hold Jason's hand.

"What in the hell happened to me? And what day is it?"

Philip leaned over him. "Jason, it's Monday. You had to have some surgery and you're less than twenty-four hours out from it."

Okay, only twenty-four hours gone, then. "But what happened to me?"

Jason's father put his hand on his cheek. "We'll talk about it when you get a little better. Now is not the right time. You get some rest."

The two fathers walked out, but Philip stayed by his side.

"Philip, you look worse than I do. You need to go and get some sleep. But will you please tell me what happened? I'm a big boy. I can take it."

Philip started crying again. Jason had never seen him this emotional. "I'm dying, aren't I?" he whispered.

Philip smiled through the tears. "No, you're not dying."

"I must be dying. You would never cry like that otherwise." Jason laughed, which caused him to wince with pain.

"I'll tell you everything later on. I promise." Philip pressed his hand. "You lost a lot of blood, but they got everything put back together, and you'll heal." He kissed him on the lips this time, lightly. "Now go to sleep."

Jason did, and it was remarkably easy. He woke up at six. Philip was asleep at his side, holding his hand. Both fathers were sitting in chairs facing him.

A tall, handsome man in surgical scrubs walked in and looked at Jason. "Well, Dr. Green, I hear you're not a very cooperative patient. You could have injured yourself, taking out that tube. That was a first for me. But you *are* doing very well, and tomorrow morning, we'll move you into a regular room. Are you hungry?"

"I'm starved. Sir, who are you?"

"I'm the guy who took that bullet out of your chest."

Jason watched as the doctor suddenly realized that no one had told Jason what had happened. "I was shot?" he said in a raspy voice. "Would someone please tell me what happened?"

"I'll leave that to Phil and your father. You're doing very well. You'll be out of here in a week or so." He nodded to the other three men and turned around.

"Wait, Doctor. What is your name?"

"Alexander Patterson." He turned back and his gray eyes crinkled in a smile. "Dr. Green, I hear you're an amazing doctor. I'm glad you're still with us."

"Am I going to be able to run again?" He remembered the tube going into his right chest. God, how that had hurt. "Did you have to remove my lung?"

"Only your middle lobe." Dr. Patterson nodded. "You'll be able to run marathons if you want. You may not set any more NCAA records, but you'll run." He turned around and walked out of the room.

Jason looked at the three men. "Now will someone tell me what happened? The rest of the details, please?"

Mr. Olsen moved to stand in front of the bed. "You were shot when you were walking home from the hospital after we returned from Camp David. Do you remember who Congressman Harrison is?"

"Of course."

Mr. Olsen spoke slowly and deliberately. "Fang's contact, the Chinese man in the pinstriped suit, contacted Harrison to tell him that you discovered Fang's spying, but as far as he knew you were the only one who knew anything. Fang said that Glassman had no idea and would not be in the lab until the next day. So Harrison decided to solve his problem by having you killed. He hired a contract killer through one of his aides, and you were shot. The wound that you had would have been fatal but you were lucky—" His voice faltered. "You were so close to the hospital that they managed to—to get blood into you and get you into surgery in time." He stopped to clear his throat.

Philip had turned his face away, Jason noticed, to hide

that he was crying again. Jason had a feeling it had been more than touch-and-go on the operating table and wondered just how many pints of blood they'd had to pour into him before the bleeding stopped. A lot, he bet.

"Anyway," Mr. Olsen went on, "Harrison had no idea that the president, FBI, and CIA already knew about the thefts, and his involvement in particular. Harrison wanted it to look like a drive-by shooting. But the shooter was caught and admitted to everything. That's thanks to your neighbor, Mrs. Holiman, who saw the whole thing and got his license plate number. The cops pulled him over minutes later," he said with grim satisfaction. "Harrison was arrested and will likely be in jail for the rest of his life. He also admitted to taking millions of dollars from the Chinese government in return for placing Chinese nationals into important scientific labs. Harrison claims that he had no idea they were stealing data. He claims that he believed the Chinese simply wanted to get well-trained scientists. He was paid over five million dollars for his good deeds."

Jason just stared at Mr. Olsen, wondering if this was all one of his nightmares.

His dad got up and came over to him. "Are you okay? We should stop talking about this."

Jason looked at his father. "No, I'm fine," he said softly. "What happened to Fang and the Chinese man?"

"They were both picked up in Seattle, ready to board a plane to Beijing." Mr. Olsen still looked grim. "They are both in custody in an undisclosed location. The other six postdoctoral fellows that you suspected have all been arrested and have all admitted to stealing information. The president told me that this is the tip of the iceberg. We'll never know the extent of the spy ring because it's a political hot potato. The Chinese nationals will all be deported, most likely. The president intimated that we have computer geniuses in this country who know how to retaliate, and apparently we have already disabled several Chinese mainframe computers that contained stolen scientific data."

Jason turned on his side and closed his eyes, brief tears squeezing out from behind his eyelids. He wondered how Fang was feeling. He had cared about their research.

Jason fell asleep almost immediately and did not wake up until five the next morning. When he woke, Philip was sleeping in the chair next to him. Jason noticed that he had changed scrub suits and had taken a shower.

He smiled, because he had intended to let Philip know that he smelled and needed to shower. Jason wondered if he smelled just as bad. He continued looking at Philip. Nothing was the same anymore. Maybe almost dying did that to you. He hoped it wasn't too late.

At six, Philip woke and looked at Jason, who was still staring at him. They both smiled, and neither said anything. At that moment, the surgical resident walked in.

"Dr. Green, I'm going to remove that chest tube. It's not draining very much, so it can come out."

"Thanks, Doctor. While you're at it, would you please take out the Foley? I will pee just fine on my own."

Mr. Olsen and Jonathan Green both walked in as both tubes were being taken out. It hurt a lot, but Jason didn't wince.

"Dr. Green, we'll be moving you to a regular room this morning." The resident smiled down at him. "I've never seen anyone recover this fast from what you went through."

Jason's father and Mr. Olsen both kissed Jason and Philip and sat down.

"Not so fast." Jason motioned for both of them to

stand up. "You both need to move. I need to get into the bathroom and have a bowel movement."

Philip stood. "Jason, I'll go get a bedpan. You shouldn't get up yet."

"Just help me up. I'm not going to use a bedpan in front of you." Jason looked over at both fathers, who were staring at them, and then turned back to Philip. "I know we've been intimate in the past, but having bowel movements in front of each other is not in our future."

All three men laughed. Jason managed to suppress a laugh, knowing it would really hurt. Philip helped Jason move slowly into the bathroom, pulling the IV pole along with them, bags of fluids rocking back and forth.

Jason sat down on the toilet and looked up at Philip, who was standing over him. "Get out of here."

"I'll be right outside. Yell if you need me." Philip left, looking worried.

A few minutes later, Jason opened the door and rolled his IV pole out. They were all standing in front of the door in a row, staring at him.

Jason smiled and shook his head. "I think it was Socrates who said, 'Nothing makes a man feel better than a good crap.'"

They all laughed and helped Jason back into bed.

An hour later, Jason was in a regular room on the surgical ward. He ate well and drank fluids, but they kept the IV in for the antibiotics. It had only been thirty-six hours since the shooting, and he found himself strong enough to walk the halls. Not that he had a lot of time for walking the halls—he had a continuous stream of visitors.

Seth was the first visitor to the new room. He came in and started crying. "You look like shit." He walked over to Jason and kissed him on the cheek. "Thank God you're okay. I know about everything, Jason. I can't believe this. It's like something out of a Clancy book."

"How did you find out?"

"The FBI found out I was your close friend. They questioned all your friends. I told them I would talk to them only if I knew the story, and so they told me. But they threatened me that if I told anyone, I would be prosecuted for a federal crime. Where's Philip?"

"I made him go home to sleep and shower." Jason grinned. "His body odor was ruining my appetite."

"I've been ordered by your father to stay no more than two minutes. He's outside screening visitors and giving orders."

Philip walked back in. Jason looked at him and to his surprise became aroused. He couldn't believe that he could get an erection after what he'd been through. He started laughing as he looked at Philip.

"What's so funny?"

"Nothing." Jason said.

Philip walked over and kissed Jason tenderly on the lips, and then hugged Seth.

"Okay, I'm leaving before I have to witness man-on-man action." Seth rolled his eyes. "I'm not ready for that."

He walked out, and, a moment later, Drs. Glassman, Stern, Berk, and Skor entered the room. Jason sat up, surprised.

"Well, Jason, you are a beautiful vision. You look a heck of a lot better than Phil here," Dr. Glassman said.

All the men smiled.

"Thank y'all for visiting me. But I'm fine. I'm planning on leaving tomorrow. Dr. Skor, I feel terrible that I've let you down. Has someone replaced me on the floor?"

"Jason, everything is fine. We pulled Seth off his elective, and he's trying his best to take your place."

Suddenly the door opened again, and in walked the President of the United States, with his young marine aide dressed in a civilian suit behind him. Jason suppressed a laugh after seeing the stunned expressions on his professors' faces.

"Jason, I'm relieved to see you looking so well," the president said with a wide grin.

"Mr. President, I hope you didn't make a trip up here just to see me. I'm fine, sir."

The president nodded at the professors. "I wanted to make sure they were taking good care of you."

"Sir, my intention is to go home tomorrow. This is no place to get any rest."

Philip and the four professors looked on in obvious shock at the conversation.

"Jason, from what I understand, thirty-six hours ago, no one thought you would live. Do what the doctors tell you. That's an order." The president shook his finger at Jason. "The sergeant here asked if he could accompany me to see you. He's been very worried."

The sergeant stepped forward. He looked like he was in his mid-twenties, with short blond hair and a very attractive but serious face. The sergeant looked at the president, Philip, and the professors and then spoke in Mandarin. "Dr. Green, the President said I could speak to you in Chinese. I'm so relieved that you are recovering. I also want you to know how courageous I thought you were, the way you talked about your sexuality to the president. It inspires me and other gay members of the military. And I wanted to tell you also that if you ever split from Dr. Olsen, I am available." The sergeant's face turned beet red.

Jason smiled and replied in Mandarin. "Sergeant, I am so grateful for your good wishes. And I am flattered by your proposition. In the unlikely event that Philip and

I break up, you will be the first man I call. Thank you so much for coming."

"Jason, I'm awarding this medal to you." The president took a medal out of his pocket and handed it to Jason. "It's the Presidential Medal of Freedom. It's the highest civilian honor that our nation has. Unfortunately, I need you and the other few around here who know what happened to keep this to yourselves." He looked around at the others in the room. "These good men, and your close friends and family, know what happened, but everyone is sworn to secrecy because of national security issues. I'm not sure how we are going to handle Harrison, but the public will not know that he was linked to your shooting. I can assure you, however, that he will spend the rest of his life in prison."

"I understand, Mr. President. All I want to do is get back to being a doctor and researcher. I have no interest in the world of espionage."

The president smiled. "Damn, I was hoping to entice you into a CIA position."

"Mr. President, I'm honored and very grateful for this medal, and frankly undeserving of it, but if the medal was a ploy to get me to join the CIA, I'm afraid you'll not be successful in that endeavor."

The president chuckled. "Jason, you're too much. Get healthy and go back to your doctoring and research. Phil, take good care of him. Gentlemen." The president shook Jason's hand and smiled. Then he turned around and the sergeant followed him out of the room, after smiling at Jason.

The four professors and Philip stood speechless. Philip broke the silence. "You must have made quite an impression on the president, not to mention the marine. What did he say to you—"

Dr. Glassman interrupted. "Jason, we wanted to wish

you speedy recovery. Do what the president told you.
Frankly, I think this is the only time I've ever agreed with
anything he has said. Listen to the doctors. We need you
back healthy."

The four men walked out.

"What *did* the marine say to you? Do I need to worry?"

"He is apparently gay and thanked me for talking openly to the president at Camp David."

"Is that all?"

"He did say that if you and I ever broke up, he would
be available." Jason laughed, and then grimaced with
pain.

Philip did not seem amused. "And what did you say?"

"I told him I was grateful for his good wishes, but that
he shouldn't hold his breath regarding any Olsen-Green
breakup."

"Jason, I'm frightened. I thought you were going to
die on Sunday. And I'm afraid I've already lost you with
my stupidity."

"Now is not a good time to talk. I'm tired, and there
are too many people in and out. But nearly dying simpli-
fies things. Things that were cloudy have suddenly become clear. For now, just know that I love you deeply."
Jason reached up and put his hand behind Philip's neck.
He slowly pulled Philip to him, just like the first time he
had kissed him. They kissed tenderly and then passionately.

CHAPTER 19

After the president's visit on Tuesday afternoon, Jonathan Green turned away all visitors except for Mr. and Mrs. Olsen, his sister Susie, and Paul and Anna, both of whom had come on Sunday night.

Philip rarely left Jason's bedside, unless Jason complained that he smelled, in which case he would run to the doctors' lounge, shower, and put on a new scrub suit. He was never gone for more than twenty minutes. Jason slept soundly on Tuesday night and refused all pain medications, although the chest incision was quite painful. The pain reminded him that he was alive.

Early Wednesday morning the stream of visitors started early. Jason's father had not yet arrived.

Jason's friend Alex Groh came at six. "Hey, Jason. God, you look great." He looked at Philip. "You must be Philip. I'm Alex Groh, one of his fellow interns. Jason has told me all about you." He smiled, still looking at Philip. "You should know I'm next in line in case you two ever break up." Philip smiled politely, but Jason could tell he didn't find the comment amusing. "We were told that you probably wouldn't make it," Alex continued. "Everyone came by to see you yesterday, but your father politely turned us all away. I just can't believe how good you look. Hey, and there's a rumor sweeping the hospital that the president visited you."

Jason smiled. "Thanks for coming, Alex. The president of what?"

"Of the United States."

"Came to visit me?" Jason asked with a look of surprise.

"The nurses swore that they saw the president visit you. He was surrounded by twenty or thirty Secret Service men."

"Oh, that's right. Yes, I remember now. He was here yesterday. I'm expecting the Pope this evening, and the Dalai Lama is on his way as well."

Philip and Jason laughed, Jason wincing with pain.

"Jason, we miss you. Get well soon." Alex hugged Jason lightly and left.

Dr. Stern and then Dr. Glassman visited him briefly, followed by dozens of interns and residents from the orthopedic and internal medicine services. Even Kevin Gray came by for a brief visit. It was clear that Jason's father had not yet arrived. He would have put a halt to the visitors. It was only eight in the morning, and Jason was already exhausted from the constant stream.

Dr. Patterson walked in just after eight. "Good morning, Jason. How are you feeling today?"

"I feel good enough to get out of here. Please let me go home today. I'll get considerably more rest at home." Jason gave him a lopsided smile. "No one leaves me alone here."

"You've been in this hospital less than three days. You suffered an almost lethal wound. You had to have fourteen units of blood."

Jason's eyebrows rose with that revelation. He'd actually guessed eight units. So the bullet must have severed a main artery.

"Most people with your kind of injury are in the hospital for weeks," Dr. Patterson said with some severity.

Jason looked directly into his eyes. "Sir, I'm eating and drinking well, and I have no respiratory problems, thanks to you." Philip was watching Jason with a slight grin. Jason sighed. "I'm pissing and shitting, I have no infections, the only pain I have is when I laugh, and everyone here is trying to make me laugh. I assume my labs look fine. So please let me get out of here." He rolled his eyes. "Save me from exhaustion by visitation. I'll be a good patient. If anything changes, I'll come running back. I live only one block from here."

Dr. Patterson looked at Jason for a long time. He came over to him, took his blood pressure, and listened to his lungs and heart. "You can't be alone. Who will stay with you?"

Mr. Olsen had walked in as the discussion was going on. "Dr. Patterson, he'll stay with us in Wilton. His father is staying with us, and if anything should happen, I can helicopter him here in twenty minutes."

"Mr. Olsen, I would never impose on you like that. My apartment is only one block from here, and there is plenty of room for my father to stay with me."

"I don't want to hear another word from you." Mr. Olsen shook his head. "It's not a point of discussion. You either stay here in the hospital, or you come to my house. Your choice."

Dr. Patterson stood silently, looking at Jason. "I've never released anyone this quickly, but I've seen you walking the halls and moving faster than most of my residents." After another thoughtful pause, he said, "Okay, you can go. But I want to see you in my office in one week."

"I'll be back at work, but I promise I will break away and visit you. Dr. Patterson, thank you so much for saving my life, and for everything you've done for me and my loved ones."

Dr. Patterson waved his hands for a time-out. "Jason, you're *not* going back to work next week. You'll go back to work when I say you're ready to go back to work."

"Sir, then I will need to see you first thing on Wednesday morning because that's when I'll be going back to work." Jason would be more than ready in a week and possibly sooner. But he'd give it a week. He met Dr. Patterson's glare.

Dr. Patterson shook his head. "Be on this floor at six-thirty next Wednesday. Is that early enough?"

Jason stood up and walked over to the surgeon and hugged him. "That's perfect, Dr. Patterson. I want you to know how grateful I am to you."

Dr. Patterson patted Jason on the back, obviously feeling awkward at such a demonstration of gratitude.

Philip went to Jason's apartment to grab some clothing and toilet articles, and in an hour, Mr. Olsen, Philip, Jonathan Green, and Jason were in a limousine on their way to Wilton.

It was just three days since the near-fatal gunshot wound. Jason pressed his face against the window, looking at the countryside on a cloudy beautiful spring day, wondering why he had been so lucky. Tears stung his eyes, and he kept his face to the glass so that the others would not see his tears. Philip took his hand, and Jason turned to him briefly, smiling, and then put his face back on the window.

Mrs. Olsen came out to greet them, gave Jason a kiss, and held his face in her hands, her eyes glistening with unshed tears.

"Mrs. Olsen," he said with a diminutive smile. "I feel I am imposing on you and Mr. Olsen."

She smiled and then took his hand and led him inside. "Jason, you and your father are family."

He looked around at the familiar space, feeling emotionally and physically drained. "I'm very tired. Would you mind if I took a nap?"

Philip took Jason's arm and led him up to his room. Without saying a word, Philip undressed him, put him into his bed, and covered him with a blanket. Then he lay next to him until Jason dropped off to sleep.

He wakened pleasantly as someone gently shook his shoulder. It was his father. "Jason, you should get up. You haven't eaten since breakfast."

Jason sat up and looked at the clock. He had slept almost six hours. "I must have been tired." He smothered a yawn. "I never nap."

Jason's father sat on the bed next to his son and kissed him on the forehead. "Philip has checked in on you every ten minutes all day." He paused, and his eyes took on a faraway look. "Philip told me what happened. You know, before you were born, I strayed once, and your mother found out. That was—a hard time. We worked through it, and we had about as perfect a marriage as I could imagine. I never recovered from the guilt I felt about what I did, and to this day I regret it and think about it often. Your mother never mentioned it again after the initial trauma. Perhaps it actually strengthened our relationship." He looked at Jason and smiled sadly. "Philip is a good man, and I know he loves you deeply. You are your mother, and you will get through this."

Jason looked at his father in total shock. His father was with another woman? Jason sat quietly for a long moment. "Thanks for telling me that, Dad."

His parents' marriage had been perfect. They were totally in love and mutually supportive. He got up and slowly dressed. They went downstairs and found everyone gathered in the living room. Dr. and Mrs. Glassman had joined the group along with Dr. Stern and his wife.

Dr. Glassman stood up and embraced Jason. "Well,

Jason, you look like you've been in a gunfight and lost. I'm sorry I didn't visit more often. I had to go to Washington yesterday to meet with the other scientists who were involved, and the FBI people."

"Don't give it a second thought, Dr. Glassman." Jason rolled his eyes theatrically. "Frankly, one less visitor was a blessing." Everyone laughed, and Jason went to Mrs. Glassman and kissed her on the cheek. He then went to Dr. Stern, who stood up and shook hands. "Dr. Stern, I hope that you didn't come up to Wilton because of me. I'm fine."

Dr. Stern laughed. "Jason, I came up here because John Olsen told me to. He gives us a lot of money, and when he says jump, I jump." Everyone laughed. "But I think that he asked me to come so that I could tell you that you are not to return to work until you have completely recovered. As your boss, I'm telling you that you are not coming back to work next Wednesday."

Jason smiled. "Dr. Stern, I'm grateful for your concern, but with all due respect, sir, you've wasted your trip. The only way I'm not returning to work on Wednesday is if you fire me. I'm really fine, and by then I'll be back to normal and bored. I'll know if I'm not ready, in which case I promise that I'll stay away. Besides, there is no way that Seth Goldberg can handle that service all by himself."

Dr. Stern harrumphed, but Jason caught a glint of amusement in his eyes.

Jason squeezed in next to Philip, who was sitting in one of the oversized leather chairs next to the large sofa. Philip had been mostly silent. The talk was lively, mostly about current events, politics, the war in Iraq, the economy, and the medical and legal professions. Jason could tell that they had all agreed to avoid talking about the events surrounding the shooting.

Jason ate a large supper. He had lost ten pounds in just the past four days and was determined to regain his muscle mass. He ate two helpings of everything and realized that everyone was watching him and smiling at each other.

"Philip, will you go for a walk with me?" he asked after the meal ended. "I want to get some exercise."

"It's getting late, Jason. How about tomorrow?" Philip actually looked nervous.

"I really feel like walking. C'mon. You're going to get fat if you don't start exercising. It's warm and beautiful out there." Jason rose and pulled Philip up. "Thank you, Mrs. Olsen, for the wonderful supper."

They walked in silence for several hundred yards. Philip kept giving him worried looks, as if he were waiting for him to pass out. Or possibly drop a bombshell. "Philip, before all of this happened we were ready to break up. I'm sure you were tired of my drama, and I don't blame you." Jason stopped to rest. His chest hurt when he took deep breaths.

"Jason, we—"

Jason put his hand over Philip's mouth. "Quiet. I have to tell you this. While I was lying in that awful hospital bed, after I got that godforsaken endotracheal tube out, looking at you sleeping with your head on the bed next to me, it dawned on me that the great lesson I had been taught by Dr. Glassman and Dr. Berk—" He paused and took a deep breath, feeling the pain of his incision and his own discovery, looking down at the ground."—well, I was ignoring that lesson in my personal life."

"What lesson are you talking about?" Philip asked softly.

Jason looked up again at Philip. "That great lesson is that it's always most important to ask the right question in problem solving." Another pause. "After the event with Lucas, I asked exactly the wrong question. The betrayal hurt, of course, but every time I think about having sex with another person, like that marine, that is a betrayal no different than what you did. The betrayal was not the problem. Sure, I was angry and I used it to make me feel better. But the question I kept asking myself was whether I was the right match for you. I assumed because of what happened, there were things you needed that I couldn't give. You're a strong person in every way, and my answer to that question was that you needed to be dominant in a relationship, sexually and otherwise, and that it was not possible for me to be the kind of person you needed." He raised his hand as Philip started to speak.

"The problem with that question is that I was answering a question that only you can answer. You are strong, and I know that if I'm not the right person for you, you would somehow let me know. The question I *should* have been asking is whether *you* are the right match for *me*." Jason paused. "Philip, you are the perfect match for me. I cannot think of an imperfection that you possess. The question of whether I'm the right match for you—well, that's your question. I can't answer that. I don't know how you'll deal with your need to be sexually dominant, or how we will deal with it, if you decide to stay with me. We'll have to come up with something."

Jason turned away from Philip to look at the beautiful countryside. "I had to get this off my chest. I love you so much. If you decide to break it off, I'll deal with it. I love you enough that I would far prefer to be your friend rather than your lover if I were not your right match. You deserve—we all deserve—to be happy."

Philip stood still for a moment. He gently turned Jason around to face him and put his hands on Jason's face. "The question I kept asking was if I could be happy in a relationship with you, when I knew that I was not good enough for you. Maybe that's what drove me to do what I did with Lucas. Jason, the domination thing is a tiny and insignificant part of me. The only imperfection I see in you as my match is that you're too good for me."

"That's such nonsense." Jason shook his head. "Maybe I can run a little faster than you, but I can't throw a football ten yards. And maybe I have certain intellectual skills in research that are a little better than yours, but I couldn't come close to doing what you do in the operating room, even if I trained for a hundred years."

Without a word, their arms went around each other, and they held one another until Jason could no longer take the pain in his chest. "Sorry, Philip, the incision is hurting."

Philip leaned away. They stood a hand's breadth apart and kissed. It was a sweet kiss, like they both remembered from better times. Hand in hand, they walked slowly back to the house. In the living room, everyone was still in a lively discussion.

Jason stifled a yawn. "Excuse me for interrupting, but I'm going to bed. I want y'all to know that I feel I'm the luckiest person in the world. I'm so grateful to all of you. Anyway, please drive carefully back to the city."

Jason slowly climbed the stairs, with Philip following closely behind.

"Jason, I'm tired as well. Would you mind if I slept with you?"

Jason smiled. "I'll sleep much better if you do. The problem is that I think I stink, and I don't know if I have the energy to shower now."

Philip laughed. "Then we can both stink together."

They crawled into bed, their bodies entwined, and both fell asleep within a minute.

CHAPTER 20

On Thursday and Friday, Philip went to the hospital but came back to Wilton early each evening. Jason recovered rapidly. He ate ravenously and had gained eight of his ten pounds back by Friday. The weather had been beautiful, in the seventies and clear, and he and his father walked for miles at a time, several times a day. His breathing was nearly normal, and other than the incision pain, he felt well and energetic. Mr. Olsen worked from home and went on several walks with Jason as well.

On one of the walks, Mr. Olsen put his hands in his pocket, and cleared his throat. "You know, Jason, I don't want to intrude on your relationship with Phil. I know it's been difficult. But I know Phil better than anyone, better than he knows himself. He's always been at the top of everything he's done, whether it's academics, popularity, looks. Everything. It was very difficult for him to admit he was gay, and coming out to us was extremely difficult for him. He was certain he'd never find someone he could be with for the rest of his life. And then he found you. This is the first time he has ever felt that he is not good enough for someone, not the one in control. It's really that simple. It's no excuse for what he did, but I'd bet my reputation and fortune that he'll never do it again." Mr. Olsen paused as they kept walking. "I just wanted to get this off my chest. We've become very fond of you and don't want to lose you."

Jason swallowed, aware of how difficult that must have been for Mr. Olsen to confide. After a long pause, he said, "I've worked through our problems, *my* problems, and I'm content. Philip is perfect for me. What he did is a nonevent in my mind." He stopped briefly. It was true, he realized suddenly, not just something he was saying. Over the past few days, and nights, he had not experienced any flashbacks or dreams about Phil and Lucas. He smiled and started walking again. "That he thinks he's not good enough for me is laughable. I've thought from the first day I met him that I was not good enough for *him*. Anyway, just know that I couldn't imagine anyone loving another human being more than I love Philip. Our relationship is now up to him."

Mr. Olsen didn't say anything, but he smiled all the way back to the house.

Friday afternoon, Paul came home for a long weekend, primarily to see Jason, he said. His hug made Jason catch his breath with pain, and he finally let go. Then he stood back with his hands on Jason's shoulders, his eyes moist. "Jesus, you look a heap better than when I saw you on Monday. I can't believe it."

"Paul, I don't remember you being there on Monday."

"Well, you hadn't pulled that tube out of your throat yet. I heard about that. You've sure got chutzpa."

Jason laughed. "You still must be with Amy Edelstein. She's making a Jew out of you."

Philip had picked Anna up at Grand Central Station and arrived at five o'clock. Mrs. Olsen prepared a Sabbath dinner and asked Jason to say the prayers. Jason suggested that Paul might want to practice, making everyone laugh. Jason's voice was still raspy and he spoke, rather than sang, the prayers.

"I have an announcement to make," Jason said during the meal. Everyone was quiet, looking at Jason expectantly. "I'm going back to the city tomorrow afternoon, and I'm making my daddy go home. Dad, I've already purchased your plane ticket. Your plane leaves at four-thirty tomorrow. I feel great. I walked ten miles today, and my energy is normal. The only reason I'm not running is because of my chest incision. I love being with y'all, but it's time for me to go back. I want to get back to the lab and back to my patients." He held up a hand before anyone could interrupt him. "I know y'all are going to protest. But don't waste your energy. I'm going back tomorrow. Y'all have been so kind to me and to my daddy. I'll never be able to repay you, and I'm so grateful to you. But you've done enough, I'm fine, and I'm going back tomorrow. Any questions?"

Heads shook, eyebrows rose, but no one said a word and everyone continued eating silently.

"Good. It's settled."

His father was going to worry about him, but he also knew that his father was anxious to get back to his business. Jason was bored, and his energy had almost returned to normal. It was time to get out of the Olsen family's hair.

After supper, Jason coaxed Philip into walking with him.

Philip was frowning and had been frowning off and on since Jason's announcement. "Do you think you're really ready to go back?"

"I really feel great, except for the incision and maybe a little loss of strength because I haven't been running." Jason touched Philip's arm. "I feel pretty normal."

"Well, I'm going with you, and you're moving in with me. And I won't take no for an answer."

"Philip—"

Philip put his hand over Jason's mouth. "Jason, it's time for you to shut up. You are not going to stay alone this soon after major surgery, and besides, it's time for us to move in together."

They walked in silence for a few minutes. "You don't know what you're getting yourself into," Jason said, breaking the silence. "We will probably have fights over the thermostat, and you're going to have to endure my music. I'm going to mess up your bathroom and bedroom. Sometimes I have really bad body odor, particularly after I run. I fart and belch a lot, I have these night terrors, I pick my nose, I sneeze a lot, I—"

"Stop it." Philip grabbed him, gently, by the shoulders. "You can pick, fart, belch, and mess up all you want. I've already moved all your things into our apartment, and your McIntosh speakers are already hooked up to the stereo system."

Jason stopped and for a second, his heart seemed to stop. "Are you—certain this is what you want?"

"I've wanted you to move in for the past ten months." Philip's voice was hoarse.

Jason put his arms around Philip and kissed him as passionately as he ever had. Then he eyed Philip with a frown. "Wait a minute. I was surprised that no one objected to me leaving tomorrow. Did you have something to do with that?"

Philip laughed. "I told our fathers that you'd likely do this, and that I had already moved your things into my apartment. So they were prepared and knew you wouldn't be alone."

Jason laughed. It felt so good to laugh, despite the pain.

On Saturday morning, Jason went for a long walk with his father and then another walk with Paul, who told Jason that Philip was his hero and how glad he was that

Philip had found someone to love. It was the first time that Paul had talked seriously with Jason.

A limousine picked Jason's father up at one-thirty p.m. to take him to LaGuardia, and it was an emotional good-bye for everyone. When he finally let go of Jason, he turned around, tears in his eyes, and got into the limousine without saying a word.

At four o'clock, Philip brought his Porsche around, and Jason said good-bye to the four Olsens. He knew that anything he said wouldn't do justice to how grateful he was, and so he just kissed and hugged all four and got into the car while Philip said his good-byes.

They drove in silence for ten minutes.

"I guess you've decided I'm an okay match for you at least for now?" Jason asked softly.

"Jason, I intend to marry you one day and grow old with you." Philip's smile was as wide as Jason had ever seen it.

They arrived at the apartment at five-thirty p.m. When they walked through the entry door, the attendant said, "Good evening Dr. Olsen, Dr. Green."

Jason startled at that and saw Philip looking at him. So it was official. In the apartment, he saw his McIntosh speakers on both sides of the huge window facing Central Park. He walked silently into the bedroom and opened the closet, and all his clothes were hanging next to Phillip's.

Jason started to undress. Philip was in the kitchen pouring sodas when Jason walked into the kitchen naked and aroused. Philip turned around and started laughing. "Jason, you were almost dead less than a week ago. I figured you wouldn't be able to have an erection for at least a few months."

Jason didn't smile. "Do you remember when Seth was visiting me in the hospital, and you walked into the room?"

"Yes."

"And I started laughing?"

"Yeah, I remember. I figured Seth had said something funny to you."

"No, Seth was crying. You walked in, I looked at you, and I got an instant erection. Believe me, I was in pain and didn't feel very well, but that's what happened."

Jason pulled Philip into the bedroom. Philip was obviously worried about his large incision and sutures. Jason slowly undressed Philip, and they made love as passionately and intensely as they ever had. No visions of Lucas with Philip intruded. There was only the desperate and inexplicable lovemaking that they had had before. They climaxed together, after an hour, and then they showered together, washing each other, Philip moving gently over the scar and sutures.

After they dried off, Jason took scissors out of the drawer. "Take them out, Philip."

"Take what out?" Philip blinked.

"The sutures. Take them out. The incision is fine, I don't need them anymore, and they're driving me crazy. They stick me all the time."

Philip looked at the incision. "Okay, it's healed, I know, but I better not. Dr. Patterson will be mad, and the incision is only six days old."

Jason went to the mirror with the scissors.

"Okay, okay. Wait." Philip grabbed the scissors. "Let me do it. When you get your mind made up, I know there's no stopping you."

When he finished, Jason turned around and kissed him. He felt Philip's erection against him. Jason got on his knees and pleasured Philip. It took only a few minutes.

"Jesus, Jason, you were dead a week ago. You're a sex machine."

They both laughed.

They both fell asleep at eight, and Jason awoke Sunday morning at seven-thirty to the smell of bacon and eggs. He had slept for almost twelve hours and felt completely rested for the first time since surgery—really for the first time since the Lucas event. Jason went into the kitchen and hugged Philip from behind.

As they were eating, Jason told Philip that he wanted to go to the lab and then to the hospital to go over patient charts. Seth had been taken off his elective rotation in cardiology to cover for Jason, and he was certain that Seth was unhappy about it. After all, he would be working twice as hard on the medical service than on the cardiology elective. So his plan was to relieve Seth starting Monday. Philip wanted to go to the hospital in order to catch up on his duties, and they planned to meet in the cafeteria at noon.

Jason walked into the computer room and there sat Dr. Glassman with someone new. A new postdoc fellow, Jason surmised. Dr. Glassman wouldn't waste time replacing Dr. Fang. After all, the bioinformatics section of the lab was crucial for the proper functioning of the other six labs he headed, not to mention the hundreds of outside labs that were depending on Dr. Glassman's computers.

Dr. Glassman looked up. "My God, Jason, you look wonderful!" He stood up and embraced Jason for an unusually long time. Jason saw the look of surprise on the new postdoc's face. "Well, John told me to expect you back, although he's not happy about it. Dr. Green, this is Eric Adelman. He's the new fellow who'll be heading this section. He knows about Dr. Fang's family problems and his abrupt return to China, and we were able to recruit him from Duke."

Jason held out his hand and smiled. Dr. Adelman stood up and shook Jason's hand. "Dr. Green—"

"Please call me Jason," Jason interrupted.

"Jason, I've heard a lot about you. I can't believe how good you look. The other postdoc fellows told me you were almost dead a week ago."

Jason smiled. "Well, they exaggerate a little bit."

"And they told me the President of the United States visited you in the hospital."

"How rumors like that get started always amazes me. I didn't even vote for the man—"

"Okay, boys, enough of this," Dr. Glassman interrupted. "Jason, I'm glad you're here. Dr. Adelman is asking questions that I'm not capable of answering. If you can spend the next hour with him answering his questions, I would be grateful. You have one hour, that's it. John Olsen and Henry Stern have both threatened me that if your recovery is delayed because of overwork in this lab, there will be severe consequences." The barest hint of a smile quirked the corner of his mouth. "I'll be back in an hour, and you best be gone." Dr. Glassman turned around and walked out.

Jason learned quickly that Dr. Adelman was a computer genius. Jason went over the computer programs, the data files, and recent downloads that had not yet been analyzed. The new fellow picked everything up instantly. Jason also showed him the computer program that he and Dr. Fang had developed and the ongoing projects that had been developed from the program. Eric became very excited by that program, and Jason assured him that it was his project to continue.

Exactly one hour later, Dr. Glassman appeared at the door. "You're out of here, Green." Jason and Dr. Glassman just looked at each other, and Jason didn't budge. "I mean it. Go. Now."

Jason reluctantly stood up and looked at Dr. Adelman. "I guess I'd better leave. I've learned to do what he says.

I hope you won't mind if I show up here, usually in the later afternoon or evening during the week and on Saturday if I'm not admitting patients. If you need help on Sundays, I'll be available in the afternoons when I don't have to work in the hospital. When you're not here, you can just leave me a note of things you want me to do."

"Green get out of here, *now!*"

As Jason walked out of the lab, he heard Dr. Adelman tell Dr. Glassman, "He's amazing."

Jason walked slowly to his hospital floor. It had been eight days since he had been there, one day before he'd been shot.

He immediately saw Seth with Gerald Shenkman and Erica Strickland. Jason smiled as he walked toward them. All three stood, staring at him. Seth hugged him without saying a word and wiped the tears from his eyes. Gerald Shenkman then hugged him and Erica Strickland gave a brief, if stiff, hug as well.

"Dr. Green, Erica, and I tried to visit you, but your father, who was very nice—" Gerald hastened to add. "—wouldn't let us in. We were really worried about you."

"Jason, what in the fuck are you doing here?" Seth broke in. "I was told you would be back on Wednesday."

Jason looked at Gerald and Erica. "Thanks for trying. I know my daddy turned most people away, but I appreciate it."

"But I guess he didn't turn the president away," Gerald Shenkman said with a grin. "We heard the president visited you."

Jason laughed. "Gerald, you know how rumors go. It wasn't the president, it was the Dali Lama." Everyone laughed. Jason continued, "There's an old saying: Don't witness with your mouth what you don't witness with your eyes. They're just rumors."

Gerald's grin widened. "Well, Dr. Green, my girlfriend was your nurse, and she witnessed it with her eyes."

Jason turned to Seth. "You can get back to your cardiology elective tomorrow. I'm coming back tomorrow full time. I hear that you are having a difficult time keeping up anyway." He winked at the students. "So it's time to get you back to something you can handle."

Seth laughed. "Very funny. But I'm going to continue on this service with you until I'm certain you're healthy enough to handle it. I've been threatened by Dr. Stern that should you be overworked and adversely affected, I will be in deep shit."

"Seth—"

"Forget it. There's no discussion. I'm here at least for the week. We've just finished rounds. Why don't you go over the charts?"

"Okay, and I'm meeting Philip for lunch. Can you join us?"

"Of course."

Over the next two hours, Jason went over the sixteen charts of patients on his service. Midway he got a tap on the shoulder and looked up. It was Craig Thomason. Jason stood up, and Craig hugged him. "I tried to visit, but your father was keeping everyone out."

"I know. I heard. And no, the president of the United States did not visit me."

Craig laughed. "I know. The rumor is widespread. I can't tell you how relieved I've been. Take it easy. You were almost dead a week ago."

At noon, Seth and Jason walked to the cafeteria.

Philip's eyes were fixed on Jason as they walked toward him. "So how are you feeling?" Anxiety edged the seemingly casual question.

"I'm feeling fine. I'm tired of everyone worrying."

Philip hugged Seth. "You're staying with him for a while aren't you?"

"I don't have a choice." Seth grinned easily. "Stern said he would have my head if I didn't."

"Look, there's Dr. Patterson," Jason interrupted. Jason got up, quickly walked over to him, and hugged him, which clearly embarrassed him. Jason just laughed. "Dr. Patterson, I was hoping I'd run into you. I wanted to give you this CD of some of my favorite music as a small token of my appreciation and just wanted to show you I'm well so that I wouldn't have to visit you on Wednesday morning. I'm back to work tomorrow."

"Jason, I told you that you couldn't go back until I saw you on Wednesday." Dr. Patterson frowned. "It's just a week today. It's ridiculous."

"Dr. Patterson, I appreciate your concern, but I'm fine and very bored. I'm anxious to get back to work. I'm starting tomorrow morning."

"Let me look at your incision."

Jason pulled up his shirt.

"Who took out the stitches?" Dr. Patterson sounded surprised.

"Oh, I made Philip take them out. Don't be mad at him. Had he not taken them out, I would have. They were annoying. The incision is fine."

Dr. Patterson looked over at Philip, who was staring at them, and frowned at him. Philip merely shrugged.

"You're a lousy patient, Jason. Okay, you can start taking walks in a week, but no running for six weeks. Do you hear me? The high impact of running could disturb what I did inside your chest."

"Of course, Dr. Patterson. Thanks again for everything." Jason hugged him briefly again, and went back to Philip and Seth.

Philip shook his head. "I told you he'd be mad about the stitches."

Jason chuckled. "Oh, he'll get over it."

Over the next three weeks, Jason went to Dr. Glassman's lab every day as well as on the weekends. Jason quickly came to like and respect Dr. Adelman. Dr. Fang had excellent computer skills, but Eric Adelman was a genius with the computer. He made huge strides with the program that Jason had developed and designed several more unique proteins that would have unique affinity to specific tumor antigens. However, each time Jason sat with Eric, he would make Jason leave after an hour. Jason would protest, but Eric explained that Dr. Glassman had threatened him several times, and he admitted he was terrified of him. After three weeks of being sent home, Jason had enough. He knocked on Dr. Glassman's door.

"Sir, I'm going running now in Central Park. Would you like to join me?"

Dr. Glassman looked at him with a puzzled expression. "Are you out of your mind? Why would you ask me such a thing?"

Jason laughed. "Dr. Glassman, I'm fine. I'm running two miles every day, and Philip can't keep up with me. Your one-hour curfew for me is not reasonable any longer. I appreciate your concern, but please tell Dr. Adelman that it's okay if I stay longer. He's scared to death of you."

Dr. Glassman looked horrified. "You're running two miles every day?"

"Yes, sir, I'm almost one hundred percent now, and one hour with Dr. Adelman is not enough time. I'm just sitting with him. There's no physical exertion. So please tell him I can stay, now."

Glassman sighed, shook his head, and then removed the curfew.

After that talk, Jason spent considerable time with Eric. The two became close working associates, and Philip and he went to dinner with Eric and his wife on several occasions. The amount of research they had accomplished during the last six weeks of Jason's internship had astonished Dr. Glassman.

Jason returned to the wards on Monday and assumed control of the patients. He had been unsuccessful at getting Seth to return to his cardiology elective until the end of the week. But by the end of the week, Seth admitted that he was superfluous, and for the next six weeks, until the end of his internship, Jason had complete control of patient care and student teaching. He continued to have a great relationship with Dr. Skor, whom he deeply respected for the questions that he asked on their daily rounds.

Philip worked long hours on the orthopedic service, teaching and performing difficult surgeries. He would be transitioning from chief residency to a professorship in a few weeks and was in the process of training the surgeon who was to become next year's chief resident.

Jason's move into Philip's apartment ended up feeling natural to both of them. Their sexual relationship resumed with all the intensity it originally had. They made love for hours, usually four or five times weekly, and sometimes on the weekends, twice daily. On Sunday afternoons, Philip and Jason would sit next to each other on their couch, reading and listening to music for the entire afternoon, looking at the beautiful view of Central Park. Jason would periodically place his book aside, lean over and kiss Philip tenderly for a few minutes, and then without saying a word, pick up his book and resume reading. On occasion, Jason would drop his book in front of Philip, and whimsically say, "Whoops."

He would then get on his knees, presumably to pick up

his book, but instead he would playfully pull Philip's pants down and pleasure him orally. Philip had no problems accommodating Jason, having a libido that equaled Jason's, and he was amused at the games that Jason liked to play. Philip would return the favor by interrupting him while he was reading intensely, putting his hands on him and arousing him, which took little effort on his part.

Philip's parents came to the city most Saturday evenings to have supper with Philip and Jason. Jason assumed that they were checking up on him, but he enjoyed their company immensely and loved them as family. Philip and Jason also had Seth and Sheri over for dinner several times. One evening toward the end of June, they announced their engagement, and Seth asked Jason and Philip to serve as co-best men with his brother.

Jason's last function as an intern was the ten a.m. conference on Saturday, July first, with Dr. Stern and the chief residents. The interns eagerly anticipated the last conference of the year. Traditionally, a very difficult case was presented, and the intern who made the correct diagnosis was given the Stern Intern Award, which was honored by placing the intern's photograph on a wall in the department of medicine next to the chairman's office. In the seventeen years that Dr. Stern had been chairman, only four interns had gotten their pictures placed on that wall, and no intern had succeeded in making a correct diagnosis in the past six years.

Jason arrived early and talked with his friend Alex, who had continued to prod him about the rumor of a presidential visit while he was in the hospital.

"Can you believe this is our last day of internship?" Jason asked after greeting Alex with a hug.

Alex smiled and raised his eyebrows. "It may be your last day, but I have to admit tomorrow—unless you'd like to take my place for the day?"

"Hmmm, let me see." Jason made a show of tapping his chin and thinking. "It's between taking your place and spending the day with Philip." He shook his head. "Nope, sorry, Alex."

They both laughed.

"Yeah, I guess my hope for a split between you two isn't going to happen." Alex pouted theatrically.

"If it did ever happen, which doesn't seem likely, I would come running to you."

"So, you know that you're the one who's going to make the diagnosis today."

"I'm not opening my mouth. I couldn't care less about that award." Jason was not pretending. He really had no desire to have his picture placed anywhere except on Philip's and his father's nightstand.

The chief resident presented the case of a woman who was admitted with a fever of unknown origin. He described a very detailed physical and neurological examination.

Over the next thirty minutes, the interns discussed the case, asking the chief residents questions that they would sometimes answer and sometimes refuse to answer. Jason sat and listened to the conversation, smiling, gratified that the interns were asking the right questions. Alex leaned over to Jason. "You know what the diagnosis is, don't you?" he whispered.

Jason answered, "You, of all the interns, deserve this award. You know the diagnosis. Speak up."

"I have no idea."

"Think of the neurological examination he told us about, and the fever, and the heart murmur. Think about it," Jason urged.

Dr. Stern looked at Jason and Alex as they were whispering. "Alex, you and Jason have been talking to each other and not contributing to this discussion." He fixed his piercing stare on them. "What do you think the diagnosis is?"

"Dr. Stern, I had no idea until Jason just basically told me. Jason knows the diagnosis."

"Jason?" Dr. Stern continued his stare.

"Sir, I just prefer to stay out of this one. I didn't tell Alex the diagnosis, but I believe he knows it."

Dr. Stern glared at Jason. "Jason, tell me what you think the diagnosis is and the basis for that diagnosis. If you refuse, you'll have to repeat the internship."

Laughter erupted. Everyone at the table knew that Jason had already figured it out.

Jason's felt his face become hot as usual. "Sir, the lady has an atrial myxoma." He went on to detail the findings on physical examination that the chief resident had described and the usual presentation of atrial myxoma, a tumor that grows in the left atrium of the heart. Pieces of the tumor break off and cause strokes in various parts of the brain, and Jason pointed out the areas of the brain that had caused the abnormal findings on physical examination.

Dr. Stern smiled. "The rest of you shouldn't feel bad. It took the interns, residents, and attending physicians—including the neurologists—two admissions and four weeks to make the diagnosis. We didn't expect anyone to make the correct diagnosis, but your discussion was outstanding, and what was most thrilling to me were the questions that each of you asked. You have all done outstanding jobs. You've worked incredibly hard this year, and I'm looking forward to next year with you. Enjoy the donuts." Dr. Stern and the chief residents got up and left, and as usual, the interns attacked the donuts and coffee.

"Alex, you knew the diagnosis." Jason stepped up next to him. "You should have said it."

"I had no idea until you told me what to think about. You deserve that award, and you know it."

Jason stayed and talked with all the interns. As he was leaving, one of the chief residents yelled at him from down the hall. "Dr. Green, could you come here a minute?"

Jason walked down to the chief resident's office, where Dr. Stern and the other chief resident were sitting.

"Dr. Green, Dr. Stern and both of us noticed that you were smiling for the entire discussion," Dr. Santiago said. "We have a bet about why you were smiling. So tell us."

"Sir, I didn't intend to smile. I didn't know I was so obvious."

"Why were you smiling?" Dr. Stern asked.

"I was just proud of the interns. They were all asking the right questions. Had y'all answered some of those questions that they'd asked, they would have all gotten the diagnosis." He paused. "That's why I was smiling."

"Thanks, Jason." Dr. Stern laughed. "The chief residents owe me a dinner. They said you were smiling because you knew the diagnosis at the very beginning."

"Oh, I did, sir." Jason grinned. "But that wasn't why I was smiling."

CHAPTER 21

On Saturday evening, Jonathan Green and John Olsen reserved the entire upper section of Trattoria Del'Arte to celebrate the completion of Jason's internship and Philip's chief residency. Everyone important to Jason and Philip was present: Jason's father and sister; the Olsen family, including Anna and Paul, who brought Amy Edelstein; Seth and Sheri; Harvey and Clara Glassman; Henry and Ellen Stern; Edward and Candace Berk; Franklin and Allison Skor; Morris and Gayle Frankel; Craig Thomason; Alex Groh; the chairman of orthopedics; four other orthopedic surgery professors with their wives; and Eric and Fran Adelman. Also present were Ellie Shapiro, Judge Lackland with his wife, Mrs. Holiman, and Mr. Grayson with his two children.

Jason and Philip sat at the main table with their families, close to each other, arms and legs touching, each feeling the warmth of the other. Jason thought this must be the happiest day of his life. He was deep in thought, completely unaware of the lively chatter about him.

He was thinking how lucky he was. He had the luck of being born with an unusual intelligence, and because of that, he'd been able to connect with other geniuses, including Philip, sitting in this room with him. He thought of the thousands, probably tens of thousands, and over the millennia tenfold that number, who had been born with the same genius but whose genius had never been allowed to blossom. They had been quashed or murdered by ordinary men like Augustus, Nero, Alexander, Khan, Godunov, Napoleon, Pasha, Pol Pot, Tojo, Stalin, Hitler, Mao, Johnson, and Nixon. Or if not politically quashed, then made infirm by poverty or starvation, their genius sapped by malnutrition, malaria, plague, influenza, or HIV. Or their genius had been subdued by infirmities of the mind: autism, schizophrenia, depression, sociopathy, or self-loathing. Or drowned by a drunken father or a coldhearted mother. Or crushed by religions that threaten death to a man who loves another man, or death for cursing a mother or father, or for not believing, or a religion that threatens eternal damnation (whatever that is) for disobeying hundreds of irrational laws devised by ignorant men. Jason shook his head. How fragile are the blossoms of genius.

And yet he had been so lucky, born in a country that allowed him to flourish; born to parents who loved, nourished, and nurtured him; and endowed with physical beauty and good health. Even so, Jason knew that he was fragile: Bold and, at the same time, insecure, his mental health at times on the fence, haunted by history and the pain of others. He had learned to confront his frailties by being bold and kind and, most of all, by immersing himself in music. He wondered if he would be tough enough to allow his genius to translate into success.

Jason looked along the table to Harvey Glassman. His genius blossomed because he was a taskmaster, demanding of all those who surrounded him. Over the years Dr. Glassman must have mentored many postdoc fellows who were geniuses but who had disappeared into obscurity because of frailties that could not be overcome or perhaps had even been quashed by Dr. Glassman himself, if they somehow threatened his ego.

Jason looked at his father. He knew his father was responsible for everything good that had happened to him.

What luck!

He looked at Ellie Shapiro. He would have never met Philip had it not been for Ellie Shapiro. Maybe Seth would have introduced them, but it had been that initial confrontation which had resulted in that perfectly struck chord.

What luck!

And still, deep in thought, he looked at Philip, staring at him, not blinking once, unaware of the toasts being given. Philip was perfection, pure and simple. Their relationship had not been perfection, but Jason wondered how many relationships had ever achieved perfection. Perfection could be found in art, literature, and music, reworked and finalized to perfection. But relationships were a work in progress, susceptible to the foibles of personality and frailties of ego. Perhaps if a relationship could survive all of those obstacles, there could be a chance of perfection in the end. Jason thought again of Tolstoy: "Those who seek perfection are never content." Fuck Tolstoy. He would be content to be discontent. He would make it his mission to achieve perfection with Philip.

Jason felt his shoulder being shaken by Philip. "Hey, Jason, are you with us?" he whispered. "They're toasting us. You seem like you're on a faraway planet."

Jason smiled, still staring at Philip. "I was just thinking how lucky I am."

Jason heard clapping. Someone just completed a toast, and Jason looked around, collecting his thoughts, mentally rejoining the gathering. He scooted closer to Philip, and as they listened to toasts from Jonathan Green and John Olsen, Jason could see all eyes were on Philip and him. Jason pressed his leg firmly against Philip's leg. Philip returned the gesture, pressing his leg even more firmly against Jason's leg. And then Jason and Philip broke out into simultaneous laughter.

EPILOGUE

In 2008, Jason received a letter postmarked in Beijing from Chao Fang. He wrote that he deeply regretted what had happened to Jason and that he was devastated when he learned Jason had been shot. He was happy to learn that he fully recovered and had read all of the papers that he had since coauthored. Fang explained that he had been forced by threats to his family to participate in the data theft. He had never dreamed that violence would be involved. He had moved back with his family and was now teaching at a small university outside of Beijing. He ended the letter by saying that he would be sad until his death that he caused harm to such a good person.

Jason finished his residency in brilliant fashion in 2008. He continued his research in Dr. Glassman's lab through his residency and the following year, and his collaboration with Eric Adelman yielded important advances in computer protein modeling and the development of unique proteins that advanced the development of immunotherapy to treat cancer.

By the end of Jason's residency, the faculty unanimously voted to award Jason a PhD based on his research and a brilliant thesis, which he wrote the last month of his senior residency. Jason joined Dr. Glassman's lab full time in 2009, and in 2010, Dr. Glassman died two months after being diagnosed with pancreatic cancer.

Jason took over Dr. Glassman's position at Dr. Glassman's request, becoming the youngest scientist to lead a major scientific laboratory in the United States.

Philip transitioned to a professorship following his chief residency. In 2012 an anonymous donor gave three million dollars to establish an endowed professorship that Philip was designated to occupy. The professorship was named the Human Rights Distinguished Professorship. The donor stipulated that this professorship was to be occupied by Philip Olsen until he retired, after which it could be occupied only by a gay or transgender professor. Four years into his professorship, Philip became known as one of the most innovative orthopedic surgeons in the country. He developed new techniques and instruments for spinal surgery and was asked to be a visiting professor at medical schools all over the world. More important to Philip was that he received the Best Teacher Award almost every year from the medical students. The years he didn't receive the award, Jason had been given the honor.

Jason and Philip continued to have an intensely loving relationship. Their sexual relationship remained as intense as it had been during the first few months of their time together.

In June 2011, same-sex marriage became legal in New York, and in August of that same year, a wedding ceremony with two hundred invited guests was held at Mr. and Mrs. Olsen's mansion in Wilton. It was officiated by Judge Lackland, who performed a combined Jewish and Presbyterian ceremony, reciting several prayers in Hebrew. Paul, who had married Amy Edelstein, was Philip's best man, and Seth, who had remained as a professor of cardiology, was Jason's best man. Jonathan Green cried unabashedly as Jason and Philip both broke glasses with their right feet, a Jewish tradition of the new husband in a wedding ceremony.

A year later, Jason and Philip adopted a beautiful newborn girl whom they named Julia, after Jason's mother. Jason's father sold his business in Mississippi and moved to New York City to be near his sons and granddaughter.

Three weeks after Jason had walked in on Philip and Lucas at his apartment, Lucas received an anonymous note. The note read: *You have a nevus next to your navel that looks like a melanoma. Your children need their daddy. Get it looked at by a dermatologist.* The mole was removed, and Lucas was cured of a potentially fatal melanoma.

Did Philip ever stray again? Jason didn't know. He never thought of asking that question.

The End

About the Author

John S. Daniels is an endocrinologist and Clinical Professor of Medicine at the Washington University School of Medicine in Saint Louis, Missouri. He was born and raised in Fort Smith, Arkansas, the son of holocaust survivors. He was married for nineteen years and has three daughters from that marriage. He has been with his partner, Lance Cimarolli, for the past twenty-one years.

CPSIA information can be obtained
at www.ICGtesting.com
Printed in the USA
BVHW01s0947190218
508438BV00032B/146/P